T0129406

**He grabbed hold and stopped the Datsun
from toppling off the road.**

"Glen!" Katie screamed. "Glen!"

He could barely see her face over the hood.

"Get—out—the—car," he managed.

"I'm trying," she sobbed. "I can't get the goddamn seatbelt, Glen—"

He looked up and saw her eyes, wide with terror. The car began to fall backward again, dragging him with it. He wasn't strong enough. When it counted the most, he wasn't strong enough. He was—

"Glen!" Katie screamed.

He looked up and met her gaze as the bumper slipped out of first his right hand and then his left.

For a second, the car and Katie hung there in space in front of him.

And then they fell.

A split-second later, the car hit and exploded in flame.

With a roar of primal fury and sorrow, Glen Kane launched himself off the side of the mountain and into the heart of that fire.

# journey into darkness

## The Unauthorized History of Kane

### a novel by
### Michael Chiappetta

World Wrestling
Entertainment™

**POCKET BOOKS**

**NEW YORK  LONDON  TORONTO  SYDNEY**

POCKET BOOKS, a division of Simon & Schuster, Inc.
1230 Avenue of the Americas, New York, NY 10020

World Wrestling
Entertainment®

This book is a work of fiction. Names, characters, places and incidents are products of the author's imagination or are used fictitiously. Any resemblance to actual events or locales or persons, living or dead, is entirely coincidental.

ISBN: 978-1-4767-3889-5

First Pocket Books paperback edition September 2005

10  9  8  7  6  5  4  3  2  1

POCKET and colophon are registered trademarks of
Simon & Schuster, Inc.

Cover design by Dave Barry

Visit us on the World Wide Web
http://www.simonsays.com
http://www.wwe.com

Manufactured in the United States of America

For information regarding special discounts for bulk purchases,
please contact Simon & Schuster Special Sales at 1-800-456-6798
or business@simonandschuster.com.

# book one:
## cursed

# prologue

"You freak," Denton said.

Glen hit him in the face.

"Hey." Denton looked surprised.

Glen punched him in the stomach.

"Ow," Denton said, and bent over double.

Glen knocked him down to the ground and twisted the boy's arm behind his back. He reached into Denton's coat pocket and took back the dollar Denton had stolen from him this morning. His lunch money. Glen took the rest of the money in Denton's coat too, just for good measure—about four dollars in change and a couple crumpled-up bills, about a week's worth of lunch money, and since Denton had been taking Glen's lunch money for most of the last month, he figured he was still a little short on the deal.

"Hey!" Denton said again. "Give that back!"

"Shut up, whiner," Glen said. He turned and glared at the rest of Denton's gang—the sixth-graders who hung out with Denton Young, who did his every wish because Denton's dad was some kind of big shot on the Marfa City Council—balled his hands into fists, and took a step forward.

"Anybody else want to fight?"

The other boys—three of them, whose names he couldn't really remember at the moment, not surprisingly, considering that he was dreaming—shook their heads and backed away from him.

Glen snarled.

They ran.

He smirked, watching them go. Not so tough now, were they? Not so ready to make fun of him because of his freaky disease, because his parents wouldn't let him play sports, because his eyes were two different colors, or because he was a second-grader. Uh-uh. They were chickenshit cowards, just like Mark had said.

A hand fell on his shoulder. A big hand.

Glen turned, and there was Mark smiling down at him.

"Nice," Glen's brother said, smacking his own fist into his other hand. "Show those chickenshit cowards a thing or two."

"Yeah."

"Let 'em know not to mess with a Callaway. Even one in second grade."

"Yeah."

Of course Mark wasn't in second grade, Mark was in fifth grade. Everyone at Marfa Elementary was scared of Mark. For real scared—not just because he was so big (bigger than anyone else in the school), but because he had no fear, not of anyone, not of anything. A couple weeks back, right before lunch, two kids from sixth grade had cornered him on the playground, gotten him down on the ground, started pounding on him. Glen heard what was happening, ran out of the school just in time to see Mark lying there on his back, not moving, the two sixth-graders just standing there laughing. Glen thought for a second that maybe his brother was dead or something.

Then Mark sat up all of a sudden, and then, like he wasn't hurt at all, got to his feet and started after the sixth-graders. They did it again—beat him down to the ground.

And again he got up. And this time, the sixth-graders weren't laughing.

And this time, Mark got in a few good shots of his own.

The sixth-graders tried to leave the playground. He went after them, and got them on the ground, first one, then the other. They didn't get up so easy.

Mark got suspended for a week.

Nobody messed with Mark anymore. Not after that. Whereas Glen . . .

Everybody messed with him. Because they knew he couldn't fight back. Except now they wouldn't mess with him. Now they'd know he could fight too, that there was a little bit of Mark Callaway in him as well.

"Guess I owe you an apology, son."

Glen turned again, to his right, and saw his dad ambling toward him, shaking his head, smiling to himself, and smoking a cigarette.

Smoking a cigarette.

Glen frowned.

His dad had quit smoking two months ago. Big celebration—Mom made a special dinner. Old family recipe. It didn't seem right for his dad to be smoking again after that.

Even if this was a dream.

"I guess I was wrong," Randall Callaway said, taking a big drag in, letting a big puff out. "I guess maybe I shouldn't have stopped you from fighting before. Doesn't look like you hurt yourself, and it seems like you made an important point with those boys." He nodded down the street, and Glen saw that Denton Young had gotten up off the ground and was running after his buddies, trying to get as far away as he could from the Callaway clan.

"Guess maybe your ma and I should rethink that whole thing about you playing sports too," Randall said.

"Really, Dad?"

"Would I lie to you?" Randall smiled and took another puff off his cigarette. The smoke blew right in Glen's face, and

Glen smelled it really strong, and he coughed, and he tossed in his sleep, and he began to wake up.

He still smelled the smoke, though.

That, he guessed—unlike his revenge on Denton Young, or his dad's decision to let Glen play sports—was for real.

Glen rolled over in his bed, not opening his eyes yet, a little bit angry, a little bit disappointed in his father.

*Dad said he was going to quit—he promised us, and he'd been true to that promise for the whole summer, and now . . .*

Glen decided he'd have to start hiding Dad's cigarettes again. Boy, did he get mad when Glen did that last time, said a seven-year-old kid had no idea how hard it was to be a grown-up, and the cigarettes helped him relax, and what was the harm. Well, Glen knew what the harm was, smoking killed you, and besides, Dad's "it helps me relax" excuse was the same one he'd used with the drinking, and how much easier was Dad to be around now that he'd quit the drinking? A lot, was how much.

*Boy,* Glen thought. *The smell was really strong now.* Dad was probably smoking right outside Glen's window. Which made sense—Glen's room was way in the back of the house, which was not just the family's home but their place of business, the Callaway Funeral Parlor. The business—the big room where they held the services, the little receiving room right off the front door, and the bigger sitting area on the other side of the entryway—occupied all of the ground floor, except for Glen's room. Down in the basement, they had the supply room, and the workroom, and the rest of the family—Glen's mom and dad, and Mark—lived on the second floor. Which was probably why Dad had come all the way down here to smoke: it was as far away from his bedroom as he could get. He was probably right outside the window lighting up, except, now that Glen thought about it, hadn't he shut that window before going to sleep tonight?

*Well, obviously not, genius, or you wouldn't be smelling smoke.*

*Get out of bed,* Glen told himself. *Go to the window. Don't make a big scene now, now is not the time for a big scene, just go tell Dad that if he has to smoke, not to do it so close to the house. How hard could that be?*

Glen rolled over and opened his eyes.

The smoke was everywhere—way, way too much of it to be coming from a cigarette.

He sat bolt upright in bed.

The smoke was coming from the hall, billowing into his room like steam out of a sauna.

The house was on fire.

Glen gasped in shock, and accidentally took in a big mouthful of that smoke. It caught in his throat, and he started coughing, hacking, just the way Dad used to. Smoker's cough. That's why you have to quit, Dad. That's why.

Glen couldn't catch his breath. He couldn't stop coughing, could barely even think over that sound and the roar of the fire coming from out in the hall. His eyes teared up.

*What do I do? Oh God, what do I do? I don't want to die.*

He was just a kid, kids weren't supposed to die like this except they did all the time, he'd seen it on the news more than one time, the last a couple weeks ago a girl up in Alpine had been in her bath by herself, hit her head on the faucet, and drowned while her mom was in the kitchen making cookies. It happened. But not to him. *Please, please, not to me I don't want to die what do I do I—*

*Don't panic. Get low to the ground. Find an exit.*

Glen heard Mrs. Prescott's voice in his head as clear as if she was standing right next to him, whispering into his ear. Mrs. Prescott was his second-grade teacher at Marfa Elementary, where they had to do fire drills once a month. They

weren't real serious fire drills (that's what Mark said anyway, in fifth grade they had serious fire drills), but they always made Glen a little nervous anyway. The big alarm bell
clanging, Mrs. Prescott leading them down the hall in single
file, being strict strict strict about the no-talking rule, and always asking one of them what they would do if they were in
a real fire. Sometimes the kid she asked had the answer,
sometimes he didn't, but Mrs. Prescott always repeated her
saying anyway.

*Don't panic. Get low to the ground. Find an exit.*

Don't panic. Okay, he was not panicking already, right? So
that one was taken care of. Number two . . .

Get low to the ground.

Glen rolled out of the bed, right onto the floor, slammed
into it so hard that the night table next to his bed bounced. His
vision blurred for a second. It didn't hurt a bit, though.

There was a dirty T-shirt on the floor next to him. He remembered something else from their fire drill all at once, and
picked up the shirt. He wrapped it around his mouth and nose
like an old cowboy bandit. It helped block the smoke, helped
him breathe a little better.

Okay. One and two done, now number three. Find an exit.

*The window,* Glen thought. The window behind him.

He started crawling toward it, dragging himself across the
floor, digging in with his elbows, pulling himself along, leaving dark red streaks in the dirty beige carpet as he moved.
Blood—so he had hurt himself falling off the bed. So what?
The sight of blood didn't bother him—he had a total disconnect from blood. A total disconnect from pain. Those things
were just words to him.

When Glen Callaway got hurt, he never felt anything.

He reached the window, grabbed the sill, and pulled himself up. The fire was in his room now, he could tell, because

the smoke was getting darker and thicker. It was getting hard to breathe again without coughing.

The window wouldn't budge. Glen would have to break it, Mom wouldn't like that but . . .

Glen's hands fell away from the window.

Mom. Dad. Mark.

Were they upstairs now? Were they trapped in the house?

He spun around, looking for the red lights of the alarm clock at his bed. Maybe Mom and Dad had gone out. They had started doing that these last couple weeks, going out like a couple, letting Mark and him stay home alone by themselves. His mom said Mark was old enough to be responsible. So if it was still early, maybe they were . . .

Glen's eyes found the clock on the wall. One-thirty.

His stomach sank—even if they'd gone out before, they were home now. Everyone was home. But maybe they'd gotten out already. Maybe they were waiting for him right outside his window. Maybe . . .

No. They hadn't gotten out. Glen knew that for a fact, no way any of them would have left him in here to burn up. They were upstairs. His heart sank.

It was up to him, Glen realized. He had to wake the others. He had to get them out.

*Don't panic. Stay low. Find an exit.*

"No," he whispered. "I have to find my family."

He turned around and looked into the heart of the fire.

It was in his room now—burning up the side of one wall, burning his posters. There went Nolan Ryan, and Danny White, and Darth Vader, and one leg of his dresser was on fire too, but more importantly the whole door frame was outlined in flames, and beyond it the main room where they held the services looked like one of those pictures of hell the deacon was always pointing out to them in Bible school, big red and orange tongues of fire.

Beyond the big room, he saw the staircase leading up to the second floor was burning too.

*Find an exit.*

*Shut up, Mrs. Prescott,* Glen thought to himself. *Just shut up.*

He took a deep breath and ran.

Straight through the door, straight through the main room, past the burning old upright piano, the stacks of folding wooden chairs that were now stacks of flame, past the bookcases full of songbooks and Bibles, and out into the hallway to the base of the stairs and—

He looked down at his right arm.

His pajamas were on fire. Heck, his pajamas were just about gone, he was really the one on fire. The skin was singed, and black. Glen, of course, didn't feel a thing.

Glen had a disease—doctors had a fancy name for it, he couldn't remember that name now but what it meant was he couldn't feel pain. Even at this moment, with his arm on fire, he couldn't feel anything. He could sure smell it though.

His stomach rolled over. Don't think about it, Glen told himself. Don't think about—

He slapped at his right arm with his left hand, trying to put out the flame. The burned skin slid off like the crusted-over cheese on pizza and underneath—

Glen's stomach heaved, and he ripped the T-shirt away from his face before he threw up on the floor.

His head was spinning. His throat was raw. He had to sit down for a second.

*Don't panic. Stay low. Find an exit.*

Maybe Mrs. Prescott was right.

*The front door,* he thought, and lifted his head, and blinked, and blinked again to clear his vision, the smoke was pretty bad down here now, and turned to his left—

And there it was. The front door, not ten feet away from him. Standing wide open.

*Why? Why was the front door open?*

He tried to think of a reason, and failed. He looked straight ahead, at flaming drywall. He looked to his right, at the staircase, which was now a wall of flame.

He started to cry.

"Mom," he whispered. "Dad."

He saw the flames around him and the smoke spreading, and he knew it was supposed to hurt, but it didn't. He felt himself coughing and struggling, but there was no pain. He felt at peace there, at home among the devastation.

His vision blurred again, and all at once, he was lying on the floor, looking up at the stairs, and then the stairs were gone, faded to black, and then the wall in front of him started to fade too, and he turned his head and looked down the hall, at the front door, his exit, but he wasn't going to make it. None of them were. The fire was going to get them all.

At that second, he heard his mom's voice in his head.

"Fire," she said. "The Kane family curse."

*No,* Glen thought. That was crazy talk. And yet . . .

Here he was, dying, the fire raging around him.

Glen saw the front door before him again, wide open, and tried one last time to get up. He failed.

He burned.


By the time the volunteer firefighters arrived from the communities surrounding Marfa, the building was completely engulfed, fire shooting angrily from the roof of the structure.

The men quickly sprang into action, whipping the hose off the truck and turning it on the house. For the next hour, they struggled to tame the fire as the dry, windy night fought for control of the moment.

As the blaze at the front of the home died down, two firemen waded through the frame and through a window into what used to be the main parlor. The burned remains of the piano faced a barely touched folding chair. The corner bookcase was scarred black, its contents reduced to dusty ash among scorched hardcovers. The ceiling drywall had splashed across the staircase.

At the bottom of the stairs, a body lay across the floor.

The firemen immediately ran toward the limp form before them. One whipped off his glove and felt for a pulse, but there was none to be found. The fireman scooped up the victim and carried him outdoors to where the EMT techs were waiting with a gurney.

"Christ. It's a kid." Michael Kemp was in his first month on the job as an EMT. In the previous twenty-three days that comprised his career, he had seen nothing more than a few basic cuts and one broken knuckle. Just a few hours ago, Kemp's colleagues were telling him that Sundays were historically the least active day of the week, as most people were either at church or at home. And now this Sunday was turning into the worst day anyone had seen in Marfa in over a decade.

Kemp bent over the child's form—it was a boy. A very, very badly burned boy.

He looked at the boy's face. It was untouched by soot, but some of the hair was singed off the top of his scalp, and there was severe blistering on his right cheek and down his neck. His torso seemed untouched by the fire, but his right arm, and the whole lower half of his body . . .

Kemp's stomach turned. It was one thing to see such damage on a television screen or in a book; on a child it was downright grotesque.

The EMT collected himself and felt for a pulse even though one of the firemen had already done it. There was none. He put his mouth to the boy's lips and administered CPR, then went back to searching for a pulse. Nothing again. He waited a few moments and repeated the routine.

"Hey." His partner put a hand on Kemp's shoulder. "Give it up, rook. The kid's gone."

Kemp ignored him, and kept working.

After a third attempt at CPR, he put his fingers to the boy's neck. Still cold.

Damn it.

Kemp sighed, and pushed away from the body.

He clasped his hands together and said a little prayer for the boy, at the same time apologizing to the Lord for missing church earlier in the day.

Then he stood up.

A crowd had gathered around Kemp while he worked; he hadn't noticed. His partner and half a dozen firemen.

"Kid was too badly burned," Kemp said. "He didn't make it."

The firemen turned away. His partner stepped up next to him.

"Not your fault, rook. No one was going to make it out of there. Not in the dead of night."

"Not with all the chemicals in that place." That from one of the firefighters, who stepped forward now and nodded in the direction of the still-smoldering building. "It was a funeral home—they got a ton of chemicals in there. All those flammables, wood-frame house, dry night like this . . . place probably went up in five minutes, if that. We're just lucky we got here in time to stop it."

"Yeah." Kemp shrugged. "I guess. Lucky."

He watched the firemen work for a few minutes, listened to them talk about what might have started the fire. Arson, one said. Another one said that that was stupid—who would want to burn up a funeral home? Kemp didn't care about how it started—he just wished he could have saved that kid.

He turned back to his partner then.

"Let's get back on the road, all right? The night's not getting any . . ."

Kemp's voice trailed off. His partner was staring in the direction opposite the house, his jaw slightly agape, his eyes wide.

Kemp followed his gaze, and felt his own jaw drop open in disbelief.

The kid who'd been lying flat on the gurney a moment ago, dead to the world, was now sitting up, staring at the two of them.

Kemp made a noise, shook his head.

"No," he said. "That's not possible."

The kid blinked. For the first time, Kemp noticed that the kid had two different colored eyes, one brown, one blue.

"There was no pulse. The kid was dead, I swear." He turned to his partner. "The kid was dead."

"Maybe he was." Kemp's partner shook his head as if to clear away the last of his disbelief. "Not anymore, though.

# chapter one

Glen Callaway was unconscious for six weeks.

The EMTs had gotten him from Marfa to Big Bend Regional Hospital in Alpine in fifteen minutes, sirens wailing the whole way down 90, but it took the ER doc there even less time than that to realize he was overmatched, that this kid needed specialized treatment. Before dawn, Glen was in San Antonio, choppered in to the burn center at Fort Sam Houston, where doctors performed the first of what would eventually be a half dozen skin grafts, harvesting flesh from the back of his legs, his buttocks, even the bottoms of his feet to replace what the fire had burned away. Glen knew nothing of his travels, the operations, his surroundings, or the attention he drew nationwide for his miraculous recovery. He was drugged the whole time, while his body healed. Drugged, unconscious.

Dreaming.

He opened his eyes to the sight of his dad, leaning over him, brushing the hair back from his eyes.

"Hey, buddy. How you doing?"

Glen shrugged. "Okay, I guess."

He was four years old again, lying in bed, in Big Bend Regional, where he'd just spent the night after having a day full of tests, of doctors drawing blood and poking him with needles and shaking their heads. At least it was over now.

Not that his parents looked any less worried. Especially

his mom, who was sitting on the edge of the bed, clasping her hands together, rocking slowly back and forth. She looked real upset. Glen had told her that no matter what the doctors said he felt fine, but that hadn't seemed to calm her any.

"You understand what the doctors were telling you?" his dad asked. "What they were talking about?"

Glen nodded. "Yes, sir. I do understand."

"They call it HSAN. That stands for Hereditary Sensory and Autonomic Neuropathy. It means you can't feel any pain."

"I know, Dad."

"Which means you have to be very, very careful about what you do. Pain is—"

"I remember," he interrupted. "Pain is the body's warning mechanism. I have to watch what I'm doing all the time, I have to be careful not to get into fights or play sports or do any of those kinds of things because since I can't feel pain I'll never notice things like cuts or bruises or broken bones."

His dad managed a smile. "That's right, son. That's right exactly."

Glen nodded, wondering how he'd known all that. All those big words. He was only four years old.

It was almost as if he'd had this conversation before.

"You can bet I'll be careful, sir. I surely will."

"This is all my fault," his mom said.

"Now don't start in with your crazy talk, Susanna."

"It's not crazy," she said. "Not crazy at all. My father. His father before him. My cousins. My aunt, my uncle, all the way back to—"

"Susanna Kane," his dad said sharply. "How many times have I asked you not to talk like that in front of the boys? Those ideas—"

"They got a right to know," his mom said firmly.

"Susanna Kane—"

"She's right, Dad."

Glen looked up and saw his brother, Mark, standing at the door.

"We got a right to know, me and Glen. We got the blood in us too, after all. Maybe we got the curse too. Just like all the people in here."

Mark held up a book before him then, a big brown scrapbook that Glen recognized instantly. The Kane family scrapbook. Kane was his mom's maiden name (that was even what everyone still called her most of the time, not just Susanna, but Susanna Kane), and the book traced her family's history all the way back to Pilgrim times. She'd been putting it together over the last few years, it had become—what was that word Dad had used?—an obsession of hers ever since . . .

Ever since he was born, Glen realized.

Now how did he know that?

"There's no such thing as a curse," his dad said. "And now I don't want to hear any more about it."

"But, Glen," his mom began. "What about this with Glen?"

"What about it?" his dad asked. "It's genetics, that's all."

"Kane family genetics," Mark said. Dad glared at him. Lately, Mark seemed just about as interested in the Kane family as his mom. He spent a lot of time looking at the scrapbook, at all the pictures and the papers Mom kept with it. He spent more time with that book than his schoolwork, in fact, that's what Dad was always saying. Too much time. Wasn't even getting outside enough to play. He was getting pale. In fact . . .

Glen looked up at his parents and his brother then, suddenly noticing how pale they all looked, how white their skin was, almost waxy-looking, like they weren't real, like—

A terrible feeling ran through him then, and he shivered.

"Please," Glen said in a small voice. "Let's not talk about the curse."

"That's right. That's my boy." His dad put a hand on Glen's shoulder. "There ain't nothin' magical about this condition you have, this HSAN. Long as you're careful, you'll be fine."

Glen nodded.

"No fightin'," his dad said.

"I got that."

"No sports."

"Yes, sir."

"And stay out of the sun. You don't want to burn. That could be dangerous. Very, very dangerous. Burning. You hear me?"

"Yes, Dad," Glen said. "I hear you."

"Because you could crisp right up, and never know it. Never feel a thing."

Randall raised his hand then, and took a drag off his cigarette.

All at once—like magic, Glen thought—a nurse appeared behind him.

"Sir, there's no smoking in here."

"No smoking?" His dad frowned. "Oh. Right. Sorry."

He dropped the cigarette on the floor. Glen watched it land, and then, as if in slow motion, bounce once, and then again before finally coming to rest next to the trailing edge of his blanket.

The edge of the cloth glowed red and began to smoke.

"Oh, no," Glen whispered. He looked up at his mom and dad. "The bed—"

"Oh, my. Look at that." The nurse put her hands on her hips and shook her head. "Your bed's on fire, I'm afraid."

His mom's eyes widened. "I knew it. You see, Randall? You

see what I mean? Come on." She stood and grabbed hold of Glen's hand. "We'd better get going."

"Well, shoot." His dad put his hands on his hips and frowned. "I guess you're right, Susanna Kane. We better get going. We better run, in fact."

Glen started to get out of bed. The nurse pushed him back down.

"No, you don't. We got some more tests to do."

"Please let me go," Glen said. "Please."

The nurse shook her head. "I'm sorry, son."

"Glen, come on!" Mark stood at the door to the hall, holding it open. As Glen watched, his dad walked through that door and disappeared.

"Dad!"

"Come on, Glen," Mark yelled. "I can't hold this door open forever!"

Glen tried again to get up. The nurse, again, pushed him back down.

His hand slipped free from his mom's.

"Oh, Glen." His mom was crying. "I wish you would come with us."

Glen started crying too.

"I'm coming, Mom! Don't leave without me."

But she was going. She was gone, out the door after his dad. With a last look back at Glen, Mark followed.

"Wait!"

Glen climbed out of bed.

The nurse stood in front of him, blocking his way.

He made a fist at her. She shook her head.

"You heard your dad, Glen. No fighting."

"But—"

"No fighting."

He shoved past her. Except now the room was so filled with

smoke, he couldn't see the door. He couldn't even see past his own hand now. He stumbled, first in one direction, then the other, and then all of a sudden . . .

He looked up, and saw he was standing at the foot of a stairway—the stairway at his house, back in Marfa. It wasn't the hospital room on fire, he realized then. It was his house.

And with that, he remembered it all, and began to scream.

At the nurse's station, in the burn unit at Fort Sam Houston, a machine started beeping. A nurse set down her *Vogue* magazine, and frowned. The boy in room 41 was moving again.

She hurried down the long hall into his room. Quickly, she adjusted the sedative drip so the boy would remain unconscious—so that his body could concentrate on healing. The doctors had scheduled him for another skin graft tomorrow as well—he'd need all his strength for that.

She moved closer to the bed, and saw the boy's hair had fallen into his eyes. She brushed it back. Thank God for small favors—at least the burns on his face were relatively minor. With any luck, they'd fade after time. He'd be able to live a relatively normal life—assuming he survived the next few weeks here. Assuming anyone could live a relatively normal life after their whole family had been killed.

"Poor kid," she whispered.

Glen rolled over in his sleep, and reached out toward the sound of her voice.

His mom was talking.

Glen could hear her speak, hear her voice coming through the door to the funeral parlor office, which he was standing right in front of. The question was, though, was she with a client? Because if she was with a client, he wasn't supposed to interrupt her. Talking with clients was serious business. Funerals (and dead people, for that matter) were very serious business indeed. But Glen wanted to tell her what had happened today at school, his first day of second grade; he had made a friend, a boy named Brian Erben, who lived just five minutes down the road and had already invited him over to play with his racing set. If his mom wasn't with a client, she could call Brian's folks and set it up, right now. This afternoon.

Glen took a step closer to the door and pressed his ear up against it.

His mom was laughing. His mom did not laugh when she was with clients. It sounded more like she was talking to a friend. Maybe Mrs. Keith, or Mrs. Larrabee, or . . .

No. It was a man, Glen heard his voice now. Dad. It had to be Dad. Glen smiled. Dad would be glad to hear about Brian too. Dad was always worried about Glen being able to make friends because he couldn't do sports or run around outside. And here it was, first day of school, and he'd made a friend already. Dad would probably drive him right over.

His mom laughed again. More of a giggle than a laugh.

Boy. Everyone was in a good mood. This was going to be great.

Glen turned the knob and pushed the door open without knocking.

The laughter stopped.

His mom was sitting on the couch opposite the desk. There was a man sitting next to her. The man had a hand on her knee.

The man was not his dad.

The man was Paul Grimm.

Grimm was a stocky little man with black hair and a mustache who worked in the funeral parlor with Glen's parents. He was the embalmer. Played around with all the dead bodies, all the chemicals in the basement. He was always trying to be nice to Glen, for some reason, Glen had no idea why. He babysat for Glen once in a while, even, when his parents had to go out. Glen always went to sleep early rather than spend time with the man.

His mom stood up quickly. Her face was a little red.

"Glen Jacob Callaway. When a door is closed, what do we do?"

"Sorry."

"What do we do?"

"Knock."

"That's right, we knock." His mom ran her hands over the front of her dress, smoothing it out. "What if I was in here with a client, Glen? What if—"

"I said I was sorry."

"That's all right. No harm done." Grimm stood up himself. "How are you, Glen? Good to see you again. You remember me, right? Paul Grimm."

"Yeah," Glen said. "I remember you."

Grimm smiled. "Good. I'm glad. So how was your school today? Big day, right? Your first day of, uh, what? First grade?"

"Second."

"Second. My, my. My, my, my. You are growing up fast. Getting to be a big kid."

Glen rolled his eyes; he hated when grown-ups talked to him like that.

His mom saw. She came around the coffee table in front of the couch, shaking her head.

"Now, Glen. You be nice to Mr. Grimm, please."

"Paul. I want the boy to call me Paul, Susanna," Grimm said, all at once sounding very serious. "You remember—like we talked about?"

"That's right. I'm sorry. Call him Paul," his mom said, putting her hands on Glen's shoulders. "You think you can do that, Glen?"

"Yes, ma'am." He looked at Grimm again. "Paul."

"That's right. That's good." Grimm looked happy now. "You and me ought to be on a first-name basis, Glen. Me working here and all. We're kind of like family, don't you think?"

His mom's hands tightened on Glen's shoulders for a second.

Glen was about to ask her to ease up when his eyes fell on the coffee table in front of the couch. There were papers spread out all over it—old-looking papers. Underneath those papers, the edge of a book peeked out. A big, brown, oversize book.

The Kane family scrapbook.

Grimm's eyes followed his. The man bent down and grabbed up a handful of those papers.

"And speaking of family—"

He straightened the papers into a stack, held the stack out to Glen.

"You might be interested in these, son."

"Oh, yes, Glen," his mom said. "I think you'd be very interested in them. They're very interesting. Look them over. That's what Paul and I were doing when you came in, honey. Looking over those papers."

Grimm smiled again. "Yes, sir. That's what we were doing, all right."

"What are they?" Glen asked.

"Copies of some things I found the other day—while I was up at Sul Ross. The university. Some information about your family, Glen. The Kanes."

"My name is Callaway," Glen said.

"Yes. It is, isn't it?" Grimm smiled. "But the name doesn't really matter, does it, Glen? Blood is what's important. Believe me, I ought to know. Considering my line of work."

"Oh, yes," his mom said from behind him. "Blood is what matters."

"The blood running through your veins, Glen," Grimm said. "Your family's blood. That's what these papers are all about, Glen. Family."

The man thrust the sheaf of papers into Glen's face.

"Go on. Take a look."

Glen couldn't help it. He glanced at the top sheet of paper. There were just two words on it.

You're Dreaming

A chill ran down his spine.

"Oh, no," he said.

Grimm nodded. "Oh, yes."

Glen spun around quickly.

His mom was gone.

Glen turned around again.

The writing on the paper had changed.

She's Dead

Grimm laughed. Glen stumbled backward, felt the office door behind him. It was hot to the touch. He smelled smoke.

He remembered everything.

"Mom," he croaked. "Dad. Mark."

Grimm was smiling, holding the paper up in one hand and pointing to it with the other.

Dead Dead Dead All Dead

Grimm's gaze bore into his. The man's eyes glittered.

"Didn't I tell you, Glen? Didn't I tell you the papers were

all about your family? Now you know everything you need to, isn't that right? About your family?"

"No," Glen said.

"Yes." Grimm smiled again. "They're dead, Glen. Dead and gone. It's just you and me now, son. I'm the closest thing to family you got left."

The man grabbed his arm.

Glen struggled as hard as he could, trying to break free.

He thrashed about so violently during what was supposed to be the fifth and final operation that he ripped away half the evening's work, ripped off a sheet of skin the size of a shirt pocket from his right arm, and made a sixth operation necessary. The nurses were given a new sedative and new instructions: make certain the boy doesn't get anywhere close to consciousness.

He didn't.

Glen had a good long sleep.

When he opened his eyes, he was lying on the floor of his house, next to the stairs. The fire was out.

The front door was still open.

He heard voices outside—strangers. A lot of strangers. He glimpsed firefighters through the open door. Footsteps sounded on the second floor above him, came running down the stairs. Mark.

His brother ran right past him, and out through the front door.

"Mark!" Glen called. "Mark, wait for me!"

Glen got to his feet and ran after him.

Just outside the door, a young man in an EMT uniform grabbed his arm. "Hey, buddy. Where you think you're going?"

"My brother."

"No, no. Come on over here and lie down on this gurney. You're dead."

"I'm not." Glen pulled away from the man and took off again.

Ahead of him, Mark was running too. And he was faster. Mark was always faster. Bigger, stronger. Better. Mark was getting away from him. Leaving him behind.

*No,* Glen thought. He's all that I have left.

"Mark!"

Tumbleweeds blew across the road, blew in front of Glen's face, obscured his vision. He shoved them out of the way with his arms, choking on the dust again, the dust and the smoke.

"Mark!" Glen yelled. "Mark! Come back!"

Paul Grimm stepped out into the road, in front of him.

"Hey, Glen. Long time no see."

"Get out of my way," Glen said.

"Now hold on a minute, son." Grimm shook his head and turned, raised a hand to his brow to shield his eyes from the dust. "Where you going?"

"My brother," Glen said, pointing down the road. "Mark. He went that way."

Grimm shook his head. "Don't think that's possible, Glen. Don't you remember?"

The man held up a piece of paper then.

Dead Dead Dead All Dead

"It is possible. It is!" Glen said, trying to shove past him. Grimm grabbed on to his arm, and held tight.

"All right, all right, simmer down. I got my car over there—we'll go look for him. Me and you. How's that sound?"

Glen looked up at Grimm. The man was smiling.

"Doesn't sound good," Glen said, and pushed Grimm away. The man's laughter followed him as he ran, heading down 17 again, running right down the middle of the road, right along the yellow line, scanning the horizon for any sign of his brother. But all he saw was scrub, the occasional mesquite tree, a row of purple mountains far, far in the distance. Where had Mark gone? He couldn't have just disappeared.

Glen's eyes fell on a signpost at the edge of the road, a few hundred yards ahead of him. He walked up to it, and around it, read the words in big black letters on the front.

Welcome to
MARFA, TEXAS

And in smaller letters underneath:

Home of the World-Famous Marfa Lights
*Giant* filmed here, 1951–1952

*Giant*. That was part of the Kane family curse too. Part of the scrapbook. There was an article in it about the making of the movie, an article about his grandpa, Robert Kane, who Glen had never met, how he'd had been hired on by the company that made the film as their local guide to Marfa. How Robert Kane got to be friends with the stars of that movie, one star in particular, who there was another article about, a star who died young, died in a terrible car accident right after he made the film . . .

Glen remembered the first time he'd seen those articles now, that day when he'd found his mom and Paul Grimm in the office. Paul Grimm had found those articles for his mom up at Sul Ross, he'd been researching the curse for her, but none of that was important right now, what was important was finding his brother.

He cupped his hands together and yelled.

"Mark! Mark, where are you?"

There was no reply.

He turned and yelled again and again, but there was nothing, and just as he was about to give up, he heard a noise behind him and turned, and zooming up the road next to him was a sports car, and in it was a young man whose face looked awfully familiar and the man smiled and gave Glen a big thumbs-up and yelled . . .

"What curse?"

And just as he did, the car flipped over and exploded into flames.

Glen tried to avoid the flames, but they started chasing him, chasing him back down the road toward Paul Grimm, who was waiting for him with open arms and smiling, and so Glen turned and let the fire catch him.

He didn't feel a thing, of course.

He just watched the fire as it consumed every inch of his body. It was everywhere he looked, on his arms, his legs, climbing up his stomach, burning him, burning his clothes, orange and red fire, yellow and gold fire, fire so bright its image was seared into his brain.

The image stayed with him a long time, till darkness took its place and swallowed him whole.

The sixth operation was a success, but it was two more weeks before the grafts were healed enough to move Glen. No rush this time, so they sent him in an ambulance back to Big Bend in Alpine. A slow-moving ambulance—the driver had instructions to keep it down to fifty-five on the highway.

"So you don't tear the skin and we have to operate all over

again," one of the doctors said. The driver nodded dutifully, but of course, once out on the highway, pushed it up to seventy without a thought until he hit the outskirts of town and came across the sign that reminded him that *Giant* had been filmed in Marfa, which reminded him of James Dean, who had died shortly after making the movie in a car crash, so he eased off on the gas a little.

Made him think of something else too, something a friend of his, a nurse down in Marfa, had told him about Dean's death. That it was because the actor had been friends with one of the locals, some family whose name escaped him at the moment, a family his friend had heard was cursed or something. Some sort of nonsense like that.

# chapter two

Glen blinked and opened his eyes.

It was dark—nighttime. He was in bed. Not his bed—somewhere else. A hospital. There were half a dozen machines at his side, blinking flashing lights too numerous to count or decipher their meaning. He tried to sit up, and couldn't. His arms and legs were restrained, held in place at his sides by strong-looking straps. There were tubes, too, running in and out of his body all over the place. His throat was as dry as the desert, and he had a terrible taste in his mouth, and worst of all—

He was all alone. Not just tonight, but forever. For the rest of his life. His parents, his brother . . . they were gone. Dead, dead, dead, all dead. The curse.

His mom had been right after all.

He blinked again, and tried not to cry.

For days, the story of the fire was repeated before him as he rested in his hospital bed, becoming part of his history like the oxygen mask over his face and antibiotics tubes hooked into his veins. Like the lights that were shined into his eyes to see if his vision was damaged. They were sad eyes now, and every time someone would approach the room to visit, they would immediately shut. The nurses and doctors were always poking and prodding, and Glen hoped that maybe, if he kept his eyes closed, they would just go away.

His room was usually bathed in silence, the quiet broken only by a nurse or doctor making rounds, checking in on him, on the machines attached to his body. Glen was covered in gauze and pads; even more than usual, he felt completely shut off from the outside world, as if what was real, what was important, were the things happening in his mind. His memories of the life he used to have.

A week or so into his stay, they moved him from the intensive care ward into the children's wing. A private room, but it didn't take long before the other kids started peering in on him, before they started tiptoeing into his room as he pretended to sleep.

"He don't look dead," one said.

"But he was. I heard the doctor talking about it—they said when they found him, he was dead," another said.

"So how come he's alive now?" the first asked.

"Well, that's the question, ain't it? Hey, you." Whoever it was at his side nudged Glen.

Glen didn't respond. He was wondering the same thing: Why was he alive? What was the point of it, anyway?

"Hey, you. You dead, or what?" The kid nudged him again, harder, hard enough that Glen moved.

All at once, there was a buzzing sound, and then one of the machines next to him went off like an alarm clock.

"Run!" one of the kids yelled. Glen opened his eyes just in time to see them disappear out the door, and a nurse come in.

He closed his eyes quickly before she could see he was awake.

The days turned into weeks. They loosened the restraints on his arms and legs. He got solid food; he was able to sit up in bed and start to walk.

The kids in the ward started coming around more often. They tried to make friends at first, but he didn't want friends.

Then the doctors took the bandages off his face, and the kids stopped being nice to him.

The doctors had done their best—they'd managed to reconstruct everything that had been scarred or deformed by the flames. But his skin was discolored—a big blotch of reddish purple on the right side of his cheek, another on his forehead. He was too sad to even cry the first time he saw himself in the mirror. He didn't know what to do.

The other kids did.

They started calling him names—freak, lobster-boy, the mummy. The comments got crueler and crueler, probably because he didn't respond to any of them. They were testing him.

When one boy said that Glen was such a freak he'd probably lit the fire himself, they found his limits.

He drew his fist back without thinking, for once ("No fighting, son, no fighting"), and hit the kid square in the mouth. There was blood right away.

There was a lot of yelling later.

Grown-ups yelling at each other, parents cursing out nurses, nurses cursing right back, a lot of kids crying. Nobody was happy, especially Glen's doctors. He'd torn the skin grafts again.

The next day, they moved Glen from the children's wing into one of the main wards.

That night he started getting phone calls.

At first he didn't answer. Let it ring five, six, seven, eight times, however long it took for the caller to hang up. Glen didn't want to talk to anyone. But whoever was calling, it turned out, sure wanted to talk to him. The phone rang every hour, almost on the hour, starting at ten A.M.

At three o'clock in the afternoon, on the third day of those calls, Glen finally answered one.

"Hello?" he said.

He heard breathing on the line. A man's breathing, it sounded like. He couldn't be sure.

"Who is it? Who's there?"

More breathing, then all at once the caller hung up.

*That was weird,* Glen thought, staring at the phone in his hand. They hung up as soon as they heard my voice. Like they were just testing to see if I was here. If I was alive.

He was pondering what that could mean when someone rapped on the door, and it swung partway open.

"Hello? Are you Glen Callaway?"

The someone was a woman—with big blond hair and an even bigger smile. She was, he realized, the first person he'd seen in a while who hadn't reacted to his appearance by looking away, even if only for a second.

Despite that, Glen wasn't going to answer her. He hadn't spoken to anyone in the hospital in a few days. But there was something about her smile . . .

She reminded him, he realized, of his mother. Just a little bit.

"Yeah. I'm Glen."

"I'm Melissa Vick, Glen." The smile got bigger still. "Can I come in?"

He shrugged. "Okay."

She shut the door behind her.

"Who was that on the phone?"

He realized he was still holding the receiver in his hand. "I don't know. Nobody, I guess. They hung up as soon as I answered."

"Huh. You don't say. Why would they do that?" The woman was carrying a thick file folder in her arms. Glen saw his name printed on the outside of it.

"I don't know."

"Well, let me know if it happens again. You certainly don't need anybody bothering you right now, do you?"

"No. I guess not."

She brought a chair up close to the bed now and sat down next to him.

"So," she said, opening the folder in her lap, "you feeling better these days, Glen?"

"I guess." He frowned. "Are you a nurse or something?"

"No, sweetie, I'm not a nurse. I'm a social worker."

"What does that mean?"

"Well, what that means is that I'm going to be here to look out for you. To help you."

"Help me do what?"

She closed the folder and laid her hands on top of it.

"Help you deal with what happened. With the accident," she said softly. "Help you move forward with your life."

He didn't know what to say to that. Move forward? Move forward to what?

"Of course we don't have to talk about any of this right now. I just wanted to meet you, now that the doctors say you're—"

"What's there to talk about?" he interrupted. "Everybody's dead, aren't they?"

Her eyes widened slightly. She took a minute before responding.

"Not everybody, Glen. You're here."

For some reason, he was getting angry.

"Yeah. BFD."

"Glen. That's not called for." She put on a disapproving expression that reminded him of his mom even more, the way she looked at him or his brother when they misbehaved, or talked out of turn, or were disrespectful. And thinking of his mom . . . all the anger, all at once, just sapped right out of him.

He sighed.

"I'm sorry," he said.

"I understand." She tried smiling again; this time, he saw sadness behind her expression. "Well, we have some time to think about things. Talk over your options. The doctors said it will be a few more weeks before you can leave." She leaned over and touched his arm lightly. "Are you in a lot of pain, honey?"

"No." Glen shook his head. "I don't feel a thing."

Out in the hall, Melissa Vick brushed the tears from her eyes.

The whole situation was so sad; no, beyond sad, it was tragic.

The fire had taken everything from the boy. He was truly all alone in the world—there were no relatives at all on his mother's side, and only a great-aunt on his father's, ninety-two years old and in a nursing home. She was going to have to find this boy a whole new family.

Not for the first time, Melissa thanked God for the fortune he'd brought her way, her own family; her husband, Jarvis; her daughter, Katie; her mother back in Kansas City—why, if she lost any of them, she had no idea what she would ever do. She couldn't imagine how Glen felt.

Down the hall, the nurses were changing shifts. Melissa saw one she knew—Beverly Cutler, who went to the Church of the Redeemer on King Street with her—and caught the woman two strides from the elevator.

"Beverly."

"Melissa. How are you?"

"Well." She shook her head. "I'm fine. But that poor boy back there . . ."

"Oh." Beverly nodded. "The Callaway boy. That is a tragic situation. Morbid, too, if you ask me."

Melissa frowned. "Morbid. What do you mean?"

"Well . . ." Beverly glanced around quickly, and then drew Melissa closer. "See . . . the police were in here the other day."

"The police?"

"Shhh." Beverly looked around again. "Yes, the police. Because the house was also the parent's business, you know, the funeral home . . ."

"Right." Melissa hadn't made that connection until now. Callaway Funeral Parlor. Glen Callaway.

"Well, when the building burned down," Beverly continued, "the police went in there and found about ten bodies, I guess."

Melissa's eyes widened. "Ten? I don't understand. There's the parents, and the brother—who else?"

"They're not sure."

"I still don't understand."

Beverly looked up and down the hall once again, then leaned closer.

"They found the parents upstairs. But downstairs, in the basement? Where they worked on all the funeral stuff? They found a whole bunch of dead bodies—folks that were dead before the fire started. And they were all . . . " Beverly made a face. "Anyway, they're having trouble identifying 'em all, on account of it seems maybe the funeral parlor was doing some illegal business. Business with folks on the other side of the border."

"Oh, Lord," Melissa said again.

"Exactly. So they can't even make positive IDs."

"Oh, my. What a mess."

"That's what I mean. Morbid."

"Well, still. My heart goes out to that poor boy. To lose your whole family just like that, your parents and your brother . . . "

Melissa's voice trailed off as all at once, she thought of something.

"Wait a minute—you said the parents were upstairs and the clients were downstairs, but what about the brother?"

"Seems like he was down in the basement too—what on earth for, they have no idea. 'Cause one of the bodies they found was a boy, but there ain't a lot left to . . . well, you know, be certain who. They're talking about sendin' the remains to Austin for a definite ID, but that's gonna cost some money too. And the council might not go for it."

Melissa nodded a final, pained thank-you for the information and made her way to the parking lot. Though she had another appointment scheduled for later in the day, she decided she was going to cancel it. Right now, family seemed a little more important. She wanted to go home and hug her daughter. And after that . . .

She wanted to start work on finding Glen Callaway a place in this world.

# chapter
## three

Melissa Vick became an everyday visitor to Glen's room, sometimes coming in the morning before starting her day, sometimes coming at night, on her way home. She wanted to establish a routine, she wanted to establish a rapport, she wanted Glen to see her as a friend.

He was a hard nut to crack.

She left him books, she left him toys, she tried to watch TV with him. She prodded him with questions about school, about his likes, his dislikes, what he might want to do once he got out of the hospital. He was distant and detached—she might as well have been talking to herself for all the information she got out of him. The boy had a lot on his mind, though, she could see that in his eyes, even if he wasn't sharing it with her, or anyone else. He was living in his mind, she could see, in his own private little heaven—or, more likely, hell.

When the doctors or nurses would come into his room to poke and prod him for tests or shots, he didn't blink. Whether they stuck him with a needle, performed scar massages on his injured body, or forced him through rehabilitation, he went through it all with a stoic face. He slept through treatments that made grown adults whimper in agony.

Of course his condition—the HSAN—was part of that. But still . . . he was a seven-year-old kid, just about the same age as her Katie. Even if she couldn't have felt a thing, Katie would have been scared. Might have cried, might not have, but she sure would have been curious. She would have had a lot of questions for the doctors, would have gotten herself underfoot, made friends with everyone. That was Katie's gift, making friends. She had a knack for it. She was just a smiling little girl, smiling all the time, the light of Melissa's life. The light of anyone's life, once they got to know her, if Melissa did say so herself. But then, she was a little biased.

Since Glen wouldn't talk to her, she went over to Marfa Elementary and spent some time with his teacher. Mrs. Prescott painted a picture of him as a shy but bright boy, capable of good grades but more prone to receiving average ones. A loner. Not at all like his older brother, the teacher said.

Mark Callaway was smart and strong, already a head taller than most in his grade, and the top athlete in his class. Full of himself too, Mrs. Prescott said. Maybe a little too full of himself, sometimes, but still . . . Mark had a real bright future, in her opinion. What happened to him . . .

"A shame," the teacher said. A terrible, terrible shame.

Melissa tried to steer the conversation back to Glen. Mrs. Prescott went reluctantly, talking about the younger brother in terms of the older one. Glen had none of the self-assurance that was Mark's hallmark at such an early age. Rather, it seemed that Glen fed off his brother, drawing strength from his affiliation with him. When they were together, Glen seemed more outgoing and social; when they were apart, he would retreat into himself.

Mrs. Prescott was no help.

Melissa got the class list from her and called the other parents, trying to find children who might have been friendly with Glen. She had the idea if she could get one or two of them to visit him in the hospital, the boy might open up to her a little. Apparently, though, Glen had no close friends at school. Nobody had anything bad to say about him, everyone was sorry for what had happened, but they just didn't see how they could help.

Melissa hung up the phone after one such call, and sighed. What could she do? She had to get to know the boy. She had to understand him better before she could think about placing him with a new family, about putting him up for adoption. And he was a good kid inside, she knew that. Even though he was so closed off, he was unfailingly polite, always did what people asked him without a word of complaint. She imagined him as a good son and a good sibling, the type of child who always did what he was told, obeyed his parents and teachers. Just like her Katie.

It was at that moment, standing in the hallway, that Melissa got an idea.

"So, honey, I was wondering," she said over dinner that night, toying with a forkful of her mashed potatoes. "Do you think you might want to help me with my work a little tomorrow?"

Katie's eyes lit up, and she leaned forward in her chair excitedly. "Me? Help you? Oh, Mama, could I?"

"I think maybe you could. See, there's this boy at the hospital—he's about your age—and I just have the feeling that he needs someone to talk to real bad."

"Well . . . isn't that what you do, Mama?"

"I do. I try to do that, but sometimes . . . people—especially children—they don't want to talk to a grown-up."

"So you think he'll talk to me?"

"Well, he might."

"Okay. I'll do it." She frowned and sat back in her chair, and got such a serious expression on her face that she looked all at once ten years older, and Melissa could see traces of the beautiful young woman she was going to grow up to be.

"But you have to tell me what to do, Mama. You have to be my coach, because I don't know what the right things will be to say."

"There is no right thing, honey. You just have to try and get him to talk to you."

"Okay." Her daughter frowned a minute, thinking. "I know. I'll bring in my dolls. We'll play with them together, and then we'll have lots to talk about."

"Well . . . I don't know about that. You bring 'em if you want, but don't be surprised if he doesn't want to play right off." She hesitated a second, remembering the sight of Glen as she'd left him this afternoon. The burns on his face, the tubing coming out of his body, the machines at the side of his bed . . .

"Now there's something I have to tell you about this boy. He was in a real bad accident—a fire. His whole family was killed, and he got hurt pretty badly."

"Oh, Mama."

"Oh, yes. So he might look a little bit scary to you, honey. But you remember, inside, he's probably scared himself about everything that's happened. Scared about what's going to happen to him now."

"I won't stare at him, Mama. I promise." Katie frowned, and looked really serious again. "But what is going to happen to him?"

Melissa frowned. "I don't know just yet, honey. That's what I'm trying to figure out. That's why I need your help."

"I'll help you, Mama. Whatever you need." Katie smiled again.

Melissa Vick reached across the table and patted her daughter's hand.

"That's my girl."

\*　　\*　　\*

Miss Efram was his nurse this morning, which Glen was happy about not because he liked her but because she, unlike the older nurses like Nurse Hunt or Nurse Somozi, wasn't always asking him a lot of questions like how are you feeling or do you think you'd like a book from the library or a special treat. No, Miss Efram was change the IV and go, take his temperature and then go, take the breakfast tray and then go. All business, like Dad used to say, which was fine with Glen because the last thing he wanted this morning was a lot of questions about why he wasn't eating his breakfast or how he had slept. The fact was, he wasn't hungry, and he didn't want to talk about it, and he'd had a bad dream last night, and he didn't want to talk about that either.

It was the same dream he'd had a few times now, the dream where he was running down the highway looking for Mark and instead kept meeting all these different people, Paul Grimm, James Dean the actor, and last night, his mom's father, Glen's grandfather, who he only knew from his picture in the Kane scrapbook.

In the dream last night, his grandfather had taken him fishing, just the way his dad used to, and then they'd gone for ice cream, and then they'd gone for a walk out by old Fort Marfa, which was pretty much deserted these days. Except in the dream, it wasn't deserted at all. There were a whole bunch of people standing around in a circle at the center of the camp, and in the center of the circle there was a big wooden stake nailed into the ground, and tied to the stake was a woman, really not much older than a girl, and she was screaming and crying and carrying on and begging for help.

As they got closer, Glen saw that all the people were dressed in funny, old-fashioned clothes. Like the drawings of the Pilgrims he'd seen in the picture book Mrs. Martinez had read them two years ago at Thanksgiving.

"Now, ain't that funny," his grandfather said, although he wasn't laughing. "There's your great-great-great-great-great-great- (he said great more times than Glen could count) grandmother, son. We ought to say hello."

His grandfather cupped his hands to his mouth and shouted. "Hey, Grandma! How are you?"

The woman tied to the stake looked at them and stopped screaming.

"How am I?" She frowned. "How do you think I am? I'm cursed, is how I am."

The woman frightened Glen. He tried to hide behind his grandfather, but somehow she swiveled her head around in a way that didn't seem like it ought to be possible so that she was looking Glen right in the eye.

"We're all cursed," she whispered. "All of us Kanes are cursed, but especially you, boy. Especially you."

Glen managed to wake himself up after that, before things got any worse.

Once he was awake, though, the dream didn't scare him as much, not as much as the dreams he had where he kept running into Paul Grimm, because after all Paul Grimm was very much alive whereas the woman in the dream he'd just had she'd been dead for hundreds of years. Her name, he knew, was Rebecca Kane. She was a witch.

The Kane curse had started with her—that's what his mom had told Glen once last year, one time when he was out from school for a few weeks after he'd fallen and broken his arm, which he hadn't even known about until he got home and his mom screamed at the sight of his arm hanging at a funny angle. Anyway, his mom had brought the scrapbook into Glen's room and tried to tell him some things about her family, about the curse, but he hadn't wanted to listen. Not then, he didn't believe then. But now . . .

What Glen was wondering now, as he stared at the congealed mass of eggs on the plate in front of him, was if he was a witch too. That would explain a lot—why it was that nothing could hurt him, for one. How he'd managed to survive the fire, which the doctors all said was a miracle, for another. If he was a witch, then it wasn't a miracle at all, because miracles came from God, and witches got their power from . . .

Someone knocked on his door.

"I'm all done," Glen called out, thinking it was Nurse Efram, come to take away his tray.

Instead, the door swung wide, and two people stepped into his room.

The blond-haired woman, Glen saw, had brought a blond-haired girl with her.

Melissa's heart leapt into her throat.

Glen looked exhausted, like he hadn't slept all night long. He hadn't eaten much of the food on his tray either.

"Glen—are you all right?"

"Fine."

"You've hardly touched your breakfast."

"I'm fine."

She decided not to push it. Not this morning—that would get things off to a bad start, and she didn't want Katie to have to fight through that as well.

"I'm sure you are," Melissa said, shifting gears. She put her hands on Katie's shoulders and moved her closer to the bed.

"Glen, this is my daughter. I thought you might want a fresh face to talk to today."

Glen shrugged.

Katie stepped forward and held out her hand.

"Hi. I'm Katie."

Her little girl smiled then, the same smile that always lit up Melissa's heart like a thousand-watt bulb.

Glen's expression didn't change.

"I can't get up to shake your hand 'cause they got this in right now," he said, nodding at the IV.

"That's okay," Katie said.

The two kids looked at each other again.

Melissa made a show of looking in her briefcase just then, and frowning. "Oh. Where is my head this morning—I need to get some papers. Would you excuse me a minute, you two? You don't mind, do you Glen, if Katie stays in here with you?"

He shrugged.

"I don't care."

"Good. I'll be right back."

She shut the door behind her then and stood with her back to it, listening.

After a moment, she heard talking. She couldn't hear what they were saying, but she heard words, and smiled. Katie had broken the ice, at least, so she'd leave them alone for a while. Get a cup of coffee at the nurse's station, maybe find Beverly and go over a few things with her—Glen's anticipated release date, any long-term medical problems he might have as a result of the fire—in fact, now that she thought about it, one of the doctors had red-flagged some bruising on his vocal cords that might present a problem down the road, and she wanted to talk about that for certain. So she'd take care of all those things, and then come back. See where they were then.

Melissa turned toward the nurse's station.

A policeman stood there, talking to the woman behind the desk. The nurse glanced up, saw Melissa, and pointed.

"There she is now," the nurse said.

The policeman nodded grimly and started walking toward her.

\*    \*    \*

The two children looked at each other.

"I brought my dolls," Katie said. "If you want to play."

Glen looked at the dolls in her hand. Two little blond dolls in matching outfits. One bigger than the other; one was probably the mother, the other the little girl. Or maybe they were sisters. An older and a younger.

"They're detectives," Katie said. "Like Charlie's Angels, on TV, you know that show? But Katie's Angels, because they work for me, not Charlie."

Glen had no idea what she was talking about.

"No. I don't like dolls."

"Okay." The blond girl looked at him a minute, looked him in the face, then up and down, looking at the IV in his arm and the blinking machines, until finally she looked back at him, looked him straight in the eye again. He expected, right then, to see the same thing in her eyes that he saw in everyone's, the pity, the sadness, mixed in with a little bit of fear. He was sick to death of it.

But she wasn't looking at him that way at all.

She was smiling.

"Your eyes are different colors."

"Yeah?" he asked defensively.

"That's kind of cool."

He blinked. Nobody had ever said that to him before.

"I guess. I don't know. It's all right. I guess."

"I never heard of anyone with different-colored eyes before."

"It's kinda rare." He hesitated. "Some kids at school tease me about it."

"Why?"

"I don't know. They just—they were sixth-graders. That's what happens at school. The big kids pick on the littler ones."

"I don't go to school. My mom home-schools me."

"You don't go to school?"

"Not yet. I'm going to go next year, though. Marfa Elementary. I'm going to be in the second grade."

"That's where I go. But I'm going to be in third grade next year. Except . . . " Glen frowned a minute, realizing something. "Except I never finished second grade. Because of the fire."

"Maybe we'll be in the same class, then," Katie said.

"Yeah," Glen said. "Maybe."

An awkward silence fell.

"I'm sorry about your house burning down," Katie said. "And your parents."

"Yeah." Glen nodded. "Me too."

"And you getting burned. My mama said you got burned pretty bad."

"I'm okay now. Except here." Glen touched the side of his face, the right cheek, where his skin was all discolored.

"That doesn't look so bad," the girl said.

"Really?"

She nodded. "No. Doesn't look so bad at all."

Even though she was saying all the same things that people always said to him, all the things that usually got him so annoyed, Glen found that for some reason, at this moment he wasn't annoyed at all. He was just sad—very, very sad.

"So what are you going to do now?" Katie asked.

"I don't know. I guess—I guess I'm going to get adopted. Have a new fam—"

The word stuck in his throat. He tried to get it out again, and couldn't. He blinked away tears.

"Sorry."

"It's okay. So—when do you get your new family? I mean, how long does that take?"

"I don't know. Thing is, I don't really want a new family."

"Yeah. I wouldn't either."

"Yeah, your mom's nice."

"Yeah. I know. We have a lot of fun together. But she's getting really busy at her job, so she's not around so much anymore. That's why I have to go to school next year."

"Second grade."

"Yeah." Katie hesitated again. "I'm a little scared about it."

"Don't worry. It's not so bad."

"You think kids'll tease me too? I don't think I'd like being teased."

Glen didn't like the idea of Katie being teased, either.

"Don't worry," he said. "Nobody'll tease you."

"You sure?"

"I'll make sure," he said.

"Okay. Thanks." She smiled again.

He smiled back.

Someone knocked on the door.

"I'm done!" Glen called out, sure that this time, it had to be Nurse Efram.

But it wasn't. It was Katie's mom again, swinging the door open all the way and stepping inside.

A police officer stepped in behind her.

After finding out what the officer wanted, Melissa had begged him to wait to talk to Glen for at least a few minutes.

"That boy in there"—she raised an arm and pointed toward the half-open door to Glen's room, beyond which the sound of the children's voices could be heard—"is talking in more than grunts for the first time in weeks. Months. Please let's leave him be for a little while longer."

The policeman—Sergeant Pete Dominguez of the Marfa PD Special Investigation Bureau—shook his head.

"We already waited a little while longer, Ms. Vick. I'm

sorry. I don't want to upset the boy either, but this investigation is a serious matter. I gotta talk to him right now."

Melissa sighed. Poor Glen—the kid just couldn't catch a break.

"Don't you have any more questions for me?"

The sergeant shook his head. "No. I have no more questions for anyone but the boy. He was the only witness."

"All right." She nodded, and knocked on the door.

Glen yelled something in response—she couldn't hear what, but took his words as an invitation to come in, and pushed the door open.

She smiled for a minute at the sight of Glen leaning forward in his bed, a light in his eyes that she had frankly not once seen from him in all the weeks they'd been talking together. That smile grew even broader when she saw Katie, leaning on the edge of Glen's bed, leaning toward him, the same glint in her own eye. They were getting along, obviously. More than getting along, in fact; if they were a few years older, Melissa would say that there was a little spark between the two of them, a little hint of romance in the air, though of course they were too young for that, at seven going on eight years old, much too young.

Weren't they?

"Glen Callaway?" Sergeant Dominguez said, stepping into the room.

The second the police officer spoke, Melissa saw the spark vanish from the boy's eyes.

"Yeah," Glen said. "That's me."

The sergeant introduced himself, taking a step closer to the boy as he did so. Melissa took Katie by the shoulders again and pulled her out of the way.

"I'd like to talk to the boy in private, Ms. Vick," Dominguez said.

"I think I should be here."

"It's your daughter I'm concerned about. I don't want to frighten the girl."

Melissa nodded. Maybe Dominguez was right—talking about the fire to Glen the way he'd talked about it to her . . . that would upset Katie.

"Sweetie," she began, "let's go out in the hall for a while."

"Why?" Katie asked Dominguez. "What do you want to ask Glen about? What do you want to know?"

Melissa couldn't help but smile. "Sir," she corrected her daughter before the officer could respond. " 'What do you want to know, *sir*,' is what you should say, honey. Mind your manners."

Katie asked the question again.

"I want to know about the fire," Dominguez said. "What happened that night."

Katie nodded, and turned to her mother. "I don't mind staying. If it's okay with Glen."

"Sure," Glen said.

Dominguez shrugged. "Fine by me. But let's all get comfortable." He looked around the room. "This might take a while."

"I don't understand," Glen said. "I talked to the police about all this before—when I first got to the hospital."

"That's right, I know you did." Dominguez pulled up chairs around the bed for himself, Melissa, and Katie. "But some new information has come up, so I need to ask some more questions. That's all."

"New information? What kind of information?"

"Well . . ." Dominguez sat. "Information that leads us to suspect that this fire may have been arson."

"Oh, my Lord." The officer hadn't said that before. "Oh, my Lord."

"What's arson mean?" Glen asked.

"It's a crime, isn't it?" Katie asked.

"That's right," the policeman said. "Arson is a crime. It means that someone deliberately set the fire that killed your parents. It means"—and here he turned his full attention to Glen—"that this fire wasn't an accident at all. It means this was murder."

# chapter
## four

Glen listened in stunned silence as the policeman explained what they'd found. It was a little complicated for him to follow—something about the chemical signatures of the different preservatives they used at the funeral home, the pattern of how the fire spread, what they'd found at the point of ignition, but it was the last thing, the simplest thing of all, which Dominguez said they'd only realized this week, that made Glen sit up straight, made a chill run down his spine just like—how did his mom always put it?—just like somebody walked on his grave.

"The front door was wide open," Dominguez said. "We missed that the first time." He glanced back at Melissa as he spoke, making sure she got the significance of what he was saying too. "You see, the fire was so big, so far along by the time the engines arrived . . . they spent their energies fighting the blaze, you understand, and not writing down what they saw. That they did later."

"I don't understand," Melissa said. "What does all that mean?"

Dominguez smiled again. "Excuse me if I'm not being clear. It means that the fact that the front door was wide open when the first engine arrived was hidden deep in the report."

"The front door being open is significant?"

"Yes. Very. The fire started between one fifteen and one thirty in the A.M. Most people don't leave their front doors standing open at that time of night, do they?"

"No, they don't," Melissa agreed.

"So this is very significant." Dominguez looked at Glen. "I have the feeling you understand."

Glen did. He'd been sitting there listening to the policeman talk, and at the same time, he'd flashed back in his mind to the very last images he had of the night his house burned down and his family died, remembering the wide-open front door and wondering how it got that why. Now he finally knew.

"Somebody set the fire," he said. "And then they walked out of the house and left the front door open."

"Exactly." Dominguez smiled. "And now we have to find out who that somebody was."

That was right, Glen knew. They had to find out. And then he had to—what? What was he supposed to do when he found out who killed his family?

"Excuse me? Did you say something?"

Glen looked up and saw that Dominguez—and Melissa Vick and Katie—were all staring at him. He must have spoken out loud.

"No," he said. "I didn't say anything."

"Okay." The policeman took his notepad out again and flipped it open to a fresh page.

"Now I have some questions for you, Glen."

Dominguez was there for almost an hour, asking Glen about what he saw that night, what he heard. Before he went to sleep, and after. What he'd done that day, what his parents and his brother had done. What he knew about his parents' business, a point the policeman kept coming back to over and over again, hammering on it far longer than Melissa thought necessary.

"Did you see anyone that looked suspicious to you around the funeral parlor the last few days?"

"What do you mean?"

"Somebody who seemed out of place, like they didn't belong?"

"No."

"What about your dad? Did he seem upset about anything recently?"

"No."

"Anybody he was fighting with? Anybody mad at him about anything?"

"Not that I can remember."

"Okay." Dominguez nodded, wrote something on his notepad. "Glen—do you know a man named Paul Grimm?"

"Yeah. I know him. He works at the funeral parlor."

"You seen him around lately?"

Glen looked like he wanted to say yes, but after a second's hesitation, he shook his head.

"No. I haven't seen him. But I don't know if he could have set the fire, if that's what you're thinking."

"Why not?"

"Because he's a weasel. He wouldn't have the guts," Glen said.

Melissa smiled at that—*weasel* was just the word for Paul Grimm, based on what she'd heard about the man from Beverly Cutler. But that was the only time she smiled during the entire time Dominguez was there. It was practically the only time she smiled all morning, in fact; the policeman's sudden appearance at the hospital had not only ruined her plan with Katie and Glen, it had thrown off her whole morning schedule. After the sergeant left, she barely had time to say good-bye to Glen herself before having to rush home to drop Katie off before her next appointment. Glen's morning had been ruined too, she could see it in his face; he'd closed right back up after his talk with Katie, having to answer all those questions, basically relive the night of the fire again.

Not that Dominguez felt good about having to ask those questions himself, judging from the occasional unguarded look of frustration Melissa had seen on his face. He was in a tough spot, the sergeant was, having to deal with a kid like Glen where he had to tread so, so carefully and try not to bruise any feelings. Not the usual kind of interrogating police did, as Melissa knew all too well from the occasional shop talk Jarvis brought home, though his shop—Jarvis was a highway patrolman—was a little bit different.

And wasn't life funny that way, how it brought the two of them together. They had opposite views on so many things, and yet they could talk those through so easily without fighting— usually, at least—well, it was a wonder to her. Like last night at the dinner table, she was talking about a man named Wendell Newton she worked with up in Alpine, an ex-con who was having a hard go of it lately, some health problems, and Jarvis listened sympathetically, but at the end pointed out that a lot of Wendell's troubles he brought on himself, living the way he had for so long. Which Melissa couldn't deny, but still, she felt it was not just her job, but her Christian duty to help those in need. Like Wendell. Like Glen. They were all God's children, and there was certainly nothing that Glen had done to bring on what happened to him. It was all just bad luck.

She'd have to see what Jarvis thought about Glen. Maybe, in fact, she could arrange to take Glen out for a meal with the whole family. Do him some good to get out of the hospital, out into the real world. She'd talked to the boy before about maybe coming to church with them one Sunday, but that suggestion had obviously made him very, very uncomfortable. Dinner would be much better. Katie would like that too. They hadn't gone out to dinner in a good long while.

She glanced at her daughter in the rearview mirror and smiled.

"You made me proud today, honey—back in the hospital. The way you got Glen to talking."

"Yes, Mama," her daughter said, distracted by the game she was playing with her dolls.

"You have a knack for making people comfortable."

"Knack?"

"Talent, I mean. You'd make a good social worker."

"Like you?"

"That's right, honey. Like me."

"I don't know." Katie frowned. "I think I might want to be a policeman, like Daddy, when I grow up."

"Well, that's all right too. Whatever you want. You got plenty of time to decide."

Melissa turned into the driveway, turned off the car.

"Now listen, honey," she said, as she let herself and Katie into the house. "I've got to run right back to the office for a few minutes. Will you be okay here by yourself until Daddy gets home, or do you want me to call Mrs. Sanders down the road?"

"Can we see if Jenny's home, Mama?" Katie asked. "If she can play?"

"Jenny's in school now, honey."

"Oh." Katie's face fell.

Melissa knelt down and touched a hand to her daughter's cheek. "I'm sorry. You'll be in school next year though. In the meantime . . ."

Her voice trailed off as she heard a car pull up in the driveway.

She frowned. Who could be coming to see her now? She wasn't usually home now, she was usually at work. She went to the window to see.

"I can't wait for school next year, Mama," Katie called after her. "That boy Glen is gonna be in my class."

"That's nice," Melissa said absently, not really listening to Katie at that moment because she'd just reached the window and saw that the car that pulled up was Jarvis's state trooper vehicle, and what was he doing home at this hour? He had the seven-to-three shift all week. What was on his mind?

She smiled all at once, because she suddenly realized that Jarvis knew she was planning on being home right about now, and that what might be on his mind, in fact, was her. That man.

She turned her head slightly to the right, to the family portrait hanging on the wall. Katie in the front, smiling her thousand-watt smile, and Melissa kneeling down next to her, and Jarvis standing behind them both, his hand on Melissa's shoulder.

Which was when Jarvis got out of the car, and her heart stopped.

Because it wasn't Jarvis, it was Jarvis's captain, Roy Egger, and it was the captain's car, not Jarvis's—it had different markings on it—and climbing out of the passenger side was Jarvis's best friend on the force, Stan Halverson. Both men wore long, long faces.

Captain Egger put a hand on Halverson's shoulder, and Stan wiped a tear away from his eye. They started down the walk toward the front door.

Melissa clutched her hand to her chest then and sat right down on the couch.

Katie walked up beside her and stood on her tiptoes to peer out the window.

"Is it Daddy, Mama?" she asked. "Is Daddy home already?"

Melissa finally found her voice. It cracked as she spoke.

"No, honey, it's not Daddy."

She had a horrible feeling in her stomach that it was never, ever going to be Daddy again.

\*     \*     \*

No one came to see him the next day. Not the blond woman, not her daughter, either. Katie.

Glen was going to ask one of the nurses what happened to them, but he had Nurse Efram all day, and she was in a foul, foul mood, something about her boyfriend stepping out on her, he guessed from little bits of conversation he overheard taking place outside in the hall. She barely looked at him all day long. Glen didn't worry about it too much; he'd see Melissa tomorrow, that was their day, and in the meantime . . . well, he had a lot to think about.

Thing number one on his mind was the fire.

From the policeman's questions yesterday, it sounded like they were trying to figure out who might have had keys to the house besides his parents. Glen couldn't think of anybody except old Mr. Blackwell, who sometimes helped around the parlor doing odd jobs, and they'd pretty much ruled him out as a suspect. Glen had been thinking hard on other possibilities since the officer left, but he just couldn't. Who would want to burn down the funeral parlor? Why? There just wasn't any reason, so Glen had decided that the police were wrong. It was an accident, although he knew it was not really an accident at all, it was the curse.

He'd also decided he was going to have to tell Melissa about the Kane family curse, and he thought that she just might believe him because one of the things he'd realized about her was that she was a God-fearing woman, as Dad always used to say. She was always talking about the Lord this, and the Lord that, and a few days ago she'd even suggested that Glen might want to come to church with her one Sunday, get out of the hospital.

Glen had been trying to figure out how to tell her he never went to church, none of the Callaways (and certainly none of the Kanes) ever went to church, but luckily she'd dropped that topic of conversation pretty quickly.

The point was, though, that she was a God-fearing woman. She believed in the higher powers up above, which meant that she'd be just as likely to believe in the ones down below. Which was where it got tricky, because although Melissa was likely to believe in the curse, if Glen told her that he was a witch, he was afraid she wouldn't talk to him anymore. And she definitely wouldn't want him and Katie to be friends— she'd probably think the evil would rub off on Katie.

Maybe he could change the story just a little bit, just tell her about the curse without telling her why the Kanes were cursed. After all, she would just have his word for it. The scrapbook was gone now, burned up in the fire, which meant that since he was the last surviving Kane, all those stories were going to die with him. Which was good.

What was better was that that night, Glen didn't dream about the fire.

Instead, he dreamed about being back in school. In Mrs. Prescott's class, and everyone was being nice to him, Jimmy Nichols wanted to know if he wanted to go to the football game on Friday night, watch Marfa High beat up on Valentine, Ty Martin came over to his desk and started telling him about the wrestling show he'd gone to last weekend up in El Paso, and did Glen want to come see a show with him and his family next month (they were all calling him Glen in the dream), and the whole time everyone was talking to him, he was aware that sitting in the seat to his right, not talking to him but just watching him, was Katie Vick, Melissa's daughter, and that even though he couldn't see her, she was smiling.

In the dream, he was smiling too.

He even woke up with a smile on his face, for the first time in what seemed like forever, and was still wearing that smile at 8:45 A.M. when just like always, Melissa knocked on the door to his room.

"Come on in," Glen called, and the door swung all the way open.

But instead of Melissa, it was a man. A short, very neat, very blond-haired man who was also smiling—why, Glen couldn't imagine.

"Hey, there, Glen. How you doing?"

Glen frowned, and stared. Who was this guy?

The man's smile wavered.

"It is Glen, right?" He looked down at the folder in his hand, and nodded. "Yeah. Of course it is. How you doing, Glen?"

The man stepped into the room, set his folder down on one chair, and pulled another up alongside the bed. He was wearing some kind of perfume, or cologne, or something. It stunk to high heaven.

"Glen, I'm Dick Beavis. I'm going to be your new caseworker."

Glen wasn't sure he'd heard right.

"My new what?"

"Your new caseworker. Gonna work on your case. I mean, gonna help you find a new home. New place to live. How's that sound?"

"What?"

"New place to live. New family. But first"—the man put his hand on the bed then, and leaned even closer—"we ought to get to know each other, doncha think? I could tell you a little bit about myself. I'm kinda new to the social work thing, but I've done a lot of work with people in the real estate business, and that's kind of the same sort of communication skill facilitatin'—"

"Wait, wait." Glen shook his head. He had a sudden sinking

feeling in his stomach. "My new caseworker? Where's Melissa? What happened to her?"

"Melissa." The blond man smiled and nodded. "Melissa."

All at once the fake smile disappeared from his face, replaced by a frown that was just as fake.

"A terrible thing happened, son. A terrible thing, and Melissa's not going to be coming back, I'm afraid." The man shifted in his chair, obviously uncomfortable. "I'm sorry."

"What happened?" For some reason, Glen felt himself on the verge of tears. "Tell me what happened!"

"Hold on, hold on. I got a note here for you." The man reached over and grabbed his folder again, and pulled out a plain white envelope with his name scrawled on the front of it, Glen Callaway.

He ripped it open and read.

*Dear Glen,*

*I'm so sorry to have to tell you this in a letter, but there's so much going on right now I just can't make it out to see you. I will try and call when things calm down a little.*

*As whoever is taking my place has probably told you by now, there has been a terrible tragedy in my family, something that makes me understand just a little bit better, I think, how awful you must have been feeling these last few months. To lose a member of your family is without a doubt the greatest trial God puts before us . . .*

Glen felt dizzy; the words started to blur. Was she talking about Katie? Had something happened to Katie?

He was scared to read on, but finally he did, and when he found out that the person in Melissa's family who died wasn't Katie, but Melissa's husband instead, he felt first relief and then shame for feeling that relief. Her husband was dead—he was a state trooper, which Glen hadn't known, and he'd been in a high-speed chase out on the highway, and his car had gone off a bridge, and that was how he died, Melissa said. A freak accident.

But Glen knew it wasn't an accident at all. It was his fault, for making friends with Katie, with her mom, for making them a part of his life.

It was the curse.

*. . . but as difficult as it seems sometimes, we have to have faith in God, in his plan for us all. I have faith in his plan for you, and I know that plan will end with your happiness.*

*I will write you once we are settled in Kansas City. I miss you already, Glen, and I will pray for you, and I wish you all the best in the world.*

*Love,*
*Melissa Vick*

"Hell of a thing, isn't it?" Beavis asked.

Glen was crying.

"No," he said. "Oh, no no no."

There was a little pink piece of paper folded up inside Melissa's note. He opened that, and found it was a note from Katie. A very short note.

*Dear Glen,*

*My dad died, so I'm moving to Kansas City. It looks like we will not be in second grade together after all. We could be pen pals, though, my mom says. Here is the address you can write me at.*

*Your friend,*
*Katie Vick*

That note made him cry even more.

At some point during his crying, he realized that Dick Beavis had sat up on the bed next to him. He patted Glen on the leg.

"It's all right," Beavis said. "It's gonna be okay."

"No, it's not gonna be okay," Glen said, wondering just how stupid this man was, because how in the world could it be okay that Melissa's husband, Katie's dad was dead? and it was his fault.

"It's a terrible thing that happened," Beavis said, "but—"

"Go away." Glen turned his back to Beavis, but the bed was small, and when he did that he jostled the man, and Beavis, who was perched awkwardly on the edge of the mattress, slipped and fell on the floor.

On the way down, one of his arms hit the little cart that held Glen's breakfast tray. The tray slid off the cart and bounced off Beavis's head.

Glen's breakfast spilled all over the man's suit.

Beavis got up cursing.

"Goddamn it!" He wiped away egg and orange juice, and glared at Glen. "I was just trying to help!"

"I don't want your help."

Beavis's eyes narrowed. "Yeah. I got that. Listen, kid, anyone ever tell you you have a bad attitude?"

"I don't care."

"Well, you ought to. Not many families gonna want a kid with a bad attitude." The instant those words left his mouth, Beavis sighed heavily. "Damn. I didn't mean that, Glen, I just—"

Glen made a show of turning away again. "Leave me alone."

He heard Beavis sigh once more. "Look, we got off to a bad start here. Let's start over, okay?"

Glen didn't respond.

After a minute, he heard Beavis pick up his folder and slide the chairs back to where they were.

"I'll leave your letters, Glen. And I'll be back tomorrow— no, Thursday. I'll be back Thursday."

Glen heard the man's footsteps walk away, and the door open and then close behind him.

He was alone again.

Dick Beavis never came back. They gave him another case-worker, Mrs. Rodriguez, who seemed nice enough, but rarely spent more than fifteen minutes at a time with him, which she kept apologizing for—"the size of my caseload"—by which Glen guessed she meant she had a lot of other people to see. That was fine with him; he was actually grateful for the lack of attention.

A week or so after she started, she brought him a big manila envelope postmarked Kansas City.

"Don't you want to open it?" she asked.

Glen held the envelope, which was stuffed full, of what he had no idea, and thought, *I do want to open it, I do.*

But it was from the Vicks. And they were better off without him in their lives.

"I'll open it later," he said, and put the envelope to the side.

After Mrs. Rodriguez left, he got out of his bed, walked down the hall to the trash chute, and threw the envelope away.

Over the next few weeks, he threw a lot of envelopes from Kansas City away.

Three months later, after being released from the hospital, Mrs. Rodriguez put him in a temporary foster home in Alpine, with six other kids. He started second grade there all over again. The Vicks' mail followed him. Mrs. Rodriguez sent a note along with it, telling him he was rude not to reply.

One day, when he got home from school, she was on the front steps of the home, waiting for him.

"I just don't want to talk to them, all right?" he said, glaring at her. "They got their lives, I got mine."

Mrs. Rodriguez looked confused.

"What?"

"The Vicks," Glen said. "I don't want to talk to 'em."

"Oh." She shook her head. "That's not why I'm here, Glen."

And then, for the first time since he'd met her, Mrs. Rodriguez smiled.

Glen suddenly realized that his suitcase, the one the hospital had given him when he left, was sitting on the steps next to her.

"We got a family for you."

# chapter
## five

It wasn't a family, exactly. It was a couple with no children. Red and Margaret Barrow. They lived in Alpine too, only not in a house, they owned a ranch.

"A working ranch," Mrs. Rodriguez said. "A hundred and thirty acres. You know how big that is, Glen?"

Glen shook his head. He didn't.

"It's big. Trust me, it's big. You'll see. Soon enough." She nodded down the road ahead of her.

They were traveling north on 118 now, following signs to the Fort Davis National Historic Area, whatever that was. Glen had never been this far out of Marfa before—the land was a little greener, and most of it was fenced in, which made sense, he supposed, if there were ranches out here.

He was in a sort of state of shock about the whole thing. A new family? Not that he'd been paying a lot of attention to what Mrs. Rodriguez was telling him lately, but he had the idea that it might take an awfully long time to find him a family, if it happened at all. He thought he remembered her saying something about how there were so many children in the Texas foster care system that many parents would refuse a kid older than five, especially a boy. Especially a boy who looked like him. Whose face was all freaky-looking, who had two different-colored eyes. He was going to ask Mrs. Rodriguez what had happened, but he didn't want to sound ungrateful.

"I think we turn here," she said suddenly.

Glen looked up. There was a break in the fence line and a sign:

Aurora

The car wheels crunched on first gravel, and then dirt, as they turned off the highway onto a long skinny road that stretched off into the distance toward a row of purple mountains.

They went down that road for a long time, past scrub and grassland and once in a while a bunch of cows standing around, looking bored. Along the way, Mrs. Rodriguez explained to him how the adoption process worked, how she would be out to see him in a couple days, and how it was his choice too about whether or not he wanted to stay with the Barrows or find another family, and Glen, who realized that she'd actually given him this speech before about how the whole thing worked and he just hadn't been listening, really listened this time, though still, it all seemed completely unreal to him.

A new family?

Finally, long after Mrs. Rodriguez had finished her talk, long after Glen had time to absorb the news (but not long enough for him to decide exactly how he felt about it), the road curved and then passed through a big wooden gate with again, the word *Aurora* on top of it—

"That's the name of the ranch," Mrs. Rodriguez said helpfully.

—and there that ranch was, right in front of them.

It was a bunch of buildings, actually, all kind of clumped together in a hollow at the base of a hill. Glen supposed they had all different kinds of buildings for the different animals on the ranch. They were just about all one-story buildings, most of them white, most with red wooden roofs, except for a gray barn toward the back and a big two-story brick house. There was a lot of fencing too, wire fencing around most of the buildings, and closest to them, coming closer as they pulled up, there was a corral with a big brown horse in it, and three people in the ring too, two men wearing cowboy hats and one woman, who was riding the horse. She had the longest, blackest hair Glen had ever seen. She turned at the sound of their car and stared at them.

She was very pretty. She was angry, too, Glen could see that not just from the expression on her face but from the way she sat on the horse.

They pulled past the corral and up to the house itself. Mrs. Rodriguez shut off the engine and turned to him.

"Nervous?"

"I guess. I don't know."

"You'll do okay, Glen. You're a good kid." She patted his leg. "Even if you don't want to answer Melissa's letters."

He blushed bright red. Not writing back to her suddenly seemed stupid.

"I'm sorry about that," he said.

She opened the door and got out. An old man was walking toward them. He had on a big cowboy hat too, and he walked with kind of a hitch in his step. He was tall for an old man, and looked to be in pretty good shape, better than the old men Glen had seen in the hospital.

Glen got out of the car too.

"Mrs. Rodriguez," the old man said. "Good to see you again."

"Mr. Barrow."

"Now, now. You know you're supposed to call me Red." The old man smiled.

"Okay. Red. Then you have to call me Helena, all right?"

"Helena it is." Mrs. Rodriguez smiled too then, and laughed, and they shook hands. Then she turned and motioned Glen forward.

"This is him," she said, putting her hands on Glen's shoulders. "This is Glen Callaway."

"Well." The man put his hands on his hips and looked Glen up and down. Looked at his face, his eyes, studying him, but in a friendly kind of way, before sticking out his hand again. "Hi, Glen. I'm Red Barrow."

"Hi," Glen said, shaking hands. "I'm pleased to meet you."

"Same here." The man looked behind them, in the direction of the corral they'd seen driving in, and frowned. "Excuse me a minute," he said, then cupped his hands together and yelled. "Margaret!"

The pretty woman Glen had seen on the way in turned her head then, saw the old man, and held up a finger. Wait one minute, Glen understood her to be saying.

The man shook his head.

"My God, that woman and her horses . . ."

He looked over at Glen.

"You like horses, Glen?"

"I guess."

"You ever ride one?"

"No."

"Haven't ridden a horse yet? How old are you?"

"Eight years old."

"Eight." The man smiled, and shook his head. "We'll have to see what we can do about that."

The woman was walking toward them now. The old man went to her, and they kissed, which was when Glen realized that she was Mrs. Barrow. His new mom, like Mr. Barrow—Red—was his new dad.

"Well, here we all are," the man said, walking back toward

Glen and Mrs. Rodriguez with his arm around the woman's shoulder. "This is Glen. Glen, this is Margaret—Mrs. Barrow."

"Hi," Glen said, sticking out his hand again.

"Hello." The woman looked him up and down then too, only in a way that wasn't as friendly as her husband's glance had been. She looked at his face and then looked away quickly. That was all right. Glen was used to that reaction. He studied her too. Up close, she wasn't as young as he'd thought, and not quite as pretty. She was too thin, Glen decided. Her skin looked kind of papery and rough.

"I'm so pleased to meet you, Glen."

She put her hand out then, and they shook. Her skin was rough, and her grip was strong, a lot stronger than Glen would have expected it to be.

She held his hand just a little longer and harder than she needed to.

"It's good to have you here. I think we're going to be great friends, don't you?"

"Yes, ma'am," Glen said, taking his hand back.

Great friends.

For some reason, he wasn't so sure about that.

They all went inside the brick house, into a big open room with a stone floor and a long wood table. They sat around the table, and the grown-ups talked for a while. A Mexican woman came in and put a plate of cookies and a glass of milk in front of him.

"For me?" he asked, looking up at the woman.

She smiled. "*Sí.* For you."

"This is Consuela, Glen," Red said. "She runs the place."

"Oh, Red," the woman said, shaking her head and smiling. "I don't run the place, Glen. I'm the cook. And I'm pleased to meet you."

"Pleased to meet you, ma'am. And thank you," he said, picking up a cookie and taking a bite. Chocolate chip, and warm.

"What am I making for dinner tonight, Red?" the woman asked.

"Well, let's ask Glen. Glen, what do you think you'd like for dinner?"

He blinked, surprised to be included in the discussion. "I don't know."

"Well, how about we just throw some steaks on the grill? That sound good to you?"

"Sure," Glen said, though he'd never had a real steak before, just chopped steak, like in the TV dinners.

"Steak it is," Consuela said.

"I'll have mine well done, Consuela," Mrs. Barrow said. "Thank you."

"Of course, Mrs. Barrow." Consuela nodded and left the room.

The adults continued their conversation until Mrs. Rodriguez said it was time for her to get back to town.

Outside, next to her car, she knelt down and gave Glen a big hug.

"I'll see you in a couple days," she whispered in his ear. "And if you have any problems before then, you call me. I put my card in your suitcase, okay?"

"Okay."

She straightened up. "Now be a good boy. And when I come back, I'm bringing you the Vicks' address, okay? And I want you to write them."

"I will," he said.

And then she was gone, and he was alone with the Barrows.

"Darling," Margaret Barrow said, putting a hand on her husband's arm. "Shiloh's still being a bit balky. I need to straighten him out before the show next week. You'll take Glen to his room?"

"I will," Red said. "See you at dinner, all right?"

"All right." She gave the man a kiss on the cheek, and then turned to Glen. "I'll see you at dinner too, Glen. We can talk some more then."

"Yes, ma'am," he said, though the words that popped into his head right then were, *We haven't talked at all yet.* But he held his tongue.

She walked back to the corral. The man watched her go, and shook his head.

"That woman and her horses. All right, Glen—what say you and me go look at your room? How's that sound?"

"Okay."

The man led Glen inside the house, through the big dining room and then up the stairs, past dozens of framed pictures. Most of them seemed to be of Red when he was younger, with a whole bunch of other men, shaking hands, holding up trophies, that sort of thing, though there were a couple pictures of Red and Margaret, and then one of Red and another woman who looked to be about Margaret's age but who had long red hair and in the picture was laughing with her mouth wide open and holding on to Red with one hand (she even, he realized, looked a little like Red), but before he could ask who any of the people were, they were upstairs and walking down a long hall lined with even more pictures.

"Your room's right down here," Red said, and he pushed open a door then, and led Glen inside.

It was a pretty small room, really not much bigger than his room back home in Marfa had been, but it had a much better view, of most of the other buildings, and the front of the ranch where they'd driven in, including the corral. Off in the distance, Glen thought he saw Mrs. Rodriguez's car pulling away. He saw a cloud of dust, anyway.

Red set his suitcase down on the bed.

"I figure you're old enough to unpack yourself," he said. "Dresser's there, closet's right there. I wasn't sure if you were gonna need clothes or not, so I went out and got you some shirts and jeans. If you don't like 'em, we can go into town later on and get others."

He slid the closet open then, and Glen saw there were three identical blue-and-white checked shirts hanging there, as well as a pair of jeans. They looked like cowboy clothes.

"You like 'em?"

"Yeah."

"Good. Tomorrow we can go out and get you some boots. You gonna work on a ranch, you need some good boots."

"Okay," Glen said. Boots sounded good to him.

He looked out the window again, and saw that down in the corral, Margaret was just climbing down off her horse. She handed the reins to one of the other men in the ring, and then ran her hands through her hair. She said something to the man, and both of them smiled, and laughed.

In the middle of that laughter, she happened to look up and see Glen watching her. The smile disappeared from her face.

Glen caught her eye and waved.

After a long moment, she waved back.

"Yeah," Red said, coming up alongside him. "We'll get you some boots tomorrow, and get you out on a horse. Let you see what that's like. If you're game."

"I guess."

"Good. Now why don't you get yourself settled, then wash up and come on downstairs in say half an hour. Dinner ought to be ready by then. Bathroom's down the end of the hall."

Glen nodded.

Red smiled at him again. "It's good to have you here, Glen."

"It's good to be here," he said, and meant it.

He looked up at Red then, and hesitated.

"What's the matter?"

"Ummm . . . I know this is probably a stupid question, but—"

"No such thing as a stupid question, son. If there's one thing I learned in my life, the only thing stupid about any question is when you don't ask it. Now what's on your mind?"

"What am I . . . I mean, what do I call you?"

"What do you call me?" Red smiled. "You call me Red. Everybody calls me Red, like I told you."

"Oh. I thought maybe . . . I don't know. Never mind."

Red put a hand on his shoulder. "You thought maybe you were supposed to call me Dad, or somethin'?"

Glen nodded. "Yeah."

"No. I hope to be your friend, Glen—hope to be more than that, actually, but I'm not your dad, am I? Randall Callaway was your dad. Ain't that right?"

Glen nodded.

"That's right," Red said. "Listen, Glen. Margaret and I read your file. We read it more than once. We know all about what happened, and all the heartache you been through. Now that heartache's behind you, I hope, but I don't think you're ever gonna forget the people you lost, and I don't want you to. Margaret and I, we don't want to replace them either. So you call me Red, and you call her Margaret, and we'll take it one day at a time, okay?"

"Okay."

"Good."

Red left him then, and Glen unpacked his stuff and washed

up, just like Red had told him to. He looked himself over in the mirror before he went downstairs. He looked okay, he supposed. The blotchy skin was fading a little—the doctors had told him that would happen, which was good, and they said that once he got outside, got his pasty-white skin a little more color, it'd be even harder for folks to pick up on the fact that he'd been burned. He hoped so. He wanted Margaret to like him too the way Red already did, and he could tell she was uncomfortable with his face. He wondered if she knew about the big patch of blotchy skin on his right side. The doctors weren't so sure that was going to smooth out as he grew. He hoped Margaret wouldn't freak out when she saw it, though he supposed she probably knew about it already. Red said they'd looked at Glen's file, they knew everything about him.

Though as Glen started down the stairs for dinner, he realized there was one thing that wasn't in the file at all. The curse.

But there was no reason they ever had to find out about that. The scrapbook was gone, the stories were all in his head, and he was going to keep his mouth shut. Period. End of story, like Dad always used to say.

He hoped.

Dinner was not good. It had nothing to do with the steak, which was delicious, but after a couple bites Glen found he couldn't really enjoy it. The problem was Margaret—she was not happy about something, and Glen had the feeling that something was him.

Conversation was strained. Red tried talking to Glen about school and what sort of things he liked to do, which went okay, but every time he tried to involve Margaret, the talk just died.

When Consuela started serving dessert, Margaret excused herself from the table, saying she had a terrible headache and was going to go to bed early. On her way out of the room, she gave Red a perfunctory kiss on the cheek and Glen an even more perfunctory pat on the shoulder.

Even the conversation between Red and him got hard after that.

"You don't like the flan?" Red asked.

"The what?"

"Your dessert. The flan there."

"No, it's good. Just ate too much steak."

"I understand that. Those were good steaks."

"Yeah."

Red cleared his throat. "Margaret had a hard day, I guess. That horse gave her a lot of trouble."

Glen nodded.

Red looked him in the eye then. "I know this is a big change for you. Understand it's a big change for us, also. Gonna take some getting used to all around."

"Yes, sir."

Red looked like he wanted to say something else for a minute, then he shook his head.

"Anyway, I'm going to call it a night too." He stood up. "If you want to read a book or something, Consuela can show you to the library. You ought to be able to find something in there."

"Yes, sir. Thank you, sir."

"Red, remember?" The man smiled, but it was a weak smile, and for the first time since laying eyes on him that afternoon, Glen thought Mr. Barrow—Red—looked like an old man. A very tired old man.

"Yep. I do. Thank you, Red."

"Thank you, Glen." He pushed back from the table. "So

feel free to go to that library if you want. But you might want to call it a night soon too. We get up kind of early around here."

"Yes, sir."

Glen ended up taking Red's advice—going up to bed, and going to sleep early. Or trying to, anyway. At first it was the silence that bothered him—no traffic noises, no people talking, just the occasional dog barking, the sound of some other animal scuffing around outside. After a while though, he got used to that.

But then there was the yelling. Margaret and Red, somewhere else in the house, shouting at each other just loud enough that he could hear the anger in their words, but not what they were saying.

He was pretty certain though, that he heard his name in there more than once.

# chapter six

Red hadn't been kidding about that early start.

Glen was woken up not by his alarm clock—which he'd set for 7:00 A.M.—and not by the sun—which this time of year was coming up around six—but by the sound of horses neighing right outside his window. He sat up bolt upright in bed, his heart hammering in his chest, and for a second had no idea where he was. He thought maybe he was having a nightmare.

Then he remembered everything that happened yesterday, and blinked and rubbed his eyes and looked at the clock next to his bed.

4:52 A.M.

He turned in bed and looked out the window.

There were men outside, walking from the outlying buildings up to the house. He heard the front door open and close a few times, and the sound of talking from downstairs. He sat in bed for a minute, unsure if he was supposed to get up or not. He smelled coffee, and all at once, was reminded of being in his bedroom back in Marfa on school mornings, when he'd hear his mom and dad out in the kitchen and smell the coffee they were brewing.

He liked that smell.

It smelled of home.

He closed his eyes for a minute and fell back asleep.

\*　　\*　　\*

When he woke again, it was light out. The clock said 7:00. For a minute, he panicked. One of the things he and the grown-ups had talked about yesterday was school—there was a bus that came to the gate out on the main road at 7:30, and Red had said that to meet the bus in time, they had to leave the house at 7:15.

Then he remembered that today was a Saturday. No school today.

Apparently it was a workday on the ranch, though. He thought about that a second, and then realized that probably everyday was a workday on the ranch.

His door swung open a crack. Red peeked in.

"Hey-ho," he said. "You awake there, pardner?"

"I guess."

"Then come on downstairs. We got breakfast on. You oughtta come meet everybody."

"Yes, sir."

Red smiled and shut the door.

Glen yawned, stretched, and got out of bed. He put on the clothes Red had shown him yesterday—the blue-checked shirt and the jeans, which fit pretty good—used the bathroom, and went downstairs.

There were three men sitting with Red at the big dining room table, passing around big plates of food—bacon and eggs and home fries and tortillas and a big basket of muffins. They were all talking and chewing at the same time, loudly, animatedly.

Red waved him over and introduced him. The men were Deke, and Lucas, and Tony; Glen heard the last names but didn't remember them. These here were cowboys, Red said. Real live cowboys. They worked the ranch for Red and Margaret. Deke was the one Glen had seen yesterday in the corral with Margaret. All three said hey, hello, how are you, didn't make a big deal about his burns, and went right back to eating and talking. Mostly eating.

Glen just sat there listening, not understanding even a tenth of what they were saying, but feeling pretty good all the same. The food was good, too: Consuela came by and gave him a big mug of hot chocolate as well.

"Not every day for this," she said, "but today—a special day. So a special drink."

"Thank you."

"Thank you is right. Thanks, Consuela, that was delicious as usual." Red dabbed at the corners of his mouth with his napkin, and stood up. "But we gotta get back to it. Day's not getting any younger, boys. Now, Glen"—he smiled—"Margaret's gonna give you a horseback riding lesson a little later, when she gets up. How's that sound?"

"Oh," he said, and then realized that might sound like he wasn't excited about it, which of course he wasn't, but he didn't want to seem rude, so he continued right away, "oh, that sounds great. That'll be fun."

The smile on Red's face wavered a second. "Good. Then I'll see you this afternoon, at lunch. Okay?"

"Okay."

After the four men left, Glen helped Consuela clean up, even though she said he didn't have to.

"I want to help," he said. "I want to pitch in."

"That's nice. But this is my job. Don't worry—you'll have plenty of other work to do around here, I'm sure."

"Like what?"

"Oh, Mr. Red, he'll find you something." Consuela smiled, and then looked over his shoulder, and all at once her expression changed.

"Good morning, Mrs. Barrow," she said.

Glen turned and saw Margaret coming slowly down the stairs, holding tightly to the railing as she went.

She looked very pale.

"Good morning, Consuela. Coffee, please, and some toast with jam—blackberry jam, if we have it, and some ice water as well. And two ibuprofen, I have a terrible headache. Three ibuprofen, in fact. Glen, I'm sure you've eaten already, but will you sit with me, please?"

He took a seat in the middle of the table. Margaret sat at the far end.

"Did you sleep well?" she asked.

"I did, thank you."

"I usually get up with Red and the others, but today I have a terrible headache."

"Uh-huh," Glen said.

She rubbed her eyes. "Consuela! That ibuprofen."

Consuela came running with pills and a glass of water.

Margaret took them without saying thank you, and handed Consuela back the glass. "I've changed my mind about the toast. Do we have marmalade? Orange marmalade?"

"*Sí.*"

"I'll have that instead of the blackberry. Thank you."

"Yes, Mrs. Barrow."

Margaret turned her attention back to Glen.

"So do you like horses?" she asked.

"I don't know. I never been around them really."

"I'm sure you'll come to like them as much as Red and I do. I grew up around horses, you know."

"Oh, yeah?"

"Yes. Back east. That's where I'm from, you know. Connecticut."

"Wow. How did you get here? I mean, what made you come out here?"

"Why, Mr. Barrow, of course. Red. I met him at a show in New York, and—" She shrugged. "We fell in love."

"Oh."

"You said you had breakfast already, Glen?"

"Yes. I had some eggs and some bacon. And some tortillas."

"Very nice," Margaret said. "Consuela is an excellent cook."

"I can tell that already."

"You'll eat well while you're here. I can assure you that," she said, as if this was a hotel he'd dropped in at for a couple days.

When Margaret's breakfast came, she stopped talking long enough to nibble a few bites of her toast. Then she leaned back in her chair and sighed.

"I have a terrible headache," she said again. "I think we'll have to postpone the lesson this morning, Glen. Consuela!"

Consuela came running out of the kitchen. "Yes, Mrs. Barrow?"

"I'm finished." She pushed the plate away from her. "I have to go lie down again, I'm afraid. Could you bring up a Bloody Mary in about—fifteen minutes?"

"Of course, ma'am."

"Thank you."

Margaret pushed her chair back, and stood.

"I'm sorry about this, Glen. Maybe we can have the lesson tomorrow, instead."

"I'd like that," Glen said quickly.

"Good. Consuela—"

"Yes, Mrs. Barrow?"

"No celery in the drink, please. There was celery last time."

"I'm sorry, Mrs. Barrow."

"That's quite all right. I just wanted to remind you." She smiled at Glen. "We're all only human, after all."

She left the table then, and went upstairs.

\*       \*       \*

Glen spent the morning with Consuela. She told him a little about herself—she'd been working for Red for almost thirty years, she had a husband and two sons who lived in Alpine, she liked to bake sweets and nobody else in the house seemed to want to eat them, so he should feel free to request cookies or cakes whenever he wanted, breakfast was at seven every day, lunch was whenever he wanted it if he was home, and dinner was at six o'clock sharp. Red liked to read, he did not like to watch TV; they only got one a few years ago and he kept it in a separate room, at the other end of the house, and refused to get an antenna so the reception was terrible anyway. Lucas was new to the ranch, she didn't know anything about him, but Deke and Tony had been around forever, they were good people, and on and on like that while she worked, and what struck Glen only later, after he'd gone outside to walk around a bit, was that she hadn't said one single, solitary word about Margaret.

Which he decided told him something in and of itself.

Red came back for lunch, like he'd promised. They went into Alpine and bought riding boots; Red said they were the best ones you could get around here, but that if Glen really ended up liking to ride, they'd drive on up to El Paso and go to the Tony Lama factory store. Go see his friend Jaime, and get him some "real boots." Glen said that sounded good to him.

When they got back, they took one of the trucks around the property. Red showed him things, and talked a little bit about the history of the ranch, and the whole ranching business, a lot of stuff Glen didn't know. If you'd asked him before if it would be interesting, he would have said no. Coming out of Red's mouth somehow everything sounded interesting.

It was just the two of them at dinner; Margaret hadn't come down the whole day, Consuela said. Red didn't look happy about that.

Red went to sleep early again; Glen stayed up in his room, thinking, reading a book he'd found in the library, and listening for the sounds of fighting, which finally started in around midnight, and lasted for an hour.

After that, he went to sleep.

The riding lesson happened the next day.

Margaret was downstairs eating with all the cowboys and Red when Glen got to the breakfast table. She seemed in a good mood. Everybody seemed in a good mood.

After breakfast, Red and the others went off to work. Margaret and Glen went out to the corral. There was a horse there, just standing in the middle of the ring, a dark brown horse with patches of white on it. It was nowhere near as big as Margaret's horse and didn't look anywhere near as imposing.

"Red and I thought we'd try you on Cortez this morning," Margaret said. "He's a very good horse."

"He looks like a good horse," Glen said.

"As long as you treat him right. That's the first rule of working with animals—treat them right, and they'll love you forever. But if you're mean to them—if you abuse them—they're likely to be afraid of you. Likely to hurt you."

She walked over to Cortez and patted him gently on the muzzle. The horse whinnied, with what looked to Glen to be pleasure.

Margaret turned and gave him a long, appraising stare. "You wouldn't abuse an animal, would you, Glen?" she asked.

"Oh, no, ma'am. Not ever."

"Good. All right, come over here. Stand here, next to me. Now—we're on which side of the horse?"

"The left side."

"That's correct. The left side." She smiled. "I almost said,

'That's right'—that would have been confusing, wouldn't it have been?"

Glen frowned. What she just said was confusing to him.

"Never mind. A little joke. Now, Glen, the first thing to re- member is that you always—always—mount a horse from the left side. Mount means get on."

"Yeah." *I could've guessed that,* he thought, but bit his tongue.

"Now. To get on"—she moved him out of the way—"you put your left foot into the left stirrup"—she put her foot into this little handle hanging down off the side of the saddle— "grab onto the horn of the saddle with your left hand"—at which point she grabbed onto the big knob at the front of the saddle, which Glen assumed was the horn—"swing yourself up, and there you are." She smiled down at him from high on the horse. "It's simple, wouldn't you agree?"

Glen nodded.

"Would you like to try it?"

"Okay."

She climbed down out of the saddle and handed him the reins to the horse.

"Oh, I almost forgot. The reins. You keep the reins in your hands while you're mounting."

"Okay."

"Now when you're up there, you'll hold these in your left hand as well. That's to keep your right hand free for other things. Opening the gates, for example. If you go riding around the ranch, we have a lot of gates."

"Okay."

"You may decide you want to help the others round up the animals at some point—probably when you're older, of course. Then you might have a whip in your right hand. Or a rope."

"Uh-huh."

"Now the right way to hold the reins is so that they pass through your fingers just so"—she pulled them through the fingers of his hand, and closed his thumb around them—"and then when you want the horse to move, you give a little tug. That's all, just a little tug. Because the reins are attached to the bit in his mouth, and if you pull hard, that will hurt him. And what's the first rule of riding horses?"

"Always mount from the left side."

"No." She shook her head. "We don't hurt them. That's the first rule."

"Okay."

"So you tug gently on the reins to make him move. If you want the horse to turn, you lay the reins on the side of the neck opposite the direction you want him to go. So to turn him left, you lay the reins on the right side of the neck. Understand?"

Glen didn't, not at all, he was pretty much completely lost at this point in the lesson, but the last thing he wanted to do was prolong this, so he just nodded and said, "I think so," which was apparently the wrong thing because Margaret shook her head and looked disappointed.

"Glen. You can't 'think' so. You have to be sure. Now— what part of what I said don't you understand?"

All of it, he wanted to say, but he had the feeling that wouldn't go over too well, so he just said, "About the reins."

"What about the reins?"

"How you turn him."

"How you use the reins to turn the horse?"

"Yes."

"It's very simple," Margaret said, with more than a little bit of an edge to her voice, and at that moment Glen just wanted to forget all about the riding lesson and go back inside, but of course he couldn't do that, that would more than likely make Margaret even angrier.

"Reins on the right side of the neck, horse turns left. Reins on the left, horse turns right. Got it?"

"Yes. Thank you."

"You're welcome." She sighed. "Glen, you're really going to have to pay attention, okay?"

"Yes. I will."

"Because this is my valuable riding time, and it's not polite to waste people's time."

"I don't mean to waste your time, ma'am, I'm sorry."

"Well, I appreciate that, and I'm happy to teach you. If you'll really put some effort into learning."

"I will."

"Good. All right now. Grab hold of the horn—with your left hand, Glen—"

"Oh right, sorry."

"—and step up."

But he couldn't reach the horn, or the stirrup.

Margaret boosted him, ended up pretty much lifting him right up into the saddle.

Once he was seated, though, there was another problem. His legs were too short to reach the stirrups.

"Get down so I can fix those," Margaret said, glaring at him like it was his fault.

Glen nodded and swung himself off the other side of the saddle.

"Glen, no!" she said sharply. "You always dismount to the left, remember? Now please pay attention."

"But you didn't say that before."

"I certainly did. And don't contradict me." She started tightening the stirrups. "It's bad manners for a child to contradict an adult."

Even when the adult is the one who's wrong? Glen wanted to ask, but didn't. Instead, he said, "Sorry," and walked around the horse to join her so he could try again.

"Stop!"

He froze in his tracks.

"Never walk behind a horse, Glen. It's very dangerous."

"I'm sorry," he said, and reversed his direction, and came around the front of the horse to join her.

"And I'm sorry for yelling. I just didn't want you to get hurt." She smiled tightly, and finished tightening the stirrups. "All right. That should do it."

She got him back into the saddle, and proceeded to spend the next five minutes lecturing him about posture, about sitting tall, keeping his heels down, stacking his body, keeping his ears over his shoulders, shoulders over hips, hips over heels, heels down, and on and on until Glen's head spun.

He went around the ring all of two times, at a snail's pace, before Margaret helped him off the horse, shaking her head.

"Well, there's a lot of work to do," she said. "But the important thing is that you enjoyed it. You did enjoy it, didn't you, Glen?"

"Oh, yes," he said, mustering up all the enthusiasm he could. "I enjoyed it a lot."

"Good." She stared at him expectantly. "Well . . ."

"Well . . . " He couldn't think of what the "well" was for. "Well, I would like to do it again?"

"Glen . . . what do you say after someone does something nice for you?"

"Oh, I'm sorry. Thank you."

"You're welcome. I think we had a good time." She took the reins and started leading the horse away from him. "You just have to apply yourself a little more, Glen. I'm sure you'll do just fine."

Watching her walk away, though, he had his doubts.

The next few months were pretty happy ones for Glen. He settled into a routine at school, had a pretty easy time of it because for one thing, the kids were really, really impressed that he was living with Red Barrow, who was obviously some kind of big deal in Alpine, which meant that the cracks about the burns on his face and the different colors of his eyes were kept to a minimum, and for another, because he was repeating second grade, and didn't have to try too hard in class. He even made a friend, a boy named Chip Walker who lived not that far down the road, and went over to his house a couple times to play. One Friday, he even had a sleepover at the Walkers', though *sleep* was not the right word to use; Glen and Chip stayed up watching TV till past midnight, Chip's parents having stuck them in the family room by themselves for the evening. They watched a movie called *Dracula Has Risen from the Grave,* which Glen was pretty sure was going to give him nightmares, and did, and after that, a little bit of a detective show called *The Rockford Files,* which was boring, so they switched to another channel, which was featuring professional wrestling. That was not boring. At first Glen didn't know what to make of it, to be honest. There was a guy dressed up like an Indian (Chief Jay Strongbow, he was called), and he was wrestling another guy who had more muscles than Glen had ever seen on anyone before, somebody called Superstar Billy Graham who turned out to be the heavyweight wrestling champion of the world.

Glen frowned. Billy Graham? He remembered Melissa Vick talking to him about Billy Graham once.

"I thought he was a preacher," Glen said. "Billy Graham."

Chip looked at him funny.

"What are you talking about?"

Glen shut up and watched for a few minutes. It was pretty wild. It wasn't just wrestling—Chief Jay and Billy Graham were throwing each other all over the ring. They bounced off the ropes, they flew through the air, they bent each other into all different kinds of shapes. Billy put the chief in a "figure four"—a little later, the Chief put him in a "deathlock." Chip got all excited when that happened. Glen asked why.

"Because when Chief Jay wins, he does this dance. This war dance. You have to see it. It's wicked cool."

Chip started doing a dance then, kind of an Indian dance, hopping all around the room, making "whoo-whoo" noises and laughing at the same time.

His parents came in, and shut off the TV.

At school later in the week, Glen found out from a depressed Chip that Chief Jay hadn't won after all, that Billy Graham was still the champion.

Mrs. Rodriguez came by every few days to see him at first, asked him a lot of questions about how things were going, though from the looks she and Red kept exchanging, he expected that she knew that things were going pretty good, with the exception of Margaret, who was kind of detaching herself from him more and more. Glen didn't know what to do about that—Red obviously didn't want to talk about it, so he was content to let it lie too. As was Mrs. Rodriguez, whose visits gradually trickled off to once every couple weeks.

And Margaret was right; he even ended up being able to ride a horse, though that had nothing to do with her. It was Red who ended up teaching him, pretty much by putting him up on the horse and letting him ride around the ranch a few times before even trying to correct what he was doing.

And late one afternoon, after he'd gotten home from school, he finally found out where the ranch got its name. Aurora.

It was, as it turned out, the name of Red's daughter.

# chapter
# seven

"So the Circle B used to be called—"

"River Run, like I told you. It was part of the Double Diamond back then, just like this place was. That was fifty years ago, though. Lot of changes since then."

Consuela was making dinner—rice and beans, and chicken-fried steak—and filling Glen in on a little bit of the local history at the same time. He was trying to figure out how all the ranchers around here related to each other. One thing he knew—a lot of them were having a hard time making ends meet. He got that from some of the kids at school, some of whom lived on ranches just like Aurora, with names like the Circle B and Talley's Canyon, which was when Glen asked Consuela where Red had gotten the name for this ranch—Aurora—from.

She was silent a long time before answering.

"He didn't tell you?"

"No."

"Well . . . I'm not sure I should be the one to tell you."

"Why not? What is it, some big secret?"

"No, but—"

"Well, come on then, Consuela. Please."

She sighed, and nodded. "Aurora is Red's daughter."

Glen just about fell off his stool when he heard that.

"His daughter? Red has a daughter?"

She nodded. "From his first marriage."

"His first marriage?" Glen suddenly realized how little he knew about Red. "When was this?"

"A long time ago." Consuela smiled at the memory. "Twenty years ago, at least, since Lucia died. The first Mrs. Barrow."

"And Aurora—is she dead too?"

"No." Consuela shook her head. "I shouldn't be telling you this."

"Why not?"

"Because this is for Red to tell you."

"Well, he's not here. Come on, Consuela. Where is she? Where's Red's daughter?"

"Dallas," the woman said finally. "She and Red don't talk anymore."

"Why not?"

Consuela bent down to check something in the oven. "You'll have to ask him about that."

"But why don't they talk?"

"It's not for me to say," Consuela repeated. "Now go. Shoo. I have to finish in here."

But Glen had an idea already.

He suspected it had something to do with Margaret Barrow.

He didn't ask Red about it right away—he wanted to wait for the right time. That turned out to be a Saturday afternoon when Margaret had gone to El Paso for the day, to go shopping. He and Red spent the morning riding around the ranch, and when they got back, Deke and Tony were in the corral, practicing for a big rodeo coming up the next week in Marathon. Tony showed him how to hog-tie a calf, which involved wrestling the animal to the ground and tying him up with some very specific knots, including something called a "hooey," the name of which made Glen laugh out loud—a "hooey," that didn't sound like a kind of knot, it sounded like something you coughed up from inside your throat.

Everybody laughed when he said that.

They had sandwiches for lunch, and then Red asked him about school, and his friends, and Glen pretty much repeated the conversation he'd had with Consuela the other day, and that led him right into the question, where'd the name Aurora come from?

Red nodded when he said that, but didn't respond for a minute.

Then he said, "Hold on a minute," got up from the table, and went upstairs. Actually, he didn't go upstairs, he went up the stairs and stopped a couple steps down from the second floor, pulled a picture off the wall, and came back down.

"Name of the ranch comes from her," he said, and handed Glen the picture.

It was of him and the laughing red-haired woman, the one Glen had noticed the first day he was here.

"Who's she?" Glen asked.

Red looked at him and smiled, like he knew Glen already knew the answer to that question.

"That's Aurora," he said. "That's my daughter."

The whole story came out then, and it was pretty much as Glen had suspected. Aurora's mom had died young; Red had raised her by himself. She'd grown up to run the ranch named after her, at least as much as Red. When he came back from New York with Margaret, the two of them didn't click from the get-go. Red implied there'd been a bunch of big, nasty fights, at the end of which Aurora pulled her father aside and said something to the effect of, 'It's her or me, Dad, 'cause I can't live with that woman,' and Red said she couldn't ask him to make a choice like that, and she said that was just what she was doing, and he said again he couldn't do it, and she listened and nodded. The next morning when Red woke up she was gone.

"She still sends a Christmas card, and a card on my birthday," Red said. "But other than that . . . nothing."

He looked very sad all of a sudden.

"I'm sorry for bringing this up," Glen said. "I was just curious."

"Of course you were. It's not your fault. It's just a bad situation, that's all. I expect it'll clear up soon enough."

"I hope so."

"So do I. For Margaret's sake, too," he added quickly. "It's hard on her, knowing that she came between me and Aurora. I've told her it's not her fault, it takes two people to make a problem this big, but—"

"I get it," Glen said. Now that he had the truth, the whole subject was uncomfortable for him. He wanted to move on to another one as quickly as possible.

"I'll tell you what," Red said. "To be honest with you, I think part of the reason why Margaret agreed to adopt you too was because she knew I missed Aurora. That might be why she's being slow to warm to you too, Glen. Because seeing you—it reminds her about my girl, too."

"Oh," Glen said, his eyes widening. "It's complicated, isn't it?"

"Sure is. But I appreciate how you're handling the situation, Glen. You're bein' real grown-up about it. I know you and Margaret have a hard time once in a while, and I appreciate you sticking with it. I really do." He smiled. "You're doin' better than Aurora did, that's for sure."

Glen didn't know what to say to that.

But on the way upstairs that night, Glen stopped by the picture, which Red had hung back up on the wall, and took a closer look at it. The two of them sure looked happy together.

Must have taken an awful lot to drive her away.

\*       \*       \*

Red ended up having to go to Austin himself a few days later, on business. Something to do with a law that they were about to pass that would make things a lot tougher for the independent ranchers like him to make a living.

He wasn't happy about it.

"Hate wearin' this damn monkey suit," he said as he came down the stairs, wearing a sport coat and dress pants. He was wearing a bolo tie, too. It was the first time Glen had seen him in anything other than a plaid shirt and jeans.

"It looks okay," Glen said.

"You look good," Margaret added, coming up behind Red and giving him a kiss on the cheek. "Very statesmanlike."

"Oh, hell." Red shook his head. "I look like an idiot, and we all know it, but me and Hallie Stillwell are just about the only two sane people left in this part of the state. We gotta remind those youngsters up in Austin who pays their salaries." He pointed a finger at Glen. "Never go into politics, son. Remember that."

"Yes, sir, I will."

"He's kidding. You be whatever you want to, Glen," Margaret said.

Glen couldn't help but smile at that. That was about the nicest thing she'd ever said to him.

Red smiled too.

"Now you two gonna be all right here without me?"

"We'll be fine," Margaret said. "Won't we, Glen?"

"Yes, ma'am," he answered, really meaning it. Margaret seemed in a really good mood today, for some reason. Maybe their relationship was about to turn a corner, he thought.

As it turned out, he was right.


Things started going bad after lunch.

Margaret wanted to give him another riding lesson. Glen

tried to beg off, but saw right away that wasn't going to be possible without hurting her feelings. Later on, of course, he realized that he should have just taken a page from her book, said he had a headache, that he didn't feel well.

Needless to say, the lesson didn't go well. Margaret kept trying to get him to "stack his body," as she put it.

"Ears over shoulders, shoulders over hips, hips over heels," she said over and over again as he rode around the ring in a tiny little circle. "Imagine a plumb line running straight through your body to the ground and stay in that position."

"Yes, ma'am."

"You know what a plumb line is, Glen?"

"Yes, ma'am."

He had no idea on earth what a plumb line was.

"Good." Glen noticed to his dismay then that she took another sip from the flask she was carrying with her. She'd been sipping at it since they got outside.

"Red didn't tell you any of this?" she asked.

"No, ma'am."

She made a noise of disgust in her throat. "Of course he's making me do the hard work. I'm sorry, Glen, that you're bearing the brunt of it, but there's a right way and a wrong way to do things. You understand that, don't you?"

"Yes, ma'am."

"Good." She took another sip and frowned at him. "Don't look at me, look ahead! Stack your body, Glen! A plumb line!"

And that was pretty much how the afternoon went.

Margaret never came down to dinner. Consuela sat with him as he ate and every once in a while glanced nervously toward the stairs.

"You sure you gonna be all right?" she asked. "I could stay here tonight, if you want."

"I'll be okay," he said, trying to sound braver than he felt. "Deke and the others are right out in the bunkhouse. Don't worry about me."

"I do worry," Consuela said. She hesitated a moment, then continued. "Mrs. Barrow—when she gets drinking, she's not really herself."

That might be a good thing, Glen wanted to say, but held his tongue.

He didn't want Consuela to stay, though. He wanted to handle things himself. What was it Red had told him?—I appreciate you stickin' with it. He didn't wanna let Red down.

Besides, what was there to worry about, really? Margaret might get angry sometimes, but she was his new mom, wasn't she? Everything was gonna be fine. And the ranch hands were right outside, if he needed them.

There was no reason to worry. No reason at all.


Sometime in the night Glen woke to the sound of knocking on his door.

"You in there, Glen?"

He rolled over and looked at the clock. Two-ten.

"Yes, ma'am. I'm in here."

"Open up. I want to talk to you."

"Ummm . . ." He didn't know what to say; could he say no to Margaret?

No, he realized. He couldn't.

"Just a minute," he called out, and turned on the light. He got out of bed and opened the door, and realized at once that had been a very bad idea.

Margaret was drunk.

Her hair was loose and falling all over the place, her bathrobe was barely closed, and Glen could tell she was naked underneath it, and worst of all, she was carrying a bottle of liquor in one hand, which meant she was still drinking.

"Just wanted to check in on you, if that's all right," she said, and took a big swig off the bottle. "Since Red's out of town. You don't mind, do you?"

And before Glen could answer, she walked into his room and sat down on his bed.

"So tell me, Glen, how's it going with you? You like living here with me and the old man? Red, I mean?" She snorted and coughed, and took another sip from her bottle.

"Yes, ma'am. I sure do like it. I appreciate everything you both have done for me."

Margaret waved a hand away. "Ahh. I ain't done shit, and we both know it."

"That's not so, ma'am," Glen said. "You been—"

She glared at him. "You contradicting me, Glen?"

"No, ma'am."

She pointed a finger at him.

"Don't contradict me."

"I won't."

"And don't call me ma'am, goddamnit. I ain't a fuckin' ma'am."

Glen felt nauseous. This whole scene, it reminded him of some horrible, horrible times he'd pushed way to the back of his mind, scenes from long ago when his dad used to get drunk and come home and him and his mom had terrible fights, said terrible things to each other.

"No. I won't."

"You're supposed to call me Mom, you know."

"Okay," Glen said quickly. "Mom."

"Ah, fuck." She waved a hand at him. "Never mind that. Don't call me Mom. I don't like that either."

"I could call you Margaret," Glen offered hesitantly.

"Yeah, sure. Call me Margaret." She took another sip from her bottle. "That's a good idea. That's a smart idea."

She sat there a minute, staring off into space, then all at once spun around to face him again.

"I make you nervous, Glen?"

"No."

"You don't want me in your room, is that it?"

"No. That's not it at all. I'm glad you're here."

"Don't lie to me Glen."

"I'm not lying."

"And don't contradict me."

"Yes, ma'am. Margaret," he said quickly, correcting himself. "I won't."

"Good." She nodded, more to herself than him, and fell silent again.

"Sorry about today, Glen. What happened in the ring."

"It's okay."

"I didn't mean to yell at you like that."

"I know."

"It's just that I'm a perfectionist, you know? I like things done right. They're not done right, why do 'em at all? Am I right?"

"Yes."

"Of course I'm right." Another pause. "Next time, you could ride my horse. Shiloh. He's a good horse. But you gotta treat him right. You want to do that? Ride Shiloh?"

"If you want."

"If I want? What do you want, boy? That's the question." She glared at him then, and Glen thought, *What I want is you out of my room,* but of course he couldn't say that.

"You after Red's money?" she asked suddenly.

"What?"

"She send you? You trying to get rid of me?"

"I don't know what you're talking about!"

"You don't, huh. The fuck you don't." She leaned toward him. "Tell me the truth, boy, did she send you? Huh?"

"I don't—" Glen started to say, which was when she grabbed his face in one hand and squeezed.

"You little bastard, you tell me the truth now, huh?" She squeezed and wagged his face from side to side, both at the same time. "She send you to spy on me? See if I was still in her dad's good graces? Is that what she did?"

Glen was crying and trying to talk and breathe all at once. "No, no, I swear to God nobody sent me. I don't know who you mean but nobody sent me—"

Margaret let go.

"Ah, fuck," she said.

Glen sniffled and wiped away tears, and tried to stop crying.

"DON'T LOOK AT ME LIKE THAT!" she yelled suddenly. "DON'T LOOK AT ME LIKE THAT!"

Glen bowed his head and stared at the floor.

Now Margaret was crying too.

"I used to be a good person," she said. "And then I moved to this shithole town, and this shithole state, and look at me now! I'm old and I'm miserable and I'm a fucking drunk!"

They were both quiet a minute.

"You're not old," Glen offered.

She reached back and slapped him across the mouth, hard.

Glen tasted blood.

"Don't you try and be nice to me," she said. "Don't you dare be nice to me."

She got up and wandered back down the hall again.

Glen shut his door and locked it, even though he was pretty sure she had a key.

He stayed up the whole rest of the night then, sitting on his bed, afraid she was going to come back.

*       *       *

He went to school the next day, but didn't talk to anybody. On the bus there and back, he stared silently out the window.

He was gonna have to tell Red, Glen knew that, and he wasn't looking forward to it.

I tried stickin' with her, Red, Glen imagined himself saying. I really did. But she's mean. She hit me. You should trade her in. You should get Aurora back.

When he got back home, as expected, Red's truck was parked in front of the house. Next to it was another car, though, one he didn't recognize.

When he got in the house, though, he surely recognized its driver, who was deep in conversation with Red.

It was the policeman from the hospital. Sergeant Dominguez.

"Hello, Glen," Dominguez said, getting to his feet. "I hope you don't mind me dropping in like this, but there's been a development in the case. Can we talk for a minute?"

# chapter eight

Dominguez wanted to talk to Glen in private. Red, after smiling and ruffling Glen's hair, asked if he could be there too. Dominguez said sure, as long as he understood that the questions the sergeant would be asking were for Glen, and not for him. Red nodded that he did.

Glen noticed no sign of Margaret anywhere.

"So you caught a break in the case," Red said.

"Yes, sir. Looks that way."

"Call me Red, okay?"

"Red. Sure. Now, Glen—you remember the last time we talked—in the hospital?"

Glen allowed as he did, at which point Dominguez reviewed the case for Red, how they were sure it was arson but they had no idea who'd done it, or why.

"And that's where the case has been these last few months. Until Friday." The policeman looked around at both of them. "We got a call from a motel owner up in Van Horn. He was cleaning out one of his rooms, and found this hidden underneath the bed."

Dominguez reached down then, pulled a brown paper bag from the floor, and set it on the couch next to him.

"You recognize this, Glen?" he asked, reaching into the bag and pulling something out.

It was a mask, deep black with slashes of red. There were

burn marks on the nose and cheek areas, where fire had cut across it.

"Yes," Glen said, feeling dizzy all of a sudden. "I recognize it. It was my father's. How did it get there?"

"Someone left it there, obviously," Dominguez said. "Is there something special about this mask?"

"I don't know. I just know he collected them," Glen said.

"It's a real piece of work. Beautiful," Red said, leaning forward and holding out his hand to Dominguez. "May I . . ."

The policeman handed him the mask, and Red looked it over carefully.

"There's some writing in here," he said, and then read aloud, *"Mascara de la Muerta Negra."*

"Mask of the Black Death," Dominguez translated. "They use masks like these in religious ceremonies, down in Mexico. Like in Day of the Dead."

"Fantastic," Red said, and handed the mask back to Dominguez. Then he frowned.

"This is what I don't get, Sergeant. How did you know this mask was Randall Callaway's?"

"I didn't."

"Well, then . . . " Red frowned again. "I don't understand. How'd you know to come here, to Glen?"

"Because of this," Dominguez said, and reached into the bag again and pulled out a big brown book. At first Glen thought it was a notebook, then he saw the papers sticking out of its sides and the edge of a photo and the writing on the front that said simply "Kane" and he felt his heart thumping in his chest so hard he thought it was going to break right through him.

It was his mom's scrapbook. The Kane family scrapbook.

"I guess you recognize this too," Dominguez said.

Glen managed a nod.

Dominguez set the scrapbook and the mask aside then. "The question I have is, how did these things get in that motel?"

He looked at Glen again.

"I don't know," Glen said.

"We've matched up signatures on the motel registry, looking at dates from the time of the fire," the sergeant went on. "We think Paul Grimm was at this motel right about then."

Somehow, Glen wasn't surprised to hear that name again.

"Who's Paul Grimm?" Red asked.

Dominguez explained.

"You think he set the fire?" Glen asked.

"We're looking for him," Dominguez said. "We're looking for somebody else too."

Glen shook his head. He had no idea what the policeman was talking about.

"The night clerk at that motel—he remembers seeing Grimm with a boy. He couldn't give us much of a description, though."

"A boy?" Glen repeated.

"That's right. Now, Glen, I have to ask you this. We have another witness too. That witness is saying he saw a man and a boy together the night before the fire. The man matches Grimm's description. We're still trying to figure out who the boy was."

"Well, it wasn't me," Glen said.

Dominguez stared at him intently. Glen realized that the man thought he was lying.

"I'm telling you the truth," Glen said.

"Okay. If it wasn't you—then who was it?"

"I don't know."

"Who else did Grimm know around here?"

"He knew a lot of people," Glen said. "Believe me, if I knew I'd tell you."

"You can't think of anyone he was particularly close to?"

"Nobody liked him," Glen said. "I can tell you that for sure."

"What about kids? Any kids he was friendly with?"

"He hated kids," Glen said. "The only ones he ever talked to at all were me and Mark, and that was only because we were there when he was hanging around."

"Mark's dead," Dominguez said.

"I know that."

"Which leaves you."

"It wasn't me," Glen said firmly.

Dominguez stared at him a moment longer before finally nodding in acceptance.

"Okay." The man got up. "Thanks. I'll be in touch."

"What about these things?" Red asked, holding up the mask and the scrapbook.

"The boy can keep them," the officer said. "They're of no use to me."

Later that night, after dinner, Glen took them up to his room. He put the mask on his bureau, sat down on the bed, and began flipping through the scrapbook. He hadn't thought about this part of his life in so long, things had been going so well, he'd almost forgotten it completely. Almost.

Which was when he realized he had forgotten completely to tell Red what happened between Margaret and him the night before.

He had a hard time falling asleep that night. He couldn't stop thinking about the curse, about Rebecca Kane, and James Dean, and his mom, and dad, and Mark, and Jarvis Vick, and Melissa and Katie, who he still hadn't written to and now decided he wouldn't, just because better safe than sorry.

Except the next morning, when Glen woke up, he realized he hadn't played it quite safe enough.

Red had been out riding first thing in the morning, and his horse, it seemed, had gotten spooked by something. A rattlesnake, some hornets, a shadow, who knew?

The point was, the horse had bucked, and Red had fallen hard.

He had a concussion. Cracked ribs. Most worrisome of all was the thin fracture in his neck. They didn't want to risk transporting him to a hospital, so the doctors set up shop in his bedroom, which was when Glen first began to get an idea of just how wealthy Red must have been, because by the time they finished putting in the machines and what-not they needed to treat him, his bedroom looked exactly like Glen's room back at the hospital had, a high-tech horror shop.

The sight of Red lying helpless there, strapped to all those machines, little wisps of hair falling over his eyes, just about broke Glen's heart. Especially since he knew it was all his fault.

That first night, after the nurse that they hired had fallen asleep in the guest room, after the doctors and worried friends and neighbors had all gone away, Glen crept quietly into Red's room and tried to explain, even though Red's eyes were closed and he was pretty sure the man couldn't hear him.

"It's the curse, Red," he began. "It's all my fault."

Halfway through his recitation of the Kane family history, he realized that there was someone standing behind him.

He turned and saw Margaret.

"What sort of crap are you going on about?" she asked, and he could smell the liquor on her breath, even from halfway across the room.

"I was just—"

"Never mind. Just shut up and get back to your goddamn bed, all right?"

"All right."

She followed him all the way down the hall to his room.

"I'm gonna lock you in tonight, so you don't go tromping around the house waking everybody up."

Before he could say a word in protest, she slammed the door behind him.

He heard the key in the lock then, and knew she'd been as good as her word.

That first week, Red came out of it a few times. Glen was lucky enough to be there once, and even though Red couldn't talk much, he was obviously happy to see the boy. He smiled, and even tried to ruffle his hair.

He whispered something, and Glen leaned close to hear it.

"Aurora," Red said, and smiled again.

Glen forced himself to smile back.

The second week, Red went into a coma. The doctors couldn't say for sure when—or if—he'd come out of it.

Margaret said they had to start cutting costs around the house, because the medical bills were so outrageous. She fired Consuela, who begged Glen to come with her. He said no, not because he didn't want to, but because he didn't want to see her or her family get hurt too. Because of the curse.

Margaret's drinking got worse. One night, Glen heard her coming down the hall, screaming his name like he'd done something wrong, and dove under his bed just before she opened the door.

"Where are you, you goddamn brat?" she yelled. "Are you hiding from me?"

He lay under the bed, breathing heavy, praying to God that

she'd think he was somewhere else in the house and go looking for him.

God, apparently, wasn't answering prayers that night.

"Gotcha," she said, lifting up a corner of the bedspread and
peering underneath.

Glen screamed and tried to get away.

She dragged him out by one leg.

"You're hiding from me? You're trying to run away? I'll
show you."

She pushed him down and grabbed him by the legs. He
tried to kick himself free, but she clubbed him downward,
keeping him facedown on the ground. Then she sat on top of
him, pinning him.

"You don't run away from me," she said, grabbing his
ankle. "I have to show you that. I have to teach you."

She twisted his ankle awkwardly inward, torquing it with
as much force as she could muster. Her body weight and
anger was scaring Glen, and he began to cry.

"You can feel that, huh?" she taunted him. "I thought you
weren't supposed to be able to feel anything? Why are you
crying if you can't feel? You fucking brat, you been lying
about that too?"

She continued bending his ankle, now moving it outward
with all her strength, not stopping after his crying reached un-
controllable wailing, not stopping after she heard a sickening
pop from his body. The angle was gruesome, and she was too
drunk to care.

She slammed his leg to the ground and walked out.

When the nurse came back the next day, she explained the
broken ankle by saying Glen had jumped off a galloping horse.

The third week, Red got better.

"You got the constitution of a twenty-year-old, my friend. I don't know how else to explain it," Doc Johnston said, standing up from his place at Red's bedside.

"And I bet he wants it back, right, Doc?" Red asked.

Johnston—who was older than Red, had been his physician since grade school—snorted, and shook his head. "Joke if you want, but you dodged a bullet here, Red."

"I know," Red replied, suddenly serious. He'd been drifting in and out of consciousness for a while now, for how long he really wasn't certain, but enough time for him to realize that whether you measured it in days or weeks or months or even years, God willing, his time here was drawing to a close, and he'd better mend fences and make peace while he was still able to. Which meant calling Aurora, for one thing, and for another . . .

He had to deal with Margaret.

Now the fact was that he loved her, and there was no logical way to explain that, but he'd been letting her get away with too much, for too long. There was no way he could excuse her behavior toward Consuela anymore, or toward the boy. Especially the boy. Glen was at a fragile place in his life, and a wrong word or two now could have some terrible implications later on.

When she came in to see him later, he tried to start that conversation with her. She tried to shush him, telling him he had to rest.

"I've been resting for two goddamn weeks now, I think it is," Red said. "Hell, I'm not even sure how long I've been resting. I want to do something, and since the doc says I can't do much walking for the next little bit, let's see if we can't iron this thing out, all right?"

He asked her to bring the boy in to see him. She said she couldn't. She said the funniest thing had happened. Another riding accident. Glen had broken an ankle. He was laid up in bed too.

The next night, Red was woken up by the sound of crying. Actually, at first he thought it might have been a wolf, or a coyote. Only after listening for a few minutes did he realize it was coming from inside the house, and who it had to be.

He shut his eyes then, and did some praying of his own.

Against the nurse's instructions, Red got himself out of bed the next day and hobbled downstairs, shouting for Consuela. She never answered.

He found Margaret drunk in the bedroom, wild-eyed and muttering something about a curse. He saw that scrapbook the policeman had brought from the motel—Glen's scrapbook—lying open on their bed.

He went looking for Glen, and found him locked in his bedroom.

He had a black eye, and a big red welt on one cheek, and hugged Red so hard when he let him out that the man thought he might have busted another rib.

*Enough is enough,* Red thought, and helped Glen downstairs. Then he went into the kitchen to phone the police.

Something hard hit him on the head then, and he slumped to the floor.

When Red came to again, it was night, and someone was screaming bloody murder.

Glen.

His head was pounding where Margaret—of course it was Margaret, who else could it be?—had hit him with whatever. He went to the gun cabinet to unlock it, to get a revolver, and found it standing wide open. One of the rifles was missing.

"Goddamnit," Red said, and called the police, and then headed out to the barn, where the screaming was coming from.

As Red neared the barn door, he heard a short, sharp whirring sound, then what sounded like a slap, followed by another scream. He followed the noises to the garage where the tractor was stored. He tried the knob. The door was locked.

He pounded his fist against the door.

"Margaret! Goddamnit, Margaret, open this door!"

"Go away, Red!" He heard the whipping motion again, followed by a brutal-sounding slap, and a wail from Glen.

"Margaret, open the door right now!"

The slapping sound came again, and again, and again, and Red realized what was going on; she was whipping the boy.

Red threw his shoulder into the door, but it didn't budge. Then he heard something that scared him to death. Glen coughing, choking, making a guttural noise that was unmistakably a struggle for air.

Red took a step back and kicked the door as hard as he could. It flung open, and his momentum carried him into the room.

There was a little moonlight spilling into the barn—enough so he could see that Glen's feet were dangling off the floor. Margaret had wrapped the whip around his neck and thrown one end over a beam so she could pull him completely off the ground, choking him. His hands were struggling to free his throat, but it was clear from the noises he was making that he was losing the fight.

Red lowered his shoulder and ran into his wife, knocking her to the ground and loosing her grip on the whip. Glen came crashing to the ground, and lay still.

Red felt around the boy's neck. It was an electrical cord, not a whip, and it had been wrapped around his neck so tightly, it was still choking him. Red dropped his gun and tried frantically to untie it.

"Leave it."

He turned around to see Margaret pointing a rifle at his head.

"Margaret, put that down," he said softly. "Don't do anything crazy now, you hear me?"

"I said leave it, Red. I gotta end it here." She was lit, Red saw, barely able to stand up on her feet without wobbling.

"End it? What on earth are you talking about?"

"The curse, Red. The curse that boy put on us."

"That's crazy talk, Margaret." He shook his head. "Now come on, honey, put that gun down."

"You gotta read the scrapbook, Red. You'll understand then, honey. It's all in there. That boy's a monster. Him and his family."

She swung the gun around and pointed it at Glen's head.

"I'm about to do the world a great big favor, believe me," she said, and pulled the trigger.

The gun jammed.

"Fuck," she said, and yanked the barrel back, which was when Red charged at her.

She raised the gun reflexively, and it went off.

Red felt something hit him square in the chest, and he flew backward, landing hard on the ground.

Definitely cracked a rib that time, he thought, and his vision blurred.

Margaret stared at him, at the softball-sized hole in his chest gushing blood, and fell to her knees.

"Oh, God. Red? I didn't even pull the trigger, I . . . "

She turned to Glen. "Damn you," she said, starting to cry. "This is your fault."

Glen tried to crawl away. She grabbed on to his leg. He kicked at her, and got free. He ran and hid in the corner of the barn.

"Where are you, you goddamn brat? I'll kill you! You hear me, I'll kill you!"

Glen tried not to breathe.

In the distance, getting closer, he heard sirens.

Margaret slumped down in the middle of the barn and started crying again.

"You did this to us," she said. "You hear me, boy? You did this to us. I hope you burn in hell."

Glen peeked out from the corner. He saw Margaret holding Red's revolver.

She sobbed again, and before he could say or do anything to stop her, she put the barrel to her forehead and squeezed the trigger.

The police got there in time to pronounce both husband and wife dead.

Aurora Barrow was there the next morning. She took charge like she'd never left.

She turned out not to be such a nice woman after all. She made noises about the adoption process not being formally complete, about having no obligation to Glen whatsoever. She let him keep the clothes he was wearing, and the boots, and the scrapbook. She tried to stop him from taking the mask. Didn't believe him when he said it was his. Consuela got there just in time to stop the two of them from having a fistfight all their own.

Dick Beavis picked him up at the ranch the next day.

"Well, this is a tragedy, no doubt about it," Beavis said as they drove away. "But it's not your fault, Glen. Not your fault at all. It's all on the Barrows, that's it. Not you at all."

Not on Red, Glen wanted to say. Not on Red.

But his throat was still sore, from the electrical cord. It hurt just to swallow. So he didn't say anything.

"Tell you the truth," Beavis continued. "Some of it's on Mrs. Rodriguez. Doesn't seem like she vetted these Barrows well enough. No, sir. The director's not happy at all, I can tell you that, Glen. Not at all. Gonna be some changes at the agency, is my guess. I think—" He seemed to realize then he was maybe saying too much, and stopped talking for a while.

Sometime later, Glen looked up to see that they had left Aurora, and Alpine itself behind. Up ahead of him was a sign.

Welcome to
MARFA, TEXAS
Home of the World-Famous Marfa Lights
*Giant* filmed here, 1951–1952

He was home.

His stay in Marfa didn't last long, though.

Within a week, Beavis (who was his caseworker once more; Glen never saw Mrs. Rodriguez again) had placed him in a foster home up near El Paso. The fattest woman he'd ever seen in his life, fat with short red hair and a mean face. Mrs. Dalrymple.

She looked him up and down.

"You a good worker, boy?" she asked.

Glen nodded.

"What's the matter, boy? Can't speak?"

Glen pointed to his throat.

"You a mute?" She glared at Beavis. "We didn't ask for a mute."

"He can speak," Beavis said. "He just got an injury, right now. He'll be fine in a little bit."

Mrs. Dalrymple shook her head.

"I ain't got a little bit. You see how many kids I got already? Sorry, Mr. Beavis, this ain't what I'm looking for. Can't parent if you can't communicate, that's what I always say."

And that was the end of the Dalrymples.

That was pretty much how the next four years of his life went. In and out of different foster homes, different family placements, Presidio County, Brewster County, up to El Paso, down to Big Bend, and then, in 1981, Beavis placed him with a couple named Wilbert and Raylene Harrison, who owned a little motel in Valentine, just north of Marfa.

Wilbert turned out to be a drunk, but not a mean drunk. Raylene was almost as fat as Mrs. Dalrymple had been, and spent her days behind the reception counter at the motel, watching TV. Glen helped out around the motel, went to school (most of the time, anyway), and watched a lot of TV himself. Somewhere along the way he stopped talking almost altogether. The kids started teasing him again, calling him freak, even though the burns on his face were almost all gone. They found other things to make fun of—his eyes, of course, the clothes he wore, the funny rasp to his voice on those few occasions he did talk.

He'd come full circle, it seemed.

Somewhere along the line Beavis lost track of him; Glen realized that only when he graduated from sixth grade into junior high school, and didn't get his usual "keep up the great work" card from the man. Not that he cared all that much; he didn't need Beavis. He didn't need anyone, in fact.

Somewhere along the way, Glen Callaway had grown into

an awfully big boy. Five feet eight inches by the time the fall of 1983 rolled around. Big enough that the teasing just about stopped, at least to his face. Big enough, Glen realized, that he could take care of himself, in every way imaginable.

It took him six more months to act on that realization, though.

# chapter
## nine

Frank Walsh sat in the teacher's lounge at Marfa High School, grading the pop quiz he'd given his eighth-grade American History class, and felt like popping someone himself. One of the kids, probably—like Buster Young. Buster was as dumb as his brother Denton had been, dumber probably, though nowhere near as nasty, but still . . .

Any kid who had come this far in life and thought that Benjamin Franklin was the first American president, and that Thomas Edison signed the Declaration of Independence . . .

He sighed and pushed back from his chair. Ah, it wasn't just Buster, or the other kids in the class. Walsh was frustrated because he was not just the history teacher at Marfa High; more importantly (to him, and honestly, to everyone else in the town), he was the football coach, and here they were, four games into the football season, and already it was clear that the team was not going to make the playoffs. Clear to him, anyway. Yeah, they were two and two, and had a bunch more games to go, but the fact was the two wins both came against Anthony, and Anthony was terrible this year, and Fort Hancock had beat them pretty handily, and last Friday night the Bucks had whipped their asses but good, 52–10, and it could have been a lot worse if Conrad—Conrad Dealey, Alpine's coach—hadn't taken it easy on them for the whole second half.

And not only was it frustrating about this year's team, but

things didn't look much better for the next few years either. He thought it must be cyclical or something; two years ago they were Division A champs for Western Texas, and in the running for the title for most of the previous half-decade, and then last year they started to slide, and this year . . .

Just thinking about it was enough to drive him back to the pop quizzes.

He worked silently for a few minutes, black marker flicking, noticing with relief that at least some of the kids knew the basics of early American history. Janie Boyd had almost a perfect score, as always, and Kathy Marin was right behind her, now that girl was gonna be a heartbreaker, and very, very soon, the boys in the class were starting to swarm around her already, and Walsh was happy to see that Luis Campos passed too, just barely, Campos was about the best athlete in the class, the only real top-notch football prospect out of the bunch, if a little bit too much of the clown for Walsh's sake.

Then he flipped to the next student's paper and frowned.

Glen Callaway.

Now this kid was a mystery to him.

For one thing, he almost never said a word. Walsh didn't think it was out of shyness, because the kid had a certain self-possession to him. For another thing, he never participated in gym class, on account of some medical condition the coach didn't understand. He looked healthy enough to Walsh, except for a patch of discolored skin on the right side of his face and down his neck. Heck, he looked like an athlete in the making: long and sinewy, the perfect body type for a baseball pitcher, and he had the height—kid had to be pushing six feet already—for a basketball center, and if he bulked up . . . by God, he would be a helluva football prospect too.

Of course you couldn't tell just by looking if the boy had any athletic ability, aptitude for success, or most importantly, the fire necessary to be a winner. You could give a kid all the ability in the world, but if he lacked the passion, it wouldn't matter.

Walsh wondered if maybe, just maybe, Glen Callaway might have a little bit of that passion to go along with his athletic potential.

The next day, after history class ended, Walsh caught Luis Campos on his way out the door.

"Luis. You got a second?"

Campos smiled.

"Sure. What's up, Coach? You need me to play halfback? I'm ready. I'm a little small, but I'm shifty, you just say the word, I'm—"

"Luis." Walsh held up a hand to stop the kid's prattling. "Tell me what you know about Glen Callaway."

"Glen?"

"Yeah. You know him?"

"Yeah . . . well, no. I know who he is, but I don't really know him."

"Who are his friends?"

"Huh?"

"Who does he hang out with at school?"

"Nobody."

"He's a loner?"

"Yeah. I mean, he don't ever talk to nobody."

"Really?"

"Yeah. I never heard him say a word."

Walsh, come to think of it, had heard the boy say precious few himself. "Do you know anything about him?"

"Well . . . " Luis frowned, then took a quick peek around to make sure no one was listening. Then he leaned in to the coach. "Some of the kids say he's got a curse on him."

"Come on, Luis. Be serious for once."

"I am serious, Coach. It's true. You know who his mom was?"

"Was?"

"Yeah. You know?"

Walsh shook his head.

"Susanna Kane."

Walsh frowned. "Who?"

"You don't know about the Kanes? About the curse?"

"No."

"Man, you ask anyone who's lived in this town for a while. Everyone in that family is dead, and every single one of them died young. His great-grandparents. His grandpa and grandma. His mama and papa, his brother—"

Sonofagun. Walsh knew who Glen Callaway was now.

"The fire," he said. "The funeral parlor."

"That's right." Campos nodded. "That was his family."

Walsh remembered. There had been a big stink about it in the *Sentinel,* not just the fire, but what they found afterward, all those dead Mexicans.

"So where does Glen live now?"

"Hell if I know, Coach. Hopefully far away from me. I don't need none of that curse rubbing off on me. I got big plans for my life."

Walsh nodded. "Okay, Luis. Thanks."

"Yeah, sure. So what—you need me at halfback this Friday? 'Cause I'm ready, Coach, I got the moves all down, I'm like O.J.'s little brother, you know? I'll be your secret weapon, how about that? I'll—"

"Who's Benjamin Franklin, Luis?"

The boy stopped. "Who's what?"

"Benjamin Franklin, Luis. Who was he?"

"Ah." Luis smiled. "I know him. He was the first president of the United States. Am I right, Coach?"

Walsh shook his head. He poked Luis's history book with his finger. "You spend some time studying this instead of worrying about football, all right?"

"Yeah, okay. Sure." Luis snapped his fingers. "I got it. He was the second president, right?"

Walsh was free the next period, so he walked to the principal's office. Mary Conseulos, the principal's secretary, was filing her nails and talking on the phone. She looked up at Walsh and smiled.

"Here's the coach now," she said, and moved the phone away from her mouth. "Hey, Coach. It's Jimmy Marin. He wants to know how much longer you're gonna go with the Parr kid at quarterback."

Walsh rolled his eyes.

"Tell him I'm just waiting for his daughter Kathy to bulk up a little so I can put her in. How about that?"

Mary smiled. Walsh could hear Marin talking loudly to her. "He says that sounds like the best idea you had all season."

"Tell him to get back to work."

She laughed. "You heard that, Jimmy. Get back to work."

She hung up the phone. "So what can I do you for?"

"Glen Callaway. Can I look at his file?"

"Ooh, this must be juicy," she said, rolling her seat back enough to get up from behind her desk. "Glen Callaway. An interesting character." She opened a file cabinet and thumbed through a drawer.

"Do you know anything about him?"

"Not much."

"The kids say he never talks. Ever."

"So I've heard. Or haven't heard, rather." She found the file she was looking for and pulled it out of the drawer.

"You know anything about his family?"

"Family. New or old, you mean?"

"Either."

"Well . . . I know about the Kanes, if that's what you're asking."

"What about the Kanes?"

She leaned closer. "Some people say—"

"Oh, for God's sake." Walsh rolled his eyes. "You're not going to start in with that curse talk too now, are you?

"A lot of people believe there's something to that, you know."

"Don't tell me you're one of 'em."

She shrugged. "Awful lot of bad things happened to that boy, and the people in his life."

"Come on. We're in an institute of learning, and you believe in curses?"

"You believe that Parr kid is going to be a good quarterback?"

"Hah." Walsh smirked and held out his hand for the file.

He took it back to his office and flipped through it. There wasn't much there. Glen had moved around a little since the fire—moved around a lot, actually—and the funny thing was, everywhere he went, bad things seemed to follow. Hmmm.

"No such thing as a curse," Walsh grumbled to himself, writing down the address of Glen's foster parents—the Harrisons, who had apparently recently moved from Valentine to Marfa: 2516 W. Waco. That was odd. No phone.

He glanced at his watch. Still half an hour before his next class.

What the heck. Marfa was a small town, and Waco wasn't far. Just on the other side of 90, down by the tracks, in fact it had to be right near the old Camp Marfa complex, which they were talking about turning into some kind of artists colony. Two five one six had to be right near there, in fact, because he remembered that there was this old senior citizens' complex that one of the kid's grandfathers lived in that they were talking about tearing down, and that number had been in the 2000s too, last buildings on the block, in fact. Number 2500.

Walsh frowned, and got up from his desk.

He suddenly had the feeling that the ride he was about to take was totally unnecessary, that he already knew exactly what he was going to find when he went to look for the Harrisons at 2516 W. Waco.

Walsh was back at school in more than enough time for his next couple classes. At lunch he went to the teacher's lounge, got the brown bag his wife Lucy packed for him out of the refrigerator, and sat down at the table with Chris Alvarez, the school's assistant principal.

"There he is. Just the guy I'm looking for. So let me ask you a question," Chris said. "That Parr kid—you think—"

"Let me ask you a question," Walsh interrupted. "Glen Callaway. What's his deal?"

"His deal?" Alvarez took a bite out of the giant sandwich in front of him and chewed thoughtfully for a minute. "Besides the curse? Besides the fact that he's been shuttled around between foster homes these past few years like a yo-yo? The kid doesn't talk much, but he gets decent grades, and he doesn't cause trouble. Tell you the truth, we could use more like him."

"What do you know about the parents?"

"The new ones?"

"Yeah. The Harrisons."

"Haven't met 'em. I get good reports from the social worker, though. Dick Beavis."

"Oh, God. Dick Beavis. Protect me. That guy is a—"

"Yeah. Tell me about it." Alvarez gulped down another bite of his sandwich. "Why the sudden interest in Glen Callaway?"

"I feel sorry for the kid."

Alvarez wagged a finger at him, and smiled.

"You want him for the team."

"Well . . . my thoughts did drift that way for a minute, to be sure. But . . . " He took a deep breath. "After what I just found out, I just want to make sure he's okay."

Alvarez was suddenly dead serious.

"Why? What did you just find out?"

Walsh took a deep breath and told him.

# chapter
## ten

He couldn't believe he was back here.

Glen thought he was done with these social services people, thought they'd lost track of him and interest in him and that he wouldn't have to deal with any more Barrows, or Dalrymples, or Harrisons, or other adults who claimed to want to help him, but only ended up bringing him pain. Yet here he was again, back in Dick Beavis's waiting room, waiting for old Dick Beavis himself to free up a moment of his valuable time to see him.

Damn.

Somebody had ratted him out, ruined the perfect situation. A whole year's worth of work down the drain. A year that had been in the brewing ever since Raylene Harrison had woken him up in the middle of the night to clean up a puddle of vomit somebody had graciously left out in front of the motel. That had been the last straw.

He waited a couple days, walked in to Raylene, and told her that Dick Beavis was coming to pick him up, because his Aunt June Callaway had moved back to Marfa and wanted Glen to live with her (which in a way was true—June Callaway was back in Marfa, albeit in the graveyard out back of the Church of the Blessed Hope; old Mr. Blackwell had forwarded him a letter along with a check for sixty-five dollars, his share of her remaining estate), so good-bye, thanks for the love and affection, and the chance to swing the mop, and good luck to you and Wilbert in everything.

"Hmmm," Raylene said, and went back to watching her show.

Glen hitched down to Marfa, and set out implementing the plan he'd made over those last couple days. His intended place of residence on Waco was just as he'd expected, in pretty bad shape, but heck, he'd just spent a couple years cleaning up far worse. So with a little elbow grease and some cleaning supplies, he soon had his house in pretty good order. Then he went to the public library and typed a bunch of letters on the motel stationery he'd stolen, a few to the school authorities, one to Dick Beavis just in case he ran into him, and that was it.

He was back home, a resident of Marfa once again, and now he was out on his own, just the way he wanted it. Nobody to bother him, nobody to tell him what to do.

And now someone had ratted him out. Deep in his heart, Glen had known that would happen sooner or later, he supposed, but that didn't make what was about to happen any less bitter.

Dick Beavis.

He was wondering just how painful that conversation was going to be when the door to the hall swung open and a girl walked in. The new girl.

Glen straightened up in his seat.

She'd started at Marfa just about a week ago—he'd seen her around the halls, but didn't know her name yet. She was the classic Texas cheerleader type—blond and tall and perky—a type he usually couldn't stand, but on her, the ever-present smile seemed right somehow.

Glen wondered what she was doing here. Was she like him? Was she a child without a family, here against her will? Maybe they had something in common, something they could talk about at school. Maybe he'd sit next to her at lunch tomorrow, break the ice. Maybe they'd get to be friends.

Maybe pigs would start flying south down 90 for the winter.

The girl walked over to Beavis's receptionist, said hello—the two seemed to know each other—and then turned around and headed for the waiting room magazine table.

She was wearing a Kansas City Chiefs T-shirt and tight blue jeans, and had her hair tied back in a ponytail that seemed to dance behind her as she walked. Her eyes were green; her face was dotted with a few light freckles.

She looked at Glen, smiled politely, then looked away.

Then she looked back. Her eyes widened, and her mouth dropped open, and she said:

"Oh, my God. I don't believe it."

Glen felt himself flush.

"Huh?"

"I know you."

"Yeah. We go to school together."

"No." She smiled, and shook her head. "You don't remember me?"

"Remember you?"

"Glen, come on, you don't remember me?"

He sat there, shaking his head like a big dumb dog, knowing he looked stupid, knowing he ought to say something, but he couldn't think of what.

She knew his name. How?

"Why didn't you ever answer any of my letters? Or my mom's letters? You got 'em, right?"

He blinked. Letters? What letters? Who sent him letters? The only letters he'd ever gotten in his whole life were from Dick Beavis, and this girl's mother was unlikely to be Dick Beavis, so what was she—

"Oh," Glen said, in a small voice not quite his own, because suddenly he knew exactly what letters she was talking about, and who she was, and felt the vacant expression on his face being replaced by what felt like the biggest smile he'd ever smiled in his whole life.

"I got 'em, Katie," he said, and he felt like laughing and crying all at once. "Most of 'em, anyway."

Right then Beavis's door swung open, and a blond woman, who looked a little bit older, a little bit sadder than the last time Glen had seen her, but who Glen did recognize immediately, stepped through, saw him, and smiled.

"Well," Melissa Vick said. "Look at you, all grown up."

"Getting there," Glen said.

"Getting there?" Melissa laughed. "You get any bigger, we're gonna have to raise the ceilings in here."

"Oh, Mom. Cut it out," Katie Vick said.

"I see you two found each other all right."

Glen and Katie both nodded.

"It's a good day, praise the Lord," Melissa said. "A very good day indeed."

She looked at Glen again and opened her arms wide.

"Well, don't just stand there," she said. "Come on over here and give me a hug."

Melissa knew everything that had happened to him. She had the records out, scattered all over Dick Beavis's office. Actually, it turned out not to be Dick Beavis's office anymore. It was hers.

She and Katie had moved back from Kansas City a week ago—they had, Glen learned, been trying to move back for some time. Melissa's mom, who had been raising Katie with her, had moved to Tucson at the beginning of the summer, and Katie was old enough now ("More than old enough," the girl interjected) to be on her own during the day while Melissa worked. And then, coincidentally enough, Melissa happened to be on the phone with her friend Beverly Cutler when she heard that Dick Beavis had been fired, and social services was looking for a replacement. Melissa called up and got the job right away. And that was that.

She was the same old Melissa, Glen could see that right away, honest-to-God (accent on the God) interested in his life, he could tell from the questions she managed to work in around her own story, questions about his time with the Barrows, and the Harrisons, and what on earth had possessed him to think he could live on his own, a fourteen-year-old boy?

"I'm not a child," Glen said. "And I've been doing it for a year, just fine."

"You had a very lucky year, young man," she said sternly. "What if you got sick? What if you got a disease? What if—"

"What if I got another family like the Barrows?"

Melissa sighed. "That was an aberration, Glen. A mistake. I don't understand how Helena let that woman slip by her, but I promise you, that's not gonna happen again."

"I promise you that too," Glen said firmly. " 'Cause I'm not going back to any stupid foster home."

"Glen . . ."

He started to open his mouth to argue again, and coughed instead. Something in his throat.

He coughed again, and rubbed his throat.

"That hurts?" Melissa asked.

He nodded.

"I want to get you to a doctor, Glen. I remember"—she picked through the papers on her desk a minute—"yep, here it is. Right when you were getting out of the hospital, the doctors were concerned about bruising on your vocal cords. Long-term damage." She looked up at him. "This is why you can't live alone. This is a serious condition."

"Mom's right, Glen," Katie said, speaking up for the first time. "You gotta have a doctor."

She put a hand on his arm then and smiled at him.

"Besides, no matter what kind of loser family you get—"

"Katie—" her mother said sternly.

"—you'll have us. Isn't that right, Mom?"

"That's right. But"—she wagged a finger—"you are not going to get a loser family, Glen Callaway. I'm going to get it right this time. I promise you."

Glen nodded again. His throat was bothering him something awful now. Probably from all the talking he was doing. He hadn't talked this much in months.

He motioned to Melissa for a pen and a piece of paper, and then scrawled out a question:

*So what do I do in the meantime? Can I stay where I am?*

Melissa shook her head. "I'm afraid not."

He frowned, and wrote again:

*So?*

Melissa cleared her throat.

"There's a group home up in Alpine, and I've been on the phone this morning trying to get you in. Now it'd only be for a little while," she said, catching sight of the look on Glen's face, "just a few nights, until—"

"Hey, we have a couch, right, Mom?" Katie said, leaning forward in her chair. "Why doesn't Glen stay with us for a little while?"

"That's against the rules, Katie," Melissa said. "You know that."

"Oh, come on, Mom. You make the rules."

"I do not make the rules."

"Well, you know the people who do—don't you?" Katie looked from Glen to her mom. "Wouldn't it be better for Glen to stay with us? Wouldn't it?"

Melissa sighed. "Would you like that, Glen?"

His smile, he supposed, gave him away.

"All right." Melissa threw up her hands. "Let me see what I can do. But it really would be temporary. Very, very temporary. You understand that?"

"I do," Katie said.

Glen nodded too.

As it ended up, temporary turned out to be only a week, because Melissa turned out to be as good as her word. She found Glen, at last, a foster situation that suited him to a tee.

Glen moved in with Sergeant Dominguez, the officer who'd been investigating the fire so many years ago, and his family.

Dominguez, though, was no longer Sergeant Dominguez. He was just Pete, having retired from the force a few years back. He and his wife, Alma, were already fostering three other kids in their house, which was just down the street from the Vicks. The kids were all in high school, troubled kids getting a second chance, older kids, so they all had their own things to do every day, but they ate breakfast and dinner together like a real family. Pete and Alma stayed on Glen and the other three about their homework, their social life, just the way Glen had always heard normal parents did. It all felt very, very normal to him. He got used to it.

He did not get used to Katie Vick.

He had a hard time looking at her. He had a hard time not looking at her, which he knew made absolutely no sense except it was the only way to describe how much of his attention she occupied. It wasn't so much that she was beautiful—although she definitely was beautiful—it was just she had this kind of glow to her, and he just had to watch it all the time. There was nothing else worth watching.

Glen wasn't the only boy at Marfa High with a Katie Vick problem.

She was without a doubt the most popular girl in the school; the normal high school hierarchy that put freshmen on the bottom of a long, long ladder didn't seem to apply to her. From the moment she arrived, the seniors all clustered around her, boys and girls. She was poised and confident, funny and smart. Sophomore year she was named captain of the cheerleading squad and elected vice president of her class, and would have been named homecoming queen too if she hadn't told everyone that it was tradition for a senior to be queen, and it would make her very upset if by some chance she won.

Needless to say, she didn't lack for suitors. Or friends. Or demands on her time; she was very, very busy.

Glen, on the other hand . . .

He wasn't exactly high on everyone's dance card. It was his own fault, he knew; he was still painfully shy, painfully quiet (the doctors said that until he stopped growing, they wouldn't even try to treat his vocal cords, it was just too risky), and perhaps most important of all, he didn't play sports.

Still, through ninth and tenth grade, he still managed to get in his fair share of Katie Vick time too.

They walked to school together every morning, and home on those days when Katie didn't have an extracurricular activity, which was usually Wednesday and Friday, although it varied from week to week.

They were walking home together on Thursday, the week before Halloween. October 25, 1986.

"So what are you going to be this year?" Katie asked Glen.

He shrugged. "I don't know. The usual, I guess. Some kind of monster."

"You'd make a good monster."

"Hey, thanks a lot."

She punched him in the arm playfully. "I didn't mean it that way. You could do big and scary really well, I bet. Like . . . I bet you'd be a good Frankenstein."

"Citizens of Marfa," Glen said in a raspy voice. "Bring me your candy. All of your candy."

"See?" Katie said. "You're a natural."

Behind them, a car horn honked.

Glen and Katie turned at the same time.

A big old Plymouth pulled up alongside them. Chris Hightower was driving. Hightower was a senior, a football player, a big shot around school. Glen didn't like him at all, probably because he'd been all over Katie from the moment he'd spotted her at cheerleading practice.

"What's up, Katie?" he called out, ignoring Glen entirely. "You want a ride?"

"No, thanks, Chris. I'm fine."

"Come on. You'd get home a lot quicker." He smiled, and raised his eyebrows suggestively. "Or not."

"No, thanks. In case you can't see, I'm in the middle of a conversation here."

"With him?" Hightower nodded at Glen. "I heard you didn't do much talking, Callaway."

"Glen. My name is Glen."

"Right. Glen. Sorry." He frowned. "You're a Kane, though, too—aren't you? I mean, your mother was a Kane?"

"Yeah. So what?"

"Nothing," Hightower said, in a way that Glen knew that the next words out of his mouth were gonna be something about the curse. "It's just that I heard—"

"Good-bye, Chris," Katie said, grabbing Glen's arm and walking.

"Let's just get out of here," she said quietly. "This guy is an ass."

Hightower wasn't done with them yet, though. He put the car in gear and cruised along next to them.

"Come on, Katie. Don't be like that."

"You make fun of my friend, and then you think I'm gonna hop in your car and leave with you? Grow up."

"Ah, I was just kidding. Right, Callaway? You know I was kidding."

"Glen."

"Glen, yeah. I was kidding."

"Good-bye, Chris," Katie said again.

Hightower pulled over and got out of the car. He jogged after them and caught up.

"So what do you think? You want to go to the movies Friday, Katie?"

"Are you deaf?" she asked. "Good-bye."

"I'm just trying to be friendly, here."

"What you're being is a jerk. Now go away."

"Hey." Hightower grabbed Katie's arm to stop her. "I'm just asking if—"

He stopped talking because the instant he'd grabbed Katie's arm, Glen had grabbed his.

"Why don't you let her go," Glen said.

Hightower smiled. It was not a pleasant smile.

"Well, look at this." Hightower looked down at Glen's hand, and then up at his face again. "I didn't know you had a bodyguard, Katie."

"I don't." Katie squeezed in between the two of them. "Both of you let go. What are you, cavemen? Let go."

Neither one did. They stood practically eyeball to eyeball. Glen was a little bit taller. Hightower was a lot bigger—more bulked up, more muscular.

"You're big," Hightower said. "You gonna play football?"

"He can't play football," Katie said. "He's got a disease."

"What's the matter, he can't talk for himself?"

"Just leave him alone, Chris."

"Leave him alone? I'm asking him a question. One simple question. He can't answer me? You say you're having a conversation, but this guy can't seem to string together two sentences in a row." He smiled at Glen. "Can you?"

Glen held his stare, but said nothing.

"What?" Hightower continued. "What you looking at? What? You gonna try to stare me down? I'm supposed to be afraid of you because of your freaky eyes?"

Glen stayed silent.

"You know something?" Hightower continued. "I never seen anyone with different-colored eyes before. That's just wrong. Dogs have different-colored eyes, not people. So what I'm thinkin' is, your mother must have been a bitch. Is that right, freak? Was your mom a bitch?"

Katie slapped Hightower hard across the face with her free hand.

"Shut up, you asshole!"

He shoved her to the ground and yanked free of Glen's grip all at once.

"Don't hit me, you stupid bitch, or I'll—"

He never finished that sentence.

Glen reared back and clocked him with all his strength, right across the jaw.

Hightower went down. A second later, he got up, rubbing his mouth. When he pulled his hand away, it was red.

"Blood." He shook his head. "Okay, freak-boy. You want to play rough? We'll play rough."

"That's enough!" Katie screamed. "Stop it, the two of you!"

Hightower charged and tackled Glen. The two tumbled to

the ground, rolling over a couple times before they came to a stop with Hightower on top. He managed to get an arm free, and swung at Glen's face. Glen caught that arm in his two hands and for a second held it there, but Hightower was stronger than him. He got the arm free again, and began hitting Glen, in the face, in the body, in the stomach.

Katie was screaming.

Glen didn't feel any pain, but he wanted the hitting to stop. He was afraid Hightower would punch him in the throat and do some permanent damage.

He got his arms past Hightower's punches, grabbed the boy around the neck with both hands, and started to squeeze.

Hightower's punches grew more frantic. Katie's screaming got louder.

Then Hightower's face started changing color—red first, then purple. The boy's punches had stopped altogether now, Glen realized, and he was making gagging sounds. His hands were grabbing at Glen's, trying to pry them away from his throat.

"Glen!" Katie screamed. "Let him go, let him go! You're gonna kill him!"

*Yes,* a little voice inside Glen's head whispered. *That's exactly what I'm going to do. I'm going to kill him.*

But of course that was wrong. That was a bad thing to do, killing people.

Glen let go.

Hightower wheezed, and choked, and pushed himself off Glen and onto the nearby grass. He sat there a minute, breathing heavily, before speaking again.

"You fuckin' freak," he gasped. "What the hell's the matter with you?"

Glen got to his feet, and wobbled. He couldn't feel any pain, but he could tell he was gonna have bruises all over his body tomorrow, probably all over his face too.

Pete Dominguez was not going to like that.

"You could have killed me," Hightower said.

Glen stared at him a minute before speaking.

"That's right," he said, and it came out in that same raspy voice he'd used before fooling around, only now it was happening without him wanting it to. Hightower must have gotten him in the throat too, bastard.

"Next time, I will. Leave Katie alone, understand? Leave Katie alone."

Hightower glared at him and backed away. Got back in his car and drove off.

Glen turned to see Katie, walking away herself, obviously angry.

He ran to catch up to her, but she didn't want to talk to him. She stayed mad for the rest of the week, all the way through Halloween, in fact.

But when Glen rang her doorbell, dressed like Frankenstein, she had a big smile for him.

"Look out, Katie Vick," he rasped. "I have come for you. And your candy."

She giggled. "One thing at a time," she said, tossing a Three Musketeers bar into his bag. "Now get out of here, before you frighten the children."

She nodded at a crowd of little kids coming up the sidewalk toward them.

And the next day, it was as if nothing had ever changed between them.

Something had changed inside Glen, though. He realized after fighting Chris Hightower that he had to be stronger. He'd just gotten lucky in that fight: if Hightower hadn't been such an idiot, he could have used his strength to win. From now on, Glen decided, he was going to be the strongest one, in any situation. In every situation.

He started staying late after school, adding in a new element to his daily routine.

Weightlifting.

Sophomore year ended; summer began. Glen and the Dominguez family took a motor home out on the highway, spent a month traveling around the Southwest, saw the Grand Canyon, the caves at Carlsbad, the Navajo reservation at Four Corners, the Painted Desert. On the way back, they drove through Van Horn, past a series of motels, one of which he just knew had to be the one the scrapbook had turned up in, and for the first time in a long while, Glen thought about Paul Grimm. He wondered where the man was, what he was doing. Why he'd stolen the scrapbook and the mask, whether or not he had anything to do with the fire, who the boy with him had been.

That night he had a dream about running down a highway, being chased by fire.

The week before junior year started, Katie got her learner's permit. The first Glen knew of it, he was walking down the street, having just come from the school gym and a long session on the machines, when all at once a horn sounded, and he just about jumped out of his shoes.

He turned and saw Katie leaning out of the window of her mom's little Honda.

"Hey, there. Want to go for a drive?"

Glen eyed the car, and himself, and frowned.

"I don't know if I'm gonna fit in there."

"Come on."

Glen got in. It was a tight squeeze.

"Watch this," Katie said, and promptly backed into a bush.

They both burst out laughing.

"Can I get out now?" Glen asked.

"Only if you promise to come with me tonight."

"Come with you where?"

"To see the lights. A whole bunch of us are going down to Mitchell Flats to see 'em. I thought you might want to come."

"The Marfa Lights, you mean?"

"Yes, the Marfa Lights, of course that's what I mean. What else would I mean?"

Glen shrugged.

"So you want to come?"

"Sure."

"All right. I'll pick you up around eight, then."

Glen frowned. "Doesn't a learner's permit mean you can't drive at night?"

"Well, who's gonna know, silly?" She smiled at him. "You're not gonna tell my mom, are you?"

"No."

"Or Pete?"

"No!"

She laughed. "Well, then?"

Glen was confused for a second. This was a new Katie—or at least, a little more adventurous Katie. Katie pushing the rules a little bit—Melissa was pretty strict about curfew.

Glen wondered what other rules she was pushing.

"I'll be out front at eight," he said, then shook his head. "What am I saying, out front? I'll meet you down the block—the corner the Marin house is on. All right?"

"It's a date," she said, and smiled again, and waved, and pulled away before Glen could ask her what, in fact, a date meant in this context.

He spent the rest of the afternoon, and into the early evening, wondering about that himself.

The Marfa Lights were one of those weird little quirks in nature no one could explain. Most nights, starting at sundown, you could park out on 90, look out toward the Chinati Mountains, and see them for yourself. Little glowing lights that appeared on the horizon for a while, sometimes jumped up in the air, sometimes rose off the ground, sometimes brightened or dimmed in intensity before disappearing. People had been coming to look at them for over a hundred years now, and still no one could explain exactly what they were. Atmospheric phenomenon, a hoax, flying saucers—scientists still had no idea. They were getting to be a pretty big tourist attraction, too. At least, that was what Glen had heard.

He'd never seen them himself.

Katie picked him up at eight, just as she promised, and within half an hour they had arrived at Mitchell Flats. Katie parked the Honda on the side of the road, next to about half a dozen other cars, then she and Glen ran through the creosote bushes and tumbleweeds to a clearing in the Chihuahuan Desert.

A bunch of her friends from school were already there. They looked at Glen at first, like he was the unexplained phenomenon they'd come to see that night.

"Y'all know Glen, right?" Katie said, and made introductions all around. She was moving too quick for any uncomfortableness to set in.

"So did you see anything yet?" she asked all around.

"Nope. We're still waiting."

She took a seat on the ground, facing out toward the purple mountains in the distance. Glen sat down next to her. The night was crisp and cool, and the sky was clear. One of the kids had some beers that were getting passed around. Glen shook his head when the bottle came to him—he noticed Katie didn't drink either. That made him feel better. He was pushing it as it was, staying out this late. Pete was definitely going to be angry, and Glen had learned, Pete angry was not a sight you wanted to see.

"I hope they show soon," Katie said.

"Kind of cloudy tonight," Glen offered.

"I don't know if the weather has anything to do with it."

Glen shrugged. Neither did he.

"I think they come out every night," he said.

"Not every night." Katie shimmied closer to him to make the conversation easier. "My uncle came to visit over the summer, and this was about the only thing he wanted to see. They didn't show all week."

"There are a lot of crazy stories about these lights." That was one of Katie's friends talking, a boy named Roberto. Short kid, had a big curly Afro.

"Like what?" Katie asked.

"Like the lights are the ghost of a wandering Apache chief."

"You are so full of it," the girl next to Roberto said, elbowing him in the side.

"It's true." He pushed her back, and she giggled. "The story goes that back in the old days, the chief and his tribe rode between here and Mexico, stealing from the local ranchers. One day he got caught. They killed him, and sold the whole tribe into slavery."

That sounded like a true story to Glen, sure enough.

"So the lights," Roberto finished, "are the chief, trying to guide his tribe back home."

Someone whistled, long and low. "Creepy."

"There's another one," Roberto said. "That the lights are the ghosts of a family who were traveling through west Texas looking for a place to settle. But they got lost and died. The lights are their lanterns, as they wander the desert in search of their new home."

"They're car headlights," someone else said. "That's what my dad says."

At which point a big long discussion started about whether or not the lights were real or fake, which degenerated into a whole big argument about whether or not UFOs really existed, which morphed into a big fight about which *Star Wars* movie was the best. Glen was lost there; he hadn't seen any of them. The whole conversation was moot anyway, he thought: an hour on, and no lights had appeared at all.

A bunch of the kids walked back to their cars and went home.

"You want to stay a little longer?" Katie asked.

"Sure," Glen said.

A half an hour later, they were the only ones left.

"Getting cold out here," Katie said.

Glen started to get to his feet.

"Hey, where are you going?" Katie asked, tugging on his jeans.

"I thought you were cold."

"I am cold. It doesn't mean we have to go."

He shrugged and sat back down.

"So what do you think the lights are?" Katie asked.

"I don't know."

"No opinion?"

"Can't have an opinion on something I haven't seen yet."

"Wait a minute." She shook her head. "You lived here how long . . ."

"Most of my life. Sixteen years, give or take."

"And you've never seen the lights?"

"Nope."

She shook her head. "You gotta get out more often, Glen."

"I guess so."

"I know so."

She smiled at him, and shimmied even closer. Then she did something that took Glen's breath away.

She put her head on his shoulder.

"You believe in God?" Katie asked then.

Glen was still too stunned to respond for a second.

"Uh—I don't know," he said.

"I don't." She was looking out at the mountains, and not at him. "Not like my mom does. She thinks that there's some force up there, responsible for everything we do, deciding whether or not we live or die, stuff like that. Which I don't buy for a second."

He looked down at her head, resting on his shoulder, and smiled.

"I believe we make our own fate," she said. "You think that?"

"I'm not sure," he said, and then, all of a sudden, he wasn't thinking about Katie Vick leaning on his shoulder, he was thinking about the curse, the Kane family curse, that killed not just the Kane family but everyone that came in contact with them.

He shivered.

"It is cold out here," he said.

She snuggled in even closer. Glen put his arm around her without thinking, and if she hadn't said, "That's nice," right away he would have pulled it back, that was how surprised he was at his own action.

They sat that way in silence for a minute.

"She talks about how it was God's will that took my dad away."

"Oh," Glen said.

"God didn't have anything to do with it," she said. "It was a wet road, and a busted guardrail. That was what killed him."

Glen had never heard her talk about her father before. He'd never heard about her feelings about God before either, or the little touch of anger in her voice when she talked about Melissa. That was to be expected, he guessed, a little teenage rebellion.

*God didn't have anything to do with it,* the little voice in his mind echoed then. *It was the curse.*

"Did you say something?" Katie asked, sitting up for a second and turning to him.

He shook his head. "Nope."

"Oh," she said, and snuggled back down.

They sat that way a good long while. Glen was thinking about a lot of things right then, about the lights, about Katie Vick, and his feelings about the strange things that had seemed to him, once upon a time, to rule his own life.

The curse, for one.

"I don't know if I believe in God either," he said finally, when he had his thoughts all in order. "But I do think there's a lot about this world that science can't explain."

He went on to tell her everything he knew about the Kanes then, from Rebecca Kane all the way up through James Dean and his mom. She didn't say a word the whole time, just listened, as he laid out his fears to her, his fears about getting close to anyone again, which he hoped she took as a sign that he really wanted to get close to her, but was scared.

When he was finished, he waited for a response.

She didn't say a word.

"Katie?"

She murmured quietly, and shifted position, which was when Glen realized she was asleep. She'd been asleep for his whole secret "confession."

If that didn't beat all . . .

Glen smiled and decided he had nothing to complain about.

The prettiest girl in Presidio County was with him right now, was with the cursed freaky kid with two different-colored eyes, and even if an Indian chief or a lost family descended from the sky, this would still be the most surreal sight for a thousand miles around.

He decided to let her rest a little longer. He'd keep watch for the lights. If they came, he'd wake her up.

"Glen. Wake up."

He was dreaming, and Katie's angelic voice was summoning him from sleep. He wasn't ready to wake up yet. It had been too perfect, and he wasn't ready to return to reality.

"Glen!"

He turned on his side, trying to force reality to the background, until he felt a prickling sensation at his back. His eyes shot open.

The sky was light.

Katie was looking at him with panic on her face.

"It's five-thirty in the morning," she said.

"Oh, shit."

"Oh, shit is right," Katie said.

They ran to the car.

Katie was grounded for a month. Glen for two.

"I hope it was worth it," Pete said as he got up from the table after a long talk with Glen about responsibility, about trust, about the importance of keeping your word. "I hope you understand how disappointed I am in you."

"Yes, sir," Glen said, answering both parts of Dominguez's statement at the same time, because though he did understand how much he'd disappointed Pete, the evening—the night he spent with Katie Vick—was most definitely worth it.

# chapter
## eleven

Frank Walsh looked over the class lists despondently, and sighed.

Hard to believe, but he missed the Parr kid already.

The quarterback situation for the upcoming season was grim, and it was fairly reflective of the whole team's prospects. Barring some sort of major miracle, this was going to be the third year in a row the Shorthorns missed the playoffs. Everybody liked him, Frank knew, everybody thought he was a good coach, but high school football in Texas was a big deal to the community. If he didn't find a way to turn the program around—and soon—he'd be looking for a new job.

Thing was, you couldn't make a silk purse out of a sow's ear. Not only was the talent pool just not there, but the kids he did have, their attitude was just not good. They didn't work the way kids used to, not as hard, not as long, there just didn't seem to be as much drive in them as before. Take today, for example.

Walsh had made arrangements with the school to keep the gym open all through summer, so the team could use the weightlifting room, and the only kid that showed up was Glen Callaway.

If that wasn't rubbing salt into the wound, he didn't know what was.

Glen was the biggest boy in the incoming senior class, probably had to be six-five now, Walsh thought, and he wasn't a skinny teenager anymore. He was a full-grown man, even if he was only seventeen, and a lot of it had to do with how hard he was pushing the weights. Walsh wished the kids on the squad would take Glen as an example.

Every morning, Walsh unlocked the gym at 8:45 A.M. then headed down to his office to make coffee before returning. And by the time he got back, he could hear the echoing clangs of plates in the otherwise-silent room.

The two of them had actually gotten to be pretty friendly; most days, Walsh would stick his head into the doorway, and Glen would nod hello. Once in a while, they would exchange small talk about the weather or some local happening, but for the most part, Walsh just watched. He watched for a while sometimes, partially because he wanted to make sure Glen had his technique down right, but also because he just couldn't believe how much weight the boy was lifting.

The other day, when Walsh had come in, Glen had been lying on the bench press. Walsh saw he'd put four 45-pound plates and one 25-pound plate on each side of the bar, which made for 455 pounds in all. The school record, Walsh knew, was only 315 pounds.

Glen did ten reps with the nearly quarter ton before setting the bar back down.

Walsh cleared his throat, said hello, and told Glen that he was proud to have witnessed the boy set the new school record, and he'd go put it on the wall right now.

"No," Glen had said.

"No? Why not? Aren't you proud of what you did? You ought to be proud."

"I am, but I don't see that a lot of people need to know about it."

Walsh shrugged. "Okay. Suit yourself."

"Thanks, Coach," Glen said, and went back to lifting.

Walsh remembered watching him a while longer that morning, and shaking his head. All that potential, and now he'd been over Glen's medical record more than once, and understood that the disorder the boy had was really not what was keeping him from playing sports, it was just that he wasn't interested. Didn't have that drive.

What a waste.

Walsh sighed, and set down his pen. It was time for him to get the intramural equipment set up for the summer rec programs. Eight- and nine-year-old girls' basketball program this morning.

Walsh hated basketball.

He was dragging two equipment bags through the hallway when he saw the shadow walking before him. He recognized it immediately, the same shadow he saw every morning, by itself, heading for the gym. Glen Callaway's shadow.

But this time, instead of walking away from him and to the gym, the shadow was headed in his direction.

"Coach Walsh," Glen said.

"Hey, Glen. What's up?"

Glen stopped in front of him, and smiled.

"I'm thinking about trying out for the football team this year," he said.

Walsh nearly swallowed the whistle that had been puckered between his lips.

It was all, as usual, because of Katie.

How he felt about her, how much he wanted to stay part of her life. Junior year had been even more of a whirlwind for her, and Glen felt himself even more on the sideline. She was involved in everything from the yearbook staff to the cheerleading squad to the school newspaper. She had more best friends than Glen could count on both hands, and she managed to spend time with every one of them, himself included. She wasn't just popular, too, she was smart. Her schoolwork drew raves from her teachers, and in the last quarter of her junior year, she'd received a perfect 4.0 grade-point average. She'd been inducted into the National Honor Society, and scored 30 out of a possible 36 on the ACT. In the past few months, she'd applied and received admission to schools such as Texas, Missouri, Louisiana State, Oklahoma, and Stanford. Her counselor had even convinced her to apply to an Ivy League school, and she was still waiting for an answer from Yale.

She was going places, Glen realized, and he could either go with her or get left behind. She said as much to him more than once, asked why he seemed to be so content with just getting by, with just standing by on the sidelines and never getting involved.

Sports, she was especially confused about.

"You're always in that damn weight room," she said. "Good God, look at your muscles."

They were driving back from Alpine, from going to see a movie at the theater there. She took one hand off the wheel and squeezed his bicep.

"Ow," he said jokingly.

"Yeah, right. Honestly, Glen, I don't understand why you don't want to try out for something at least. Are you afraid you're uncoordinated or something?"

"No," he said. "I just don't really think of myself as a team player kind of guy, that's all."

She shook her head. "Well, how do you know till you try?"

She had a point there, he decided.

It didn't take long for the word to get out about Glen Callaway.

Not in the school, not in Marfa, not in Texas.

It started the first day of practice, when they couldn't find a uniform big enough to fit him. One of the kids had a dad who played semi-pro; he ran home and got the old man's permission to use that.

On the second day of practice, he broke a tackling sled.

On the third day of practice, playing at defensive end for the first time, he burst through a triple-team, got into the backfield, and tackled the runner and the quarterback at the same time.

Frank Walsh was so stunned by what he saw, he forgot to whistle the play dead.

By the end of the first week, Walsh and his assistant, Ducky Thomas, were designing plays for Glen. He was going to play running back on offense, and linebacker on defense. Unless he wanted to play somewhere else.

In Marfa's first game of the season, he gained 310 yards rushing, and scored six touchdowns. In the first half. Walsh took pity on the other team and rested him for the second part of the game.

There was a write-up on him in the *Sentinel* that week, and one the next week too. It got to be a regular feature, practically. The *Chronicle* out of Austin picked up the blurb about him after the third game of the season, a 99–10 rout of Marathon.

Dusty Boggs picked up on that one.

Boggs was one of the most famous names in Texas football history. A state legend who played semi-pro ball at sixteen before going on to an All-Pro career as a safety with the AFL's Dallas Texans and Kansas City Chiefs, Boggs quit playing at twenty-seven after a catastrophic knee injury ended his career. He worked now as an unofficial scout for the University of Texas Longhorns, and as such, saw and heard about literally hundreds of prospects a year.

In all his years, he'd never heard of anyone like this kid, Glen Callaway.

He was six-foot-nine; he could bench-press 500 pounds; he was fast enough to play any position on the field, big enough maybe to play two at one time. It was a joke. It had to be a joke. Marfa? In all his travels, Boggs had never been to Marfa. Hell, he wasn't even sure he could find it on a map.

How could he not have heard of this Callaway kid before? Kids his size didn't just appear out of nowhere. If he'd transferred from another school, Boggs would've heard those rumblings. If he'd simply experienced a growth spurt, he was likely a major project. If he was any good, Dusty Boggs would've known about him already. World-class athletes don't just fall out of the sky. And if they did, they wouldn't land in Marfa, Texas. He was sure of that.

And yet . . .

He was on the road to Big Bend country the following Friday, for the Marfa Shorthorns game against neighboring Alpine.

This was the big one, everyone said, the big rivalry, Marfa vs. Alpine, and this year it was bigger than usual, because both teams were at 7-0, and whoever won would be top seed in the upcoming playoffs. The stadium was going to be packed, beyond packed—school officials had already made special arrangements with the local station to do a live broadcast, because there simply wasn't going to be room for everyone who wanted to see the game to fit in.

Glen was excited to be part of something so important, but if he was honest with himself, after what—half a dozen games?—he was getting pretty tired of how easy football was for him. It didn't involve any real skill on his part; he was just bigger and stronger than anybody. Standing on the sidelines, waiting for the game to begin, he looked over at Alpine's bench, saw them pointing at him and staring, and knew they had no way to stop him. There was no one within half a foot of his size on their team. He'd crush them—Marfa would crush Alpine—just like they'd crushed everyone else this season.

Where was the fun in that? There was no fun in that.

Luis Campos came by and smacked him on the arm.

"You the man, Glen! You the man!"

Glen nodded. "Yeah," he said. "I'm the man."

Luis looked at him funny, and moved on.

What was the matter with him? Glen thought. This was no time to rain on everyone's parade. This was the big game, everyone was so excited, and he . . .

He just couldn't get up the energy.

Maybe he was just tired. Maybe he'd gone from class freak to school hero just a little too fast. Maybe he needed a little downtime to adjust. A little break from football.

Or maybe it was something else entirely, he thought. Maybe it had to do with what Pete Dominguez had told him yesterday after dinner, when they were doing the dishes to-gether.

"Talked to some friends of mine at the department today, Glen," Pete had said.

"Yeah?"

"They're officially closing the case."

For a second, Glen didn't know what he was talking about.

"Oh," he said, in a very small voice, suddenly realizing what the man was referring to.

"Yeah." Pete shrugged. "Well, no surprise there. It's been ten years—well, almost ten years now—and there's been no progress for the last seven, since we got that tip about Grimm in Dallas."

Glen remembered that—that had been one of the first

things Pete had told him on taking Glen in. Grimm—or some-one who looked like him, anyway—had been spotted near the Sportatorium, this old arena where they had boxing matches, pro wrestling shows, things like that. But that sighting—never really confirmed—had been the last. The only one.

Paul Grimm seemed to have disappeared off the face of the earth.

"It's going down in the books as an unsolved arson," Pete said.

"Ten years," Glen said, suddenly finding the number a little hard to take in. Ten years, his parents and Mark had been dead. And how long since he'd really thought about them? About the fire? About Rebecca Kane, and the curse, and the scrapbook under his bed, and the mask, and—

"Hey."

Glen looked up.

Coach Walsh was standing in front of him, clipboard in hand.

"You all right?"

"Fine."

"Then let's go get 'em!" Walsh yelled suddenly, and just then the guy on the PA introduced the starting line-ups, and Glen jogged out onto the field with the rest of the team, and the cheers went up. The cheerleaders went up too, into a pyra-mid with Katie at the top. She smiled at him, he smiled back, and at least a little bit of the cloud he'd been feeling following him around all day lifted.

They had the coin toss—Marfa won, and elected to receive. That was the most suspenseful part of the game.

Luis Campos returned the kickoff for Marfa all the way out to the fifty. On the first play from scrimmage, the quarterback—Ty Crowell, the only black kid at Marfa High—handed the ball to Glen.

He went straight up the middle for thirty yards before six of the Colonels dragged him down.

The next play was a fake to Glen. Luis was wide open in the end zone, Ty hit him with a nice easy pass, and it was 6–0. They missed the point after. That was the weakest part of Marfa's game—the kicking squad. Not that it mattered.

At halftime it was 33–14, and the game was nowhere near as close as it sounded. One of Alpine's touchdowns came from Ty being intercepted in the end zone, and their defensive back running it all the way down the field for a touchdown.

The second half was more of the same. Glen didn't play most of it. He sat on the bench and watched. Near the end of the third quarter, Luis made a nifty run off a short pass from Ty, and got in the end zone again: 39–14. Glen went in on the kickoff team, the returner caught the ball, saw him coming, and fumbled. Marfa recovered. Ty scored on a quarterback run: 45–14.

Glen stood and cheered with the rest of the team.

"Excuse me."

He looked over to see a man in a University of Texas sweatshirt standing next to him.

"Just wanted to say hello. The name's Dusty—Dusty Boggs. You been playing a helluva game, son. Helluva game."

"Thanks."

Glen had gotten used to this part too. Grown-ups coming by to introduce themselves, tell him how good he was, how he should think about playing ball in college too, get a scholarship. That was something Glen hadn't thought about before, he had to admit. A way to go to college without paying, which was probably the only way he ever would get to go, Pete and Alma certainly didn't have the kind of money to send him to college. He'd been wondering if he could get a scholarship to some of the schools Katie was applying to; Yale had a football team, he knew.

"Excuse me."

Glen had almost forgotten the man was there.

"Sorry."

"Just wanted to ask you a question. I heard you bench-pressed five hundred pounds, boy. Is that true?"

"No."

"Yeah. Didn't think so."

"Four-fifty-five's my record."

Boggs blinked. "Four-fifty-five?"

"Ten reps."

"Ten?"

"Uh-huh."

Boggs shook his head. "Damn. That's a lotta weight. What do you do the forty in?"

"The forty?"

"Forty-yard dash. What do you do it in?"

"I don't know. Never done it."

"You ought to get a time. A lot of people are gonna be asking you that. If you want, we can do it later. If Coach Walsh says it's all right."

It was Glen's turn to frown. "Who are you, anyway?"

"Dusty Boggs, like I said."

"But who are you?"

The man smiled now. "You mean, what do I do?"

"Yeah."

"I'm a scout. For the Texas Longhorns."

After the game, Coach Walsh introduced the two of them formally.

"Dusty here came all the way from Austin to see you, Glen."

Glen didn't know what to say to that. "Thanks."

Boggs nodded. "Gotta say, son, you got the physical tools to do very well for yourself. You're what—six-five, six-six, about three hundred pounds?"

"Six-six, two-eighty."

"I played with Buck Buchanan, Ernie Ladd—you're about the biggest player I seen since them. Buck, he went I think six-seven, two seventy-five, and Ernie"—Boggs shook his head—"he went about six-nine, three-fifteen, as a player, got even bigger when he went on to wrestling. You might end up bigger than either of 'em. You're a heck of a prospect, boy. I gotta say. Heck of a prospect."

"Thanks," Glen said, not knowing what else to say.

"I'd be interested in talking to you and your folks a little bit about the university," Boggs said. "If you got the time. If you're interested."

"Sure."

Boggs handed him a card. "This is my number. Now, Coach Walsh here gave me yours, so would it be all right if I called you tomorrow?"

"Sure."

"What time is good?"

"Whenever," Glen said.

"Okay." Boggs took out a little pocket calendar. "Saturday the seventh of November, whenever. It's a date."

The man smiled.

Glen's expression froze on his face.

Saturday the seventh. November 7, 1987.

Ten years to the day of the fire.

And all at once, he knew at least part of the reason why he'd been so moody all week, so preoccupied, even if it was just subconsciously. Ten years.

"You know," Glen said suddenly. "I don't think tomorrow's gonna work after all. Maybe Sunday."

"Sunday?"

"Yeah," Glen said.

"Okay." Boggs drew a line with his marker. "Sunday the eighth, it is."

"All right."

The three of them talked for a while longer then, about the game, about Glen's potential, about the proud tradition of Texas Longhorn football, the Torchlight Parade, the Red River Shootout, the great players who'd gone through the program and gone on to success in the pros, starting with Tom Landry himself, of course, and going on up through Night Train Layne, and Earl Campbell, and Steve McMichael, who Boggs thought that Glen reminded him a little bit of, and the whole time, even if he didn't entirely get Boggs's references, or what the man was talking about, Glen nodded, and smiled at not just Boggs, but Coach Walsh too.

Except that he was only half-listening to the conversation going on around him. The other half of the time, he was focused on what tomorrow meant, focused on his parents, on his brother, and the thing, Glen realized, he'd been putting off for the better part of the last ten years.

On the bus ride home, everyone else was laughing, and having a good time, passing around big hunks of this six-foot-long sandwich that Jimmy Marin had bought for the team, and Luis was doing his version of some of the cheerleaders' moves, which was about the funniest thing Glen had ever seen in his life, except that he couldn't really find it in him to laugh.

*Ten years ago, tomorrow,* he thought, and remembered Mark beating up Denton Young, and his mom brushing the hair out of his face, and his dad taking him to the observatory out in Jefferson Davis Park, and showing him the stars and then he thought of Paul Grimm's beady little face, and weaselly little eyes, and Pete Dominguez telling him, "Case closed . . ."

And his jaw tightened, and his hands clenched into fists.

"What's the matter with you?"

Katie was standing over him, hands on hips.

"It's nothing."

"It's something." She frowned. "Slide on over."

He moved over in his seat.

"So?"

He shrugged.

"Who was that guy talking to you?" Katie asked.

Glen explained about Boggs.

"Hey, that's great, Glen. Sounds like a scholarship offer to me. Probably the first of many, right?"

"I don't know."

"You can go to college. Probably have your choice of a lot of different colleges."

"Yeah, I guess."

"You guess. Don't you want to go to college?"

"I'm not really thinking about that right now."

"I can see. What are you thinking about?"

He hesitated.

"Come on," Katie said. "You been in a mood all week. What's the matter?"

He took a deep breath and told her.

"Ten years. It doesn't seem possible."

"I know."

She smiled.

"What?"

"Just thinking about that first time I saw you—in the hospital."

Glen shook his head. "You remember that?"

"Of course—don't you?"

"Yeah. Sure. Katie's Angels."

"Oh, God." Katie bowed her head in mock embarrassment. "Please, please, don't tell anyone about that."

"Don't worry." He leaned closer and whispered, "Your secret is safe with me."

"Thank you."

They were both silent a moment.

"Your parents would be proud of you, Glen," Katie said suddenly. "Everything that you've overcome, the person you've turned into . . ."

"Thanks." He smiled. "Don't take this the wrong way, but you're starting to sound like your mom."

She punched him in the shoulder. "Hey!"

"It's a compliment, relax." He was laughing now.

"So what's the next step with that college guy?"

"He's gonna call me Sunday. I guess I'll talk to him—me and Pete and Alma. See what he's offering."

"Don't rush into anything."

"I won't."

"So what are you doing tomorrow?" Katie asked. "A bunch of us are going up to Alpine. Hang out, maybe see a movie, get something to eat . . ."

Glen shook his head. "Can't."

"Why not?"

He took a deep breath then, exhaled before answering.

"I'm going to go see them. My parents, and Mark."

"Oh." Katie nodded. "Sure, I understand."

Another moment of silence.

"Which cemetery are they in?" she asked.

"I don't know."

Katie turned to him in surprise. "You don't know? You mean—you've never been to their graves?"

"No. I was in the hospital for so long, and when I got out . . . I don't know. Nobody ever said anything. I should've thought of it."

"Well . . . you're thinking of it now," Katie said.

"I am." He shuddered. "It seems kind of creepy, though."

"It is creepy, believe me," Katie said. "My mom goes to my dad's grave like every month."

"You go?"

"Sometimes." She looked over at him. "I'll go with you tomorrow, if you want. If you want company."

"That'd be great." He frowned. "But what about Alpine?"

She smiled. "Alpine isn't going anywhere."

Glen smiled back.

Luis came walking on his hands down the aisle then.

"Hey, Katie, what do you think? Can I be on top of the pyramid next time?"

Everyone on the bus cracked up, even Glen.

When he got home, he asked Pete where his parents and Mark were buried.

"I was wondering when you were gonna get around to that," Pete said. "Marfa Cemetery." He gave Glen directions.

"Okay, but where in the cemetery?"

"You'll find them, don't worry." Pete put a hand on his shoulder. "You can't hardly miss the Kanes in that place."


The next day, Glen saw what Pete meant. A whole corner of the cemetery was taken up by his blood relations—all the names that were so familiar to him from the scrapbook, like Robert Steven Kane, first of the family to settle in this part of the country, a soldier assigned with his unit to Marfa at the turn of the century, during the Mexican War. Kane and his wife Elizabeth had stayed in Marfa at war's end, raised a family that included three sons and two daughters, all of them buried there, including the eldest son, Robert Jr., his mom's dad, his grandpa. Including his mother's cousins, Wayne and Louise, fraternal twins, killed in a kitchen fire themselves at the age of fifteen, including his mother's only sibling, an older brother, Robert III, killed in a firefight in Vietnam, including his grandmother, who he'd never met, burned up in a car accident out on old State Route 118, the road to the McDonald Observatory.

*Fire,* Glen thought, and turned his attention to the three graves in front of him.

Susanna Kane Callaway. Randall Callaway. Mark Callaway.

He'd been thinking about this moment all night long. He had expected to be crippled with anger and sadness, but his mind was as tranquil as the breeze blowing through the cemetery. He heard crickets chirping, saw tree branches dancing in the breeze, and felt something he had never expected to feel: tranquillity.

"It's kind of nice," Katie said.

Glen nodded. It was nice; peaceful. He hoped that was what they were all feeling too, his family.

He knelt down in front of his mother's grave, next to her headstone.

*Are you there, Mom?* he asked silently. *Can you see me? I hope you can. I hope you're looking down, and you can see that I'm doing all right. That I'm in a good place, that I found some people to take care of me, some people who like me, care for me, some that I—*

He glanced around then, and smiled at Katie—

*—care for myself. I'm happy, Mom—or close to it, anyway. I hope you are.*

He knelt there a minute longer—why he wasn't quite sure, because obviously there wasn't going to be any reply—before moving on to his father's grave.

*Hey, Dad. I'm sure you're up there with Mom, too, that you're doing all those things now that you wanted to do down here but never got the time to. A lot of fishing. Hunting, even, if they have hunting up there. I hope you're happy. I miss you.*

*I'm gonna come here more often now, talk to you. Hope you don't mind.*

And then he moved on to his brother's grave.

MARK CALLAWAY

1968–1977

THE STAR THAT SHINES BRIGHTEST BURNS FASTEST

*They got that right, didn't they, bro?*

Glen smiled, remembering his brother charging through the house the way he charged through life—full speed. And suddenly, it felt like with Mark, remembering the past was the wrong thing to do. Mark wasn't one for looking back; he was always charging ahead, looking forward. He wouldn't want to reminisce about the things they'd done, him and Glen; he'd want to talk about the future. About what Glen was doing, what he should have been doing.

*So, where would you be right now, bro? Up in Austin, with Dusty Boggs? Playing football, on a scholarship yourself? I could see that. You always wanted to play football. You liked just about every sport, didn't you? The more hard-core, the better. You'd be doing some kind of sports thing now, wouldn't you, even if you hadn't gone to college? Can't see you working a regular job, or helping out around the funeral parlor, no sir. Mark Callaway, undertaker? That'd be the day.*

He reached out then, and put a hand on his brother's headstone—

And all at once, he felt something. A presence, like there was someone nearby. Someone watching him.

He looked up, and saw a man standing at the far end of the cemetery. The man wore a long, dark coat that hid his shape, and the collar was folded up so that it hid his face, too. He wore a hat, so Glen couldn't see his hair.

All he could see of the man, in fact, were his eyes. Even at this distance, he felt them boring into him, measuring him, appraising him, going over every inch of his body.

Glen was suddenly very curious. He wanted to know who the man was.

In fact, for some reason, he needed to know who the man was.

He rose up slowly from the grave, and stared.

"What is it, Glen?" Katie asked.

"Hold on a second," he said, and took a step toward the man.

The man took a step toward the car next to him.

Glen broke into a trot.

The man got in his car and started it. Glen heard the engine rev, and broke into a full-on sprint, running as fast as he could, jumping over footstones, flowers, dodging headstones to try and reach the man before he pulled away, to try and get a glimpse of the license plate, but he was too late.

By the time he reached the road, the car was turning onto the highway, too far away for him to even be sure of the make or model.

He walked back to Mark's grave.

"What was that all about?"

"Did you see that guy? He was watching me."

"I saw him, but . . . " Katie frowned. "You sure he wasn't here himself—visiting somebody's grave?"

"Pretty sure," Glen said. "Otherwise, why would he run?"

Katie shook her head and smiled. "Excuse me, but if I didn't know you and I saw you coming at me for no reason, I just might run too."

Glen had to smile at that too, but just for a second.

"No, he was watching me. I'm sure of it."

"Another one of those football scouts?"

"I don't know." Glen thought about that for a second. That would explain why the man was watching him, and why he'd run too, if he didn't want Glen to be mad at him, or his college for sending him, later on. Except . . .

There was something about the guy that made Glen pretty sure he wasn't a football scout, that the man had a whole different set of reasons for spying on Glen. Glen had no idea what those reasons could be, though.

"Doesn't matter," Glen said finally, turning back to Katie.

"So are you ready to go?" she asked.

"Yeah, I guess so."

They got back into Katie's car, and then, on the drive back home, had their first big fight.

Neither of them said anything at first, not until the cemetery was far behind them. Glen was thinking about the man, more than anything else.

"So?" Katie asked.

He turned to her, unsure what she meant. "So . . ."

"So how did it feel, to go there? To be there?"

"It was strange at first. But after a while . . . I understood why there are cemeteries, why people have graves. It was peaceful, kind of."

"I think most people feel that way about cemeteries," Katie said.

"Most people." He turned to look at her then. "You?"

She shook her head. "When I go to my dad's grave, I don't feel like he's there."

She seemed to want to say more then, but hesitated.

"Sure are a lot of Kanes back there, though," she offered a few seconds later.

"All of them, in fact," Glen said.

"Huh?"

"They're all dead, the Kanes," Glen said. "All of them—except me."

Katie shook her head. "Oh, for pity's sake, Glen—you're not going to start in with that curse stuff now, are you?"

"No, but in case you hadn't noticed, I am the only one in my family left alive."

"Glen, come on."

"I don't want to believe in it—"

"Well then, don't."

"But I can't ignore it."

"Can't ignore what? That accidents happen? That people die sometimes, in ways that don't seem fair, that don't make a lot of sense? Believe me, I understand that. I mean, my father—"

"Exactly."

Katie did a double-take.

"What?"

Glen sighed. He hadn't meant to say anything about that, but now it was out, and so what could he do but forge ahead.

"I know this is going to sound crazy, but—"

"Oh, it sounds crazy already," Katie said. "It sounds way, way crazy."

She was angry.

"Well, I'm just gonna say it."

"Please do."

"I meet your mom, and I meet you, and then not long after that, your dad gets killed."

"Yeah? So?"

"I get adopted by the Barrows, and then—then they end up dying. Margaret kills herself, you know. I mean . . ."

Katie was shaking her head. Glen could see she was trying to keep her temper in check.

"Glen, that's so much bad luck, that's so much tragedy, I

can understand why you might think that way sometimes, but honestly—it doesn't prove that there's a curse. You can't go through life that way, Glen, thinking that anybody you meet or try and become friends with is going to—"

She stopped talking all of a sudden.

"What?"

She started shaking her head back and forth slowly.

"Oh, my God," she said, in a tone of disbelief. "Oh, my God."

"What?" Glen asked again.

"Is that why you've never asked me out on a date, Glen?"

It was his turn to do a double-take.

"Huh?"

"It's a pretty straightforward question. Is that why you've never asked me out on a date? Because of this curse?"

He felt himself blushing, and shifted uncomfortably in his seat.

"It is, isn't it? That's the stupidest thing I ever heard of."

They were just coming to his street now, to where Katie was going to turn.

Except she didn't. She put on the brakes.

"Get out."

"What?"

"Get out."

"Katie . . ."

She turned to him, and he saw she had tears in her eyes.

"I've been hoping that the two of us—I mean for four years now I've been waiting, and all this time you—"

"Katie—" He was trying hard not to smile, he knew that was the wrong thing to be doing, but this was unbelievable, she wanted to date him? "I didn't know you—"

"If this is how you run your life, Glen Callaway, if you let some fucking curse govern everything you do—"

Glen's mouth dropped open—that was the first time in his life he'd ever heard Katie Vick swear.

"—then I don't think our friendship has much of a future."

"Katie, I—"

"Please get out of the car, Glen."

"No, wait, don't do this. I—"

"Get out. Please."

She was staring straight ahead, down the road.

He got out.

She drove away without looking back.

# chapter
## twelve

He tried calling the next morning to apologize; she wouldn't come to the phone.

She didn't walk with him to school that day; when he tried corralling her after class, she just stomped away. It continued like that for a week; then one afternoon, waiting for her to walk home, he saw her coming out of the school holding hands with Scott Ransom, who was the class valedictorian, who had already been accepted early decision to Yale University in Connecticut, the first kid from Marfa to go to Yale in half a century.

Glen moped home by himself that afternoon.

He stayed home sick for the next couple days, and called again. Melissa answered the phone; said Katie wasn't there. Glen left word for her to call.

After a week, she still hadn't. He tried again. Nothing. And after that . . .

Well, he got the message. He let her go.

He didn't ask Katie's friends how she was doing, he didn't ask her mom, he didn't ask the other girls on the cheering squad. He thought he could see the answer for himself; she was doing fine, she and Scott Ransom were together all the time. It was for the best, Glen told himself in his room at night, after he'd finished his homework, after he'd talked out a few things with Pete and Alma regarding his plans for next year. After all, Katie was moving on in a few months anyway, into a world where he would never be at home, she was going on to a big college, and four years of hard studying, and moving up in the world, and meeting all these other boys, who were all going to be just as much in love with her as everyone in Marfa was, and there wasn't going to be time or room for Glen in her life then, so why not just cut it off now? It was for the best, for her, for him, for all those reasons, he thought, and maybe also, maybe because, this little voice in the back of his mind told him . . .

The curse.

He threw himself into football practice, and when that was done, he went and joined the basketball team. Success there didn't come as quick, but it came; by the end of the season, he was not only starting, he was starring, though Marfa lasted only one round in the playoffs before losing to Valentine, a team with five players who worked together, as opposed to Marfa, a team that didn't really work at all, largely because of him. He'd been poorly coached, Glen realized, barely coached at all; the coaches just threw him out there on the court, as if his size and strength could make up for his lack of skill. But he'd ended up hurting the team, not just on the court but off the court. They never came together because he drew so much attention. It had been the same way in football, he felt, looking back; the excitement, the craziness, had been about him, not the team. That wasn't fair to the other players, he decided. Maybe team sports weren't for him after all. Maybe an individual sport.

He wondered about wrestling.

He went to the gym one day during a wrestling practice, just stood there by the door and watched as the team—all eight of them—broke off into groups of two and practiced holds, throws, did a drill of two-minute matches where the coach, a man named Pete Loeb who Glen knew because he was also an English teacher, got down on his hands and knees with the kids and kept correcting their technique.

What Glen found interesting was that the best wrestler on the team was also the littlest, a kid named Manuel Santos who must have been all of five-foot-three, but kept throwing around the bigger kids, who included Ty Crowell and one of the linemen from the football team, effortlessly, pinning them time and time again. Glen wondered how he did that, and started edging closer to the mats to see Santos work.

"Hey, Glen."

That was Ty, who'd turned around while Glen was absorbed in watching Santos and another kid wrestle.

"Hey, Ty," Glen said, suddenly self-conscious.

The whole team stopped what they were doing, and turned to look at him.

"You interested in wrestling?" Ty asked.

Loeb stood up too now, and looked at Glen.

"Just watching," Glen said. "Don't let me interrupt."

He scooted as fast as he could out the door.

Okay, so maybe not wrestling.

He applied himself a little more to his homework; he applied himself a little more to making friends.

He got his own license, and one day Pete let him borrow the car to drive up to Aurora Ranch. He wanted to see if Consuela had come back; ask for a picture of Red, maybe ride Cortez.

Consuela wasn't there. She'd moved to El Paso. None of the others—Deke, Tony, or Lucas—were there either. Aurora was there; she didn't recognize him. Most of the animals were gone too; Aurora was selling off a big chunk of the land, and turning the place into a dude ranch, a tourist attraction. She seemed old herself now; the house seemed very small. He found the picture of Red and Aurora on the staircase, same place it had always been: Red looked different than he re-membered. After a few minutes, all he wanted to do was leave, before the few good memories he had of the place were completely erased.

On the way back, he decided to stop and see the Marfa Lights. They were there all right; it wasn't such a big deal.

Spring came; baseball season started, and Frank Walsh was all over Glen to try his hand at pitching. Glen deferred; football was enough for him. He still hadn't accepted any of the schol-arships that had come his way; now he was thinking about traveling after high school, maybe joining the army, maybe heading across Texas to Galveston and signing on with the Merchant Marines. One day in the school library, looking up different places he might want to see in the atlas, he struck up a conversation with a junior named Noreen Roy. He'd seen her around school before; she was hard to miss, as she was almost six feet tall, captain of the girls' basketball team, and the only girl he'd ever seen in the weight room. They became friends; went to the movies one Friday night to see *Dirty Dancing*.

Katie was there too, not with Scott Ransom, who he'd heard she'd broken up with, not with Paul Crockett, who he heard she'd gone out with two Fridays in a row, but with Billy Porter. In the balcony, in the back. They were kissing when Glen and Noreen came in, they were kissing during the movie, they were kissing when the lights came up.

He made sure Katie saw him with Noreen; he smiled at her, though his stomach was rolling the whole time.

He drove Noreen home; he kissed her at her door. His first time kissing a girl; it wasn't bad. It wasn't anything special.

He saw Noreen a few more times; they kissed a lot more. They did a little more than kissing; Glen began to get an idea of what all the fuss was about.

Noreen was nice. She was smart; she was pretty; she knew more about football than he did.

But being with her felt wrong to him, somehow.

One afternoon in May, he went to see Melissa for his monthly check-in. She had on a very fancy dress, and some nice jewelry. After she finished asking him all the usual questions about how he was doing, he asked her why she was all dressed up.

"I'm going to church later today," she said. "It's the anniversary of Jarvis's death."

"Oh," Glen said.

"I'd ask you to come, but I know you don't go to church, Glen."

He was about to say, "That's right," when he looked out the window and saw Katie coming up the steps to her mom's office. She was dressed for church as well.

"It's for your husband?" Glen asked.

Melissa nodded. "That's right."

"I'll go then," Glen said. "I'd like to go. If you don't mind."

He was surprised by a few things once he got inside the church, once the memorial service started. How comfortable he felt in the building, how much comfort Melissa seemed to take in the words of the minister, how much sense the minister made, and above all, how awkward he felt around Katie.

When the service was over, Melissa got involved in a conversation with Beverly Cutler, who had come as well. That left Katie and Glen standing next to each other.

He cleared his throat.

"Hey."

"Hey yourself, stranger."

"How you been?"

"Okay."

She seemed preoccupied to him; like she had someplace else to be. But he didn't want to let her leave before saying something.

"You know, I've been thinking," he said. "About what happened after the cemetery, and I—"

"I'm sorry, Glen, I can't talk now," she said.

"Oh."

"I have an appointment, and it's gonna take a while, and I've got to be back in school for cheerleading practice in two hours. I'm sorry."

*Probably a Billy Porter appointment,* Glen thought. Well, at least he'd tried.

"Okay. Well maybe we can talk in school, or—"

"Or you could come with me."

He wasn't sure he'd heard right.

"I could come with you?"

"That's what I said."

"Where are you going?"

"Another little ritual," she said. "Same purpose as this one, only . . . it's more private. More personal."

"I wouldn't be intruding?"

"No." She shook her head. "In fact, I'd really like it if you would come."

That settled it for him.

"Sure."

They headed north on Route 17, in the direction of old Fort Davis, and the McDonald Observatory. It was a flat road at first, going through the desert, past scrub and a few isolated ranches, before heading up into the mountains and getting steeper—a whole lot steeper, and windy, and in a few places, downright dangerous, just a narrow guardrail separating the road from the side of the mountains and the desert floor far below, but Glen didn't mind.

Katie was talking to him again.

After the first few, awkward minutes, it was like slipping into an old, comfortable shoe. He learned how she'd been doing in school, how her friends had been, Janie Boyd, Kathy Marin, Betty Lou Sanderson, how they were all working together now on the school yearbook, and how they all, not just her, agreed that they definitely, definitely, needed a better candid of Glen than the one he'd submitted because it just did not do him justice.

Glen laughed at that. "I'm not sure a good picture of me is possible, to tell you the truth."

She shook her head. "Don't be stupid, Glen."

But she was smiling as she said it.

He was about to tell her how much he'd missed her over the last few months when they came around a particularly sharp bend in the road, and she pulled the car to a stop.

"We're here," she said. "This is where my dad died."

They'd done a little work on the road, Glen saw, made the turn a little wider here than it had obviously been before, put in some fill and extended the guardrail too—Glen could see where it was new steel, replacing the old—so that it encircled not just the road but a little grassy spot, where there was a bench, and next to it, a plaque.

The two of them got out of the car, and walked to the bench. On the way, Katie stopped at the plaque, and ran a hand over it. The plaque read:

IN MEMORIAM
PATROLMAN JARVIS VICK
1948–1978
DIED IN THE LINE OF DUTY

She walked to the bench then, and sat down. Glen followed.

The bench had a magnificent view of the desert below, and beyond that you could see all the way down Route 17 to Marfa in the distance.

Katie leaned forward, hands on her chin, and sighed.

"I don't even know the whole story," she said. "Some guy was running drugs over the border, I don't know, something like that, and my dad recognized the car, and they went on this chase that seemed to last forever, only it didn't obviously, it ended here. No curse involved."

She said that without looking over at Glen, but he knew she was waiting for him to respond anyway.

"Of course not," he said firmly. "No curse involved."

The wind gusted as he said that. A chill ran down his back.

"I don't believe in God," Katie said. "I guess I told you that before."

"You did."

"But the thing is, whenever I come here . . . I feel something. Part of my dad, maybe, maybe just part of everything out there—" She waved in the direction of the desert, and the town below. "Part of life, I guess."

"Hard not to feel part of something bigger when you look out there," Glen said.

She nodded, and then turned on the bench to look at him.

"So, how have you really been, Glen? These last few months?"

"Good. Okay, I guess."

"Uh-huh. You hear any more from the football guys—the scholarship guys?"

"Some. Still haven't made up my mind."

"Uh-huh." She looked down at the ground. "And how's Noreen Roy?"

Glen smiled. "She's all right. How's Scott Ransom?"

"I don't know. Okay."

"And Billy Porter?"

She turned to him and made a face. "Billy is fine, thank you."

He leaned closer.

"And what about Paul Crockett? How's he?"

"Hey!" She chucked him on the arm. "That's enough."

"Yeah. Enough."

They were both silent a minute.

"I love you, Katie," Glen said.

She smiled.

"Hey," she said, getting to her feet quickly. "You want to go to a party?"

And that was how their first—and only—fight ended.

# chapter
## thirteen

The party Katie had been talking about was the following Friday, Senior Skip Day, a Marfa High tradition held on the last Friday in May, where the whole senior class skipped school for an all-day party. This senior class of fifty-two students was the biggest in the high school in a decade, and they were determined to make their party one to remember.

Glen had heard about it before, but hadn't really planned on attending. For one thing, he knew Katie was going to be there with Billy Porter, and he didn't want to sit through that. That part of it had changed now, of course, because whatever happened between Katie and Billy, he'd told her how he felt, and so . . . what else could he do? He couldn't not be with her, even if it was just as a friend. Besides . . .

He remembered what had started their whole argument in the first place, and thought that maybe, just maybe, as impossible as it sounded, Katie would rather be with him than Billy Porter, or Scott Ransom, or Paul Crockett, or any of the dozens of other boys waiting for a chance to ask her out on a date.

After all, she was driving him there, wasn't she? In the new car her grandfather had bought for her. Yes she was, and she was picking him up for the party in about five minutes, he realized, and started gobbling down the eggs and bacon Alma had put in front of him so fast that he actually made a slurping noise as one particularly big bite went down.

"Excuse me," he said.

"Slow down there, son," Alma said, taking a seat. "What's the big rush?"

"Last Friday in May, let's see, let's see . . . " Pete set down the *Sentinel* on the table and took a sip of his coffee. "Could it be—Senior Skip Day? The big party? Am I right, Glen?"

"Yes, sir," Glen said. "The big party."

"Of course." Pete set down his cup and eyed Glen carefully. "There won't be any alcohol at this party, because the drinking age is now twenty-one, isn't that right?"

"That's right," Glen said.

"And even if there is alcohol," Pete said, "I know you'll be smart enough not to drink any of it."

"Pete," Alma said, laying a hand on her husband's arm, "it's Skip Day. You remember Skip Day, back when we were kids?"

"Back when the drinking age was eighteen."

"And I was seventeen, as I recall, and you were—"

Pete shook his head. "The point is that things are different now. Glen, I want you to promise me—"

Alma cut him off. "I want you to promise *us,*" she said to Glen firmly, "that you'll be responsible. That's all. Responsible. I'll let you judge what that means."

"Yes, ma'am," Glen said. "Sir. I won't let you down."

"That's all we can ask," Alma said, and sat back in her chair.

"Hmmm," Pete grumbled, and went back to reading his paper.

Outside a car horn honked.

"Gotta go," Glen said, pushing back from the table.

Alma stood up and looked through the kitchen window to the driveway.

"Why, it's Katie Vick." She turned back to Glen and smiled. "Guess you two are over your little spat, huh?"

"That's right," Glen said, smiling.

"About time." Alma gave Glen her cheek to kiss. "Be good."

"I will. Bye, Pete."

"Dishes in the sink, please," Pete said.

Glen scraped what was left of his food into the garbage and hurried out the door, and then stopped in his tracks.

He'd obviously gotten the story wrong, somehow. Because Katie wasn't driving a new car, she was driving her grandfather's old car, a beat-up old Datsun that looked even smaller than her mom's Honda.

He walked up to the car, and frowned.

"What happened to the new car?"

"What do you mean?"

"I thought you were getting a new car."

"No, silly." She shook her head. "My grandfather got a new car, and so I got his old one."

"Oh."

"So what do you think?"

Glen walked around the car. It looked in pretty good shape, except for a piece of chrome trim that had come loose around the fender, and a few rust spots above the back wheel wells. It was sure cleaner than Glen had ever seen it; the banana-yellow exterior shone.

"So?"

"It's loud, that's for sure."

"What do you mean, loud?"

"Bright."

"But do you like it?"

He nodded. "Yeah. It suits you."

She made a mock frown. "I'm not sure that's a compliment. But what the heck—get in. We gotta stop and pick up chips."

"I don't know, Katie."

"What?"

"I don't think I can fit in there unless you cut me into pieces first."

She rolled her eyes at him. "Glen?"

"What?"

"Shut up and get your goofy ass in the car."

"I think I can only fit half of my goofy ass in here. Which cheek do you prefer?"

"Oh, for God's sake," she said, and took a swat at his butt, and missed. "Get them both in here before . . ."

Her voice trailed off.

"What?" Glen asked.

"Your mom and dad are watching."

Glen turned and saw Pete and Alma looking through the kitchen at them.

"See you later," he mouthed, and smiled and waved at them, and got in the car.

But Glen was wrong about that.

He would never see Pete or Alma Dominguez again.

The party was being held outside of town, at a campground in Jeff Davis National Park, out the same road—Highway 17—that Glen and Katie had traveled the day before. By the time they stopped for chips, and got all the way up the mountain to the campsite, it was close to eleven, and at least twenty people were already there, including Ty Crowell and Luis Campos.

"Oh, damn," Luis yelled as Glen unfolded himself out of the car. "Look who it is. The man is here, baby. The man himself is here!"

Luis ran over to Glen and gave him a high five.

Then he handed him a plastic cup full of beer.

Glen shook his head. "Not yet, Luis. It's not even noon."

"Oh, come on, it's party time, Glen," Luis said.

"Not yet, it isn't."

Luis shrugged and drank the beer himself in one gulp.

Glen glanced around. Things were obviously just getting started. Three kegs sat at one end of a row of picnic tables, a couple grills stood at the ready, and a pair of coolers housed several packs of hot dogs, hamburgers, and buns. There was a boom box playing a Michael Jackson song—Glen hated Michael Jackson—and a stack of tapes next to it.

Well away from the beer, a couple of Katie's friends—Janie Boyd and Kathy Marin—sat, deep in conversation with each other across another picnic table. Janie looked up, saw Katie, and waved her over.

"See ya," Katie said, touched his arm lightly, and was gone.

"Yo, Glen!" Ty Crowell was standing by one of the grills, holding a beer in one hand and a can of lighter fluid in the other. "Check this out, man."

He shot a stream of lighter fluid at the grill. Flames shot into the air, big enough that they sent Ty scurrying backward.

"Jesus Christ!" Luis shook his head. "What are you trying to do, man, burn the whole fucking forest down? Take it easy."

"You take it easy," Ty said. "Just having some fun, that's all."

And Ty did it again.

Flames leapt into the sky again, red and orange tongues of fire.

Glen stared into that fire, and a chill went down his back.

"Stop it, Ty," he said, and Ty took one look at his face and stopped.

Glen took the lighter fluid from him.

"I'll handle the grill," he said.

\*          \*          \*

Wasn't it funny how things worked out sometimes?

Here Katie had thought that she'd be spending this whole day with Billy Porter, and now he wasn't even here, he was the only one in the senior class who wasn't coming, which of course was her fault, she'd shattered the boy by breaking up with him, but he'd get over it. He was smart, he was funny, he was handsome, he'd be fine, and he was being stupid by not coming. Probably half the girls here would have had sex with him tonight, if he really worked the sympathy angle. Poor Billy, Katie treated you so bad, let me help you feel better . . .

Well, not to be harsh about it, but it wasn't her problem. Katie didn't have a problem in the world.

Except of course, that her friends thought she was crazy.

Janie and Kathy had a Boone's Farm wine cooler out on the table, and a stack of the same red plastic cups the boys were drinking beer from. As Katie sat, Janie poured wine into a cup and handed it to her.

"So, Kate," Janie said (Janie was the only one in the school who called her anything but Katie). "You broke up with Billy Porter."

"Yeah."

"To go out with him." She nodded in the direction of the grill.

"His name is Glen."

"Whatever."

"And we're not going out. We're just friends." She smiled. "Right now."

"Kate, Kate, Kate." Janie shook her head. "Isn't he a little—"

"A little what?"

"A little big, that's what," Kathy Marin said, smiling and leaning across the table. "Katie, now tell the truth—how big is he?"

She and Janie giggled.

Katie shook her head. "Get your mind out of the gutter."

"Don't be so sensitive, Kate," Janie said.

"She doesn't have to be—not with somebody that big," Kathy said.

"Honest to God," Katie said, draining her cup and joining in the giggling.

She reached across the table, and poured herself some more of the Boone's Farm.

Glen worked the grill all through lunch without a break. It was hot work, thirsty work, and he had Luis bring him a beer—two beers, actually—while doing it. They felt good going down—he got a little buzz going too, that felt good as well. But he remembered Alma's words—Be responsible—and stopped at two.

When the requests for burgers and dogs ended, he wandered over to the parking lot, where a bunch of the guys were playing touch football. He stood and watched for a while, until Luis noticed him.

"You want in?" Luis asked, holding out the ball.

"Nah." Glen waved him off. "Just gonna watch."

Which he did for a while. Everyone was so good with the ball . . . it made him realize that without his strength and size, he wasn't much of a football player either. Strength and size, he knew, would only take him so far. He needed training. He needed the skills—he was going to have to work hard to be a real player. Which made him realize that scholarship was not going to be as much of a free ride as it had sounded.

"Hey."

He looked down and saw Katie standing next to him.

"Aren't you gonna play?"

"Nah."

"Why not?"

"Just don't feel like it, that's all."

"Well, don't go getting all moody on me."

"Don't worry. I'm not."

He smiled at her to prove it. She smiled back.

"Want to take a walk?" Katie asked.

"Sure," he said, and they turned their backs on the crowd and headed into the forest.

Neither of them said anything for a while. They just walked, till they'd left the sounds of the party far behind, and the sounds of the woods—the occasional bird chirp, a small animal darting through the brush, the wind rustling through the trees, quiet, peaceful sounds—surrounded them.

"It's nice out here," Katie said. "Peaceful."

"Uh-huh."

Somewhere along the walk they had started holding hands—Katie let his hand go now and turned to face him.

"Glen," she said.

He drew her close, and they kissed.

It was a long, slow kiss.

It was everything that every kiss with Noreen Roy hadn't been—warm and soft and magical and meaningful in a way that Glen couldn't put into words, except that of course he could put it into words, two words in fact, those words being: Katie Vick.

In the dark, bitter torment of the years that followed, Glen would long remember that kiss as the best moment of his life.

"I didn't think that was ever going to happen," Katie said.

They kissed again, and then they both smiled, and joined hands, and walked a while longer.

Glen talked a little bit about his plan to maybe go to Galveston. Katie asked how he was gonna get there, and when he answered, "I don't know, bus, I guess," she smiled and said she'd drive him.

Then they stopped and kissed again.

"This is habit-forming," Glen said, and smiled.

Katie frowned.

"What?" Glen asked.

"Somebody's calling my name."

Glen listened close—then he heard it too.

"Fuck 'em," he said, and kissed her again.

She laughed and pushed him away.

"No, really, someone's calling my name."

"I hear it," he said, and then he heard something else as well. His name being called too.

"Sounds like Luis."

"And a couple others," Katie said. "I guess we ought to go see what they want."

"I guess," Glen said reluctantly.

Katie smiled, a different kind of smile than the one she'd offered him before.

"Don't worry," she said, taking his hand and dragging him back in the direction of the party. "The night is young, Glen."


As it turned out, the voices had been calling for Glen, after all, only calling Katie as a way to find him.

It seemed there was a bet in the offing.

"You want me to do what?" Glen asked.

"Lift a car, man," Luis said. "These guys"—he pointed to the Whitfield brothers, Jake and Ronnie, who Glen barely knew, and Paul Crockett, who'd been giving Glen the evil eye the whole party, for obvious reasons—"don't think you can do it."

"Luis . . . " Glen shook his head and smiled. "Lift a car? What are you, out of your mind?"

"Not the whole car, man, just a part."

Glen frowned. "I don't know."

"Come on!" Luis said. "Fifty bucks says you can!"

He flashed a wad of bills.

Crockett stepped forward, flashing another one. "I say he can't."

Glen and Crockett glared at each other.

"You can get hurt doing that kind of thing," Janie Boyd said. "You could strain a muscle."

"You can't lift a car, Glen," Ty Crowell said. "Be serious."

"You guys are all drunk," Kathy Marin said.

Glen stared at Crockett a second longer, then at Luis, and then finally at Katie.

"What the heck," he said. "I'll give it a shot."

It was decided a small car would serve. Katie's car, in fact.

Glen turned his back on the crowd and started to loosen up.

"You're going to do this?" Katie asked.

"You don't want me to?"

"It's up to you. I mean . . . just don't get hurt."

"Why would I get hurt?"

"Trying to lift the car."

"Trying?" He smiled now. "There is no try. There is only do."

"Ha-ha."

The crowd—most of the people at the party—walked over to the parking lot, and Katie's yellow Datsun.

"That car?" Crockett asked. "That don't look too heavy."

He walked up to the back bumper and pulled upward with all his might, barely budging the car. Ronnie Whitfield joined him. The car didn't move. Jake came over too, got his hands under the rear bumper as well, and the three of them got the back wheels to finally clear the ground.

"Satisfied?" Luis asked.

"Okay," Crockett said. "Took three of us to get it off the ground. I know he's strong, but he ain't that strong."

"It's on, Glen," Luis said. "Whenever you're ready, big boy. Make me some money!"

Glen marched confidently to the back of the car, bent at his knees, and found a section of the bumper he could grip. He took a deep breath, exhaled, then took another, shorter breath.

His backers began cheering him on; other classmates tried to break his concentration.

*Just like back in the weight room,* he thought, and then let out a deep breath, and grunted, and exploded upward.

The muscles in his arms strained; the veins in his neck and foreheard throbbed.

The Datsun's tires floated free from the earth, and a cheer went up. Glen continued to push upward until he was standing completely erect, his arms and knees locked underneath the load.

"You the man, Glen!" Luis yelled. "You the freakin' man!"

He inched the car back to the ground, and Luis and the rest of those that had bet on Glen mobbed him.

Luis gave Glen a wad of bills.

"What's this?"

"Your share of the money, man. You did all the work."

Glen smiled, but a minute later gave the wad to Katie.

"Huh?" she asked.

"Gas money," he said. "For Galveston."

She tucked it into the pocket of her jeans.


The afternoon vanished, and turned to night. Katie had wandered off somewhere with Kathy Marin. Glen found himself sitting at the table with the boom box, next to Scott Foley, who had taken charge of the music.

"Check this one out," Foley said, slipping another tape in

the boom box. "Guns," he said, and pressed a button, and all at once, this noise came out of the tape player, nasty guitars, big drums, and the singer, he sounded as though he had nails in his throat, like he was singing through pain and he enjoyed it.

Glen liked it.

"Guns?"

"Guns N' Roses," Foley said. "*Appetite for Destruction.* 'Welcome to the Jungle.' Fuckin' revolutionary, man. This fuckin' record"—he nodded at the boom box—"revolutionary."

Glen jumped off the table and got him and Foley two more beers.

They sat and listened to the whole record in silence. Glen helped Foley guard the boom box from Janie Boyd, who wanted them to put the Michael Jackson tape back in. When the Guns tape was done, Foley slipped another from his pocket into the machine. Even more guitars, even louder.

"Dirty deeds," Foley sang along with the record. "Done dirt cheap!"

"Hey, man." Tom Beathard wobbled in front of the table, and swayed on his feet. "Play some Aerosmith, dude."

"Aerosmith." Foley shook his head in disgust. "That shit is gay."

"Fuck you," Beathard said with a smile. "You're gay."

"Fuck you. You're the gay one," Foley shot back, and Beathard leaned closer, about to fall.

Glen grabbed Beathard and helped him sit down.

"You guys work it out," he said, and left the two of them sitting there, arguing.

He wandered around the party a little while longer, before realizing he'd had enough. He'd had four beers, and that was plenty for him. He didn't feel like smoking any pot, and he was tired of talking about football, and he was worried that the cops were going to find this place any minute now and shut them down, and he did not want Pete all over his case about that. It was time to go, as far as he was concerned.

He went looking for Katie, and found her with Kathy at the same picnic table she'd started out at. She was giggling and drinking something from a plastic cup. More wine cooler, Glen saw.

"There he is," she said, getting to her feet. "What's going on, Glen?"

"I'm ready to go," he said.

"Boo. Hiss." Kathy made a face. "Come on, Glen, hang out a while. The night is young."

"You tired?" Katie asked.

"Not at all."

They smiled at each other.

"Right," Katie said, getting to her feet. "Let's get out of here."

It took another half hour for them to say their good-byes. Glen watched Katie wobble over to her car, and shook his head. "I don't think you should drive."

"Yeah, you're right." Katie smiled and handed him her keys. "You drive."

"I can't drive that car. It's a stick."

"Ah." Katie waved a hand dismissively. "All you have to do is get it in gear, and we can coast down the mountain."

"And when we're down the mountain . . ."

"Then we take it slow. All we have to do is keep an eye out for the cops."

"All right." It sounded easy enough, and he certainly wasn't going to let her drive.

He squeezed into the driver's seat, put the key in the ignition, and turned. Nothing happened.

Katie laughed. "Put one foot on the brake, and with the other foot, push the clutch to the floor. Then turn the ignition."

He did as she said, and sure enough, the car fired up.

"See?" She smiled. "This is going to be easy."

It wasn't, though. The road down the mountain was dark, and lit only in a very few places. Glen had to tap on the brakes to keep his speed down. He had to concentrate too, which wasn't easy, because Katie was going on and on about something Billy Porter had apparently said to Kathy Marin about her, and she was going to give him a piece of her mind the next time the two of them talked, if they ever talked again, and meanwhile Glen was keeping his eyes glued to the road, because some of these curves were nasty, downright dangerous, whose stupid idea had it been to hold this party on top of a mountain anyway?

"So what do you think?" Katie asked.

"About what?" Glen realized that she must have switched conversational gears while he'd been preoccupied with the road.

"About my idea, silly. About going to Kansas City before we hit Galveston?"

"Oh." Glen shrugged. "Yeah. Sounds good."

"You're damn right it sounds good," Katie said. "My uncle Bob—my dad's brother—he lives there. They have the most amazing house you've ever seen. It's got a pool, and a guest cottage, where I bet we can stay . . . "

Her voice trailed off for a second.

"He's a big-shot businessman, Uncle Bob is. He's gotta be worth a million dollars. Really focused on money, you know, always asking me what my plans are after college, if I'm going to go into business, that sort of thing . . . "

"He must be proud of how you're doing in school."

"Oh, yeah. He's proud. The whole family's proud." She shrugged again. "God. He's the total opposite of my dad."

Glen was curious. "What do you mean?"

"Like, my dad . . . he never cared too much about money. I vaguely remember him having some argument with Mom about how she really didn't need to go back to work, they'd manage just fine without her doing that. 'We'll get by,' he always said. I remember that—'We'll get by.' "

Glen thought that was a little unrealistic, having been without money for so long, having seen how little Pete and Alma had and how just a little bit more cash—a couple hundred bucks a month, even—would make their lives a whole lot better, easier, a dishwasher, a new car for Alma (or a new used car anyway), a new coat of paint in the living room—but he didn't want to rain on Katie's parade.

"He sounds like a guy who had his priorities straight," Glen offered.

"Yeah," Katie replied, shifting in her seat. "I remember the only thing he ever asked me about was, 'Are you happy?' Of course, that was a long time ago, but . . . I still remember it."

She put a hand on Glen's arm.

"I'm happy now, Glen. You know that?"

He smiled. "I'm happy too."

They rounded another curve on the mountain road, a little too fast for Glen's taste. He rode the brake a little harder.

"I bet my dad would've liked you," Katie said.

"I don't know about that." Glen laughed. "Fathers can be pretty protective of their daughters."

"My dad—" Katie began.

Which was when they came around another bend in the road, this one seemingly longer and sharper than any of the others, and Glen saw the cutout, the bench, the plaque, the new section of guardrail glinting in the moonlight, and he thought—

Your dad.

Cursed.

And as he thought it, the wheel hit something slick, and the back wheels of the car began to slide.

"Glen!" Katie screamed.

He wrestled the wheel, spun it hard in the direction of the skid. Didn't make a damn bit of difference.

The car continued to slide, and Katie continued to scream, and Glen swore and slammed on the brakes and the back end of the car slammed into something and his head hit the windshield and all at once, he was flying through the air.

Then he hit hard for a second time, and the world went black.


Glen came to lying facedown on something hard. He peeked at it. The road. What was he doing lying on the road? And for that matter, why couldn't he see out of his right eye, it was all crusted over with gunk, sticky gunk like syrup, actually it felt like his whole forehead was crusted over with the stuff. He wiped at it and it came off in flakes, and then in sticky globs, just like syrup. It was in his mouth too, tasting not a bit like syrup, tasting dark and coppery and raw and—

*Blood.*

The car.

*Katie.*

It all came roaring back in his mind in a split second, and he pushed to his hands and knees and wiped away the crust from his eyes and found himself facing the mountain, staring down the road, and the car was nowhere in sight.

"Katie!" he yelled, and staggered to his feet. One of his legs, his right leg, there was something wrong with it, his knee actually, it buckled underneath him, and he fell to the ground again, and stuck out his right hand to break his fall, and when he did he saw that there was something wrong with that hand too, the pinky finger was sticking up at a ninety-degree angle to the others. Broken.

He didn't care. He couldn't feel it. He got to his feet and managed to turn around. His vision blurred for a second as he did so, then came back into focus.

He saw the cutout in the road, and the clearing where the bench had been, only now the bench was lying twenty feet past that, rolled over onto its back, and the signpost holding the plaque to Katie's father was bent in half, and the new guardrail was broken too, and what had broken it was the car, which was facing Glen head-on, the engine still running, one headlight still shining, and the windshield gone, thanks to his head, or his forehead, he didn't know which, and there was Katie, slumped in her seat, not moving.

Glen staggered toward her.

"Katie!" he shouted, and staggered faster, and shouted again, "Katie!"

And her head moved, and she looked up at him and started to cry.

*Thank God,* he thought. *She's alive. Thank you, God.*

"Glen," she said. "Oh, God, Glen—"

—and the car wobbled then, up and down, and whatever iota of relief he had been feeling disappeared and a hole opened up inside his stomach because he saw that the car hadn't just gone through the railing, it had just about gone off the mountain.

The rear wheels weren't even on the road.

"Get out of the car!" Glen yelled, waving frantically. "Get out of the car!"

Katie nodded weakly, get out of the car, yes, and tried to open her door even as Glen saw she had no idea what was going on, and he just waved her on, waved her to get out, as he stumbled toward her, shouting her name, get out, get out, why wasn't she getting out, and then he was fifteen feet away and saw her door was jammed up against the crumpled edge of the guardrail there was no way she was going to get it open, and he saw her look out of her window and suddenly realize what was happening and then the panic was in her eyes too, and he was ten feet away, dragging one leg behind him, five feet away, his hand was on the hood of the car he was going to reach through the windshield and pull her out he extended an arm she extended hers—

And the car wobbled again, and began to fall backward.

"Glen!" Katie screamed.

And he grabbed hold of the car bumper with both hands and stopped the Datsun from toppling off the road.

Oh, God it was heavy.

"Arrggghhh," he grunted, and pulled. God it was heavy, it was so heavy but he'd held it before he'd lifted it why couldn't he do it now oh God—

"Glen!" Katie screamed. "Glen!"

He could barely see her face over the hood.

"Get—out—the—car," he managed.

"I'm trying," she sobbed. "I can't get the goddamn seatbelt, Glen—"

He would have laughed. The seatbelt, he hadn't worn his and he was fine and she was—

No, she wasn't.

But he couldn't get a grip. It was his right hand his pinky finger his fucking pinky finger. He couldn't get a good grip. The bumper was slipping.

"Come on, Katie," and now he was crying too. "Come on."

He looked up and saw her eyes, wide with terror.

"Goddammit," he said, and the car began to fall backward again, dragging him with it.

He dug his feet into the ground and held for a second, the

muscles in his arms trembling, the veins popping out, but that was all. He wasn't strong enough. All those weights, all that time pumping iron, and he wasn't strong enough when it counted the most he wasn't strong enough he was—

"Glen!" Katie screamed.

He looked up and met her gaze.

"Please," she said.

"I'm trying," he said, and then he was crying too.

The bumper slipped from his right hand. It slipped from his left.

For a second, the car and Katie hung there in space in front of him.

And then they fell.

Glen Callaway screamed and launched himself off the side of the mountain after them.

# first interlude

*August 1, 1988*
*Marfa, Texas*

The police report was specific about some things, vague about others. Alcohol had been a factor in the accident—that determination was based on anecdotal testimony from students at the party (Senior Skip Day was thus forbidden in Marfa for the next half dozen years). There was enough forensic evidence, even given the badly burned condition of her body, to determine that Katie Vick had been alive when the car tumbled off the mountain and exploded into flames. Pieces of the windshield found near the shattered guardrail, and the condition of the driver's-side seatbelt, made them fairly certain that Glen Callaway had not been wearing his seatbelt when the crash occurred and had probably been hurled to his death off the side of the mountain. Rescuers searched the area near the crash for days, looking for his body, but were unable to find it.

Pete Dominguez and Luis Campos, among others, searched a whole lot longer.

Eventually, they gave up. A grave was dug for Glen near his parents, and his brother Mark. They buried an empty casket.

Alma was inconsolable at the service, blaming herself for what had happened, for not taking a firmer stand against the boy's drinking. He was just a boy, after all, no matter how big he was. She should have done more; she had failed him, she went around telling her friends, though behind her back they whispered that nothing Alma could have done would have made a damn bit of difference. It was the curse, they said. Blood will out, and the Kane blood had. The boy was the last of them, so now it was done. A tragedy, though, that the Vick girl had perished with him.

A week after Glen's service, Pete Dominguez went up to the boy's room to clean it out. He gathered the schoolbooks, the scholarship letters, the clothes, the trophies, and boxed them up for Goodwill, and for storage, which he did sullenly, angrily, furious at Glen for throwing away not just his life, but Katie Vick's, the way he had. Alcohol. Driving a car he couldn't handle.

And underneath that anger, of course, was a deep, inconsolable sorrow all his own.

A sorrow that blinded Pete to the fact that missing from Glen's room were the two things the boy had owned the longest, the only two things Glen brought with him to the Dominguez's from his Camp Marfa hideout, the only two things that remained to him of his life with Randall and Susanna Callaway, the two things that Pete himself had brought to Glen that day long ago at the Barrows' ranch.

The death mask, and the Kane family scrapbook.

# second interlude

*September 1, 1988*

The man in the long, dark jacket parked at the edge of the cemetery and made his way to the grave.

GLEN CALLAWAY
1970–1988

Someone had tried to deface the headstone already; he could see where the paint had been washed off, where the stone was now discolored. It would happen again, again and again, the man was fairly sure, if the talk he'd overheard at the diner this morning was indicative of the town's mood. They blamed Glen for the death of the Vick girl; it didn't seem to matter that the boy had lost his own life in the accident as well. "Drunken monster" were the words the woman who'd given him his coffee had used. Georgia Keith. He'd recognized her instantly.

"Do I know you?" she'd asked the man suddenly, after he'd paid for the coffee and was about to go out to the car.

"Not likely," was all he said, though of course she did, she just couldn't put two and two together now any more than she could eighteen years ago. Of course he looked a little different now than he had back then, the weight, the hard, hard miles he'd traveled, more miles than he supposed anyone else in this two-bit town had covered.

The trip this morning from Dallas had been as hard as any, but it was the only time in the past few months he'd been anywhere near Marfa, and the only free time in the schedule he was likely to get for another few, given the way Von Erich was working them. Match after match after match; town after town after town. It was a living, but more than that, it was preparation. Training, not so much for him but for his companion. His partner, even if Von Erich insisted on using Akbar as the man's manager during matches. That was all right, for now. They would be a team again, soon enough. It was all part of the plan, although this—

—the man shook his head, and knelt down next to Glen Callaway's grave—

This wasn't.

He traced his fingers over the headstone and sighed, and sent out an honest, heartfelt prayer to whatever powers there were that wherever he was, the boy would find peace.

Then his eyes wandered to another nearby stone—

SUSANNA KANE CALLAWAY

1947–1977

BELOVED MOTHER AND DAUGHTER

—and Paul Grimm shook his head.

God, she'd been a beautiful woman. Shame to think of her body moldering and decomposing under the ground. Of course, only about 75 percent of the body Grimm still remembered so fondly had even made it into the ground (that was a rough guess on his part of how much of her the fire had consumed, based on what he'd read in the paper about the extent and severity of her burns), but still . . .

A shame. A waste. He recalled the first time he'd seen Susanna Kane—his first afternoon working at the funeral parlor, he'd been down in the basement for hours, working on a girl who'd been in a car accident whose parents wanted an open-casket funeral. There was this gash in her face that just wouldn't close up right. Very frustrating.

He'd come upstairs after finally getting the skin to adhere (first time he'd used Superglue in that kind of situation, very ingenious of him, he thought), come up sweaty and stinking of chemicals, and gone into the kitchen looking for something to drink. In the refrigerator, he found a pitcher of lemonade and poured himself a glass, which even though Callaway hadn't given him permission to do, Grimm felt he was entitled to, considering all the effort he'd just put in. He downed that glass, and took a second, and then a third, finishing the pitcher, and then helping himself to a few slices of ham as well, and then decided to get some fresh air before returning to his chores down in the basement.

He'd pushed through the front door, and stopped in his tracks.

There was a woman sitting on a wicker chair on Callaway's front porch. She had a letter in her hand, and tears were running down her face.

Her skin was porcelain white. Her hair long, strawberry blond. Her body . . .

She looked up at Grimm.

"My aunt died," she said.

He blinked. Not the usual way to open a conversation with a stranger.

"I'm sorry," he replied, because that was all he could think of to say. "I'm Paul Grimm."

"I know. My husband told me you were starting work today. I'm Susanna Kane—Susanna Callaway. Forgive me. It's just . . ." She wiped away a tear.

He pulled up another wicker chair, and sat next to her.

"I understand completely," he said, taking her hand in his. "An unexpected death. Always a tragic thing."

"No," she said, shaking her head. "Not unexpected. Not in my family."

And that was how it all started between them.

Of course that was a long time ago, Grimm thought, rising from her grave. A lifetime since he'd worked in the funeral parlor, since he'd gone home to his apartment stinking of Callaway's chemicals, and sometimes, of his wife. The drunken fool, Grimm thought, glaring at Randall Callaway's stone. Served him right.

He looked now to the final headstone in the group—

MARK CALLAWAY
1968–1977
THE STAR THAT SHINES BRIGHTEST BURNS FASTEST

—and Grimm shook his head at the irony.

The authorities had never been able to sort out all the messy bits of body they'd found in the basement—and no wonder, after all the experimenting he'd done, Grimm could barely have sorted them out himself—and so they'd buried an empty casket instead, just as they had for Glen.

*The joke was on them,* he thought.

Footsteps sounded behind him. It seemed his traveling companion had gotten bored of sitting, just as Grimm suspected he would.

He rose to his feet and turned.

The man that faced him was bigger even than Glen had been, the one time Grimm had seen him, here at the cemetery last November. Bigger than any man Grimm had ever met in his life. Strong too. Ridiculously strong. Grimm had found a way to use that strength to his advantage. Over the last few years, in fact, that strength—this man—had been Grimm's meal ticket, had rescued him from a succession of dead-end jobs, put him on a path toward a future of some kind, a future completely divorced from the life he'd led in Marfa. At times, though, Grimm wondered if the man shared his vision of that future. At times, the man seemed preoccupied with the past. Which was understandable, but hardly profitable. Luckily the man was young enough that he was still quite malleable. Quite open to suggestion. Like his mother, in that way. A believer.

Grimm stepped in front of Glen's tombstone now, so the man couldn't see the dates on it. Grimm had told the man Glen had died in the same fire that killed Randall and Susanna—let him go on thinking that. But the man wasn't interested in Glen's grave. He moved past that, past Susanna's, and Randall's, to the one on the far end of the four.

"Mark Callaway," the man said, and made a rumbling noise deep within his body.

It took Grimm a moment to recognize it as a laugh.

"My grave," he said, and then laughed out loud.

Grimm put a hand on Mark Callaway's arm. "Yes, Mark, your grave."

"Nothing in my grave," Mark said, smiling.

"No," Grimm said. Nothing, and no one.

Which was, of course, their little secret.

# book two:
## avenged

# chapter
## fourteen

Two years passed.

Life in Marfa, Texas, resumed its course, albeit along a slightly different path. The loss of the homecoming queen and the football star stabbed the town in the heart; everyone just flopped along for a while, going through the motions of living. But by the time the sophomores had become seniors, the immediacy of the event had passed. Glen and Katie's story turned into a version of Beauty and the Beast; the tragedy of the star-crossed lovers became part of the town lore, like *Giant,* James Dean's death, the Marfa Lights, the fire at the Callaway funeral parlor. Gradually, everyone came to terms with it. Everyone finished their mourning, and moved on. Everyone except Melissa Vick.

On the anniversary of her daughter's death, Melissa was at the Marfa cemetery, putting flowers on Katie's grave. Not a morning went by that she didn't wake up and for just a single, fleeting second imagine that she heard her daughter downstairs in the kitchen, making the coffee, or baking muffins, or walking out to get the *Sentinel,* because that's the way her Katie was, always thinking of others, not herself, always smiling, always happy, always wanting to help. And then the warm, comforting embrace of that sleepy daydream would disappear, and reality would set in all over again. Katie was dead. Katie was in her grave, Katie was not coming back, not in this lifetime anyway, and it would be all Melissa could do to drag herself out of bed and start her day.

But Melissa had found a way to move on too. Her work. Since Katie's death, she'd thrown herself into it, a little frantically at first, which scared her friends and even Melissa herself, to tell the truth, eighteen-, nineteen-hour days those first few weeks after the funeral, but now she had a balance. She allowed herself seven hours of sleep, and on the weekends, time for church and church-related activities.

Other than that, it was all about her job. She'd been promoted: she was traveling all over the state now, more frequent flier miles than she knew what to do with. North to El Paso, east to Houston, several times a month to Austin and the state bureaucracy, but always circling back around to Marfa and the Big Bend country. Home to an empty house, an empty bed, and sometimes a terrifying dream of fire, of her daughter's last, agonized moments on earth.

Paul Grimm was traveling too.

Not under his own name, though, and not alone.

By 1990 he was officially Paul Bearer—his driver's license (an Oklahoma license, one of many other papers in his possession that identified him by his new name, including a passport) said so. He was particularly proud of that driver's license, had spent hours on the inks for it, getting just the right blend of chemicals and pigments so that the colors wouldn't fade. And the paper too—you had to use (and find, the hard part sometimes was finding) just the right grade of stock, or the fakery was evident. It was all very precise. That was what he liked about working with chemicals. You knew that when you mixed together X, and Y, you got Z. It was an exact science.

Working with people was always a little more difficult. Still . . .

Grimm (no, Bearer, he really had to even stop thinking of himself as Grimm, the authorities were looking for Paul Grimm, and even though it had been more than ten years, they were probably still looking, people had died after all, extra body parts had been found, messy messy messy, no sense getting involved in all that) thought he was getting the hang of people.

Especially people who worked in the entertainment business. In sports. In, for example, pro wrestling. Grimm (no—Bearer—Bearer, Bearer, Bearer) surprised himself by how quickly he had picked up the essentials of the business. He would never have expected it of himself. He had wrestled once or twice, back in high school, back in the day, but the pro circuit was a different animal entirely. It was sport, and it was entertainment. Occasionally staged, yes, but more often than not the violence was real. People really got hurt. Badly hurt. Once in a while very, very badly hurt.

Maybe that was why he liked it.

Although to tell the truth, even if he liked it as much as, say, working with chemicals, he would have been long gone from the business by now, having spent the last three years in an endless succession of small-time arenas, motel rooms, and fast-food joints. Not that he minded fast food. There was nothing like a good burger, or two, just the right amount of ketchup, the right mixture of tastes. But all the burgers in the world wouldn't have been enough to keep him in the business if it weren't for the promise of a much brighter future. A future of clean sheets and steak.

Mark Callaway was going to make that future a reality for him.

Mark Callaway was going to be the best wrestler in the world.

The boy's skills had first become evident a few years back,

when Paul and Mark had spent some time with his cousin Leonard in Dallas. Leonard worked the ticket booth at a small Dallas sports arena. One night he got Mark and Grimm free tickets to that evening's show. A pro wrestling card—local stuff, the CIW. Big men bouncing off each other. Grimm hated it. Mark's reaction was exactly the opposite. He was fascinated. He got Leonard to take him backstage to meet some of the wrestlers. One thing led to another, and the next thing Bearer knew, Mark was hanging out down at a gym near the arena, working there, working out there, learning some of the wrestling moves he'd seen at the show for himself. The boy had never quite forgiven Grimm for taking him away from organized sports (which was gratitude for you, Bearer thought; here he'd saved the boy from reform school or even jail, and all he did was complain), so Paul—despite his initial distaste for the sport—let Mark continue at it. It kept him out of trouble. It kept him away from the authorities, who might think it strange that a boy Mark's age wasn't in school, though considering Mark's size at that point, those questions usually didn't get asked.

Certainly no one at the gym asked them. A few weeks after Mark began hanging around there, Bearer/Grimm got a call from a man named Von Erich, who was apparently something of a big deal on the local wrestling circuit. He understood Bearer was Mark's guardian; he wanted to let Bearer know that Mark had great potential in the wrestling ring. Unlimited potential. All he needed was training. The right diet. A good manager.

At which point Bearer interrupted. Mark has a manager, he told the man. Me.

The two of them—Bearer and Callaway—spent the next few years working for the Von Erichs and the CIW. Mark wrestled under the name Commando and the Punisher, he was

Texas Red and Mark Callous. They were hard times; they were often one step ahead of bankruptcy, one meal away from starvation. Bearer put on weight—a lot of weight. He lost control of his temper more than once, and almost got them thrown off the CIW circuit in Dallas, when he got into a fight with an unruly fan. Mark had troubles too. Problems sleeping—dreams of his family, of the fire that killed them, and his own memories of the stories his mother had shared with him, the stories of the Kane family's long, troubled history.

Listening to those stories, Bearer couldn't help but think of poor fragile Susanna Kane, and her troubles, and wondered if he should get the boy help—psychiatric help. That might involve revealing his own history, risking his own safety. He couldn't do it, Bearer decided. Besides . . .

There was something to be said for the light that came on in Mark's eyes when he talked about the Kane family curse. Gave him a little edge. A little something extra. *Which they were going to need,* Bearer thought.

In just a few weeks, Mark Callaway was going to make his debut on the biggest wrestling circuit in the country: The World Wrestling Federation. Bearer had several discussions with that organization's president, Vince McMahon, regarding what name Mark should wrestle under. They'd thrown a few ideas back and forth—but none of those ideas, none of those names, had really excited either of them. Or Mark, for that matter. And that was maybe what was most important of all, that Mark be excited about climbing into that ring. That he was charged up, ready to rumble, as they said in the business. That he had a little something extra that was uniquely him.

*Uniquely him,* Bearer thought. Now what was uniquely Mark? He was a Kane, and he was a Callaway. Part mental defective, part—

Ah.

Bearer smiled to himself, and reached for the phone.

One hot September night in 1991, Melissa Vick was in Alpine, having dinner with some friends from Sul Ross, listening to a lot of theoretical discussions about social work, which always drove her crazy, and some talk about how hard it was for a small rancher to make a go of it these days, which made her frown, when one of the guests started in with some wild tales about some kind of monstrous bear, or mountain lion maybe, nobody seemed quite sure what it was, a thing that lived up in the mountains by Jeff Davis Park, that came down every once in a while to steal a sheep or raid a chicken coop.

Those stories, for some reason, sent a chill down her back, made her excuse herself early from the meal and drive home slowly, and very, very carefully.

That night, Melissa dreamed of Glen Callaway, running down a highway, chased by fire. The highway, she realized, was in Texas, running through the Chihuahua desert, leading up into the mountains, into acres and acres of forest just like she'd seen in Acadia. Glen ran along the road until it reached that forest, and then at some point broke from the highway and found a place to hide, until the fire had passed, till it was safe for him to come out again, and walk the earth.

She bolted upright in her bed, sweat running down her forehead, heart hammering in her chest.

She couldn't get back to sleep all night.

Mark Callaway's debut was every bit the success Bearer had hoped for.

By mid-1991, Mark was one of the company's most recognized up-and-comers.

By November, he was the World Champion. His signature

move in the ring—the Tombstone Piledriver—was almost as famous as he was, though of course no one but Bearer knew him as Mark Callaway. To the other wrestlers and to all the fans, he was known only by the name he fought under, the identity he assumed when he entered the ring.

He was Undertaker.

In March 1992, Pete Dominguez was diagnosed with lung cancer. By mid-April, he was in the hospital, on a respirator; on May 23, four years to the day after the crash, he was dead. Alma passed six months later.

Melissa went to both funerals. She was tired of funerals. Tired of burying people. Tired of being reminded of the past everywhere she looked.

That afternoon, she went home and called her boss. She quit her job. A week later, she moved to Tucson, moved in with her mother, got part-time work there, and as best she could, forgot all about Marfa, about the people there she had loved and lost, and especially those she had loved who she feared had survived.

Early in 1994, the mysterious sightings in Jefferson Davis State Park stopped. A few months later, hikers in a more remote region of the almost-three-thousand-acre park found a cave littered with the bones of small animals, and human feces. Ashes were found scattered just outside the cave, evidence of several small fires set sometime over the last few years. Buried deep in one such pile of ashes, they found a scrap of paper, burned black around the edges. Only one word on the page was legible:

Kane.

The hikers were from New Mexico. The word meant nothing to them. They left the paper where they'd found it, and moved on.

# chapter fifteen

Charlie Latrell walked along the pier, swinging the bat and whistling. The smell of the ocean was strong tonight; a particularly low tide, a particularly warm day. He didn't mind. Charlie liked the ocean, the smell of it, the sounds of it, the way looking out across the Gulf made him feel. There was one thing about the ocean he hated, though: the gulls. Filthy flying rats, shitting everywhere. They were at their worst right now, at sunset, when they all seemed to come out at once, for one last shot at whatever they could scavenge before calling it a night. A flock of them flew above him now, diving and cawing and cackling madly; one dropped a turd a foot from where he stood.

Charlie stopped and looked up, swinging the bat lazily back and forth.

"C'mon, birdies," he said softly, making the closest approximation in his throat he could to the gull's own raucous call. "Come on. Come to Papa."

None of the gulls listened to him. Probably they'd learned from last week, when one gull had dive-bombed him just a little too closely, and Charlie took the bat and did his best Willie McCovey impersonation, hit that bird a country mile, clean over the pier and into the channel between Galveston proper and the mainland. A home run, for sure.

Charlie was night watchman at Pier 12, Port of Galveston, Texas. Came on at 4:00 P.M. sharp, went home at midnight, when Frank Brody took over. Charlie spent most of his time in a little hut at the entrance to the pier, where he had a portable heater and a hotplate and a fridge and a TV. But once an hour he got up to walk the pier, make sure no kids had snuck past him to try and stow away on the cargo ships, or just make a ruckus, or more important yet, that no one of criminal intent had gotten by and made their way into the terminal building proper.

Because Pier 12 was where most of the big cargo ships berthed to unload their cargo (except for the Del Monte ships, which used the terminal at Pier 14 more often than not, as it had specially refrigerated storage areas), said cargo often being comprised of valuable electronics, high-ticket, easily fenceable items like television sets, and computers. There'd been a big break-in on Brody's shift a few months back, almost cost the man his job till they found out the thieves had had inside help from someone at the Port Authority, knew exactly where the containers were and how to get into the terminal itself.

But still, Charlie didn't want anything untoward happening on his watch, which was why he stuck like glue to his appointed hourly rounds, even when waiting half an hour, till five-thirty, meant he would have missed the fucking gulls entirely.

He walked on now, out along the length of the pier, past the front of the terminal building, and stopped.

There was something hiding in the shadow of the vast building, something he'd almost missed in the gathering darkness. A shape that didn't belong. A lump.

He drew closer. The lump resolved itself into a blanket, out from under which a head suddenly peered.

A very ugly head, Charlie thought to himself. Belonging to what looked like a very ugly old man.

Bums. Charlie hated these guys. Sometimes they snuck out

onto the pier to try and get on ships too, but they always got caught, and hauled off by the police or the social services folk. What made dealing with bums so bad was that they always left a stench wherever they'd been, sometimes even just used the pier as their own private Porta Potti like bigger versions of the gulls, and whenever that happened, somebody from the Authority was always calling him in for a tongue-lashing, "Charlie, you gotta keep your eyes open, Charlie, you gotta make sure the gate is locked, Charlie, this ain't too hard a job for you, is it, because if you can't handle it . . ."

"All right, Pops," Charlie said, poking the blanket with his bat. "I don't know how you got here, but let's move along."

The man grunted.

Charlie took out his flashlight and shone it in the man's face.

The man raised a hand to shield his eyes.

"Come on, Pops," Charlie said. "I'll give you five minutes before I call the cops."

The man grunted again, and gathered the blankets around himself.

"Hey." Charlie frowned. "Don't make me—"

A huge clattering sound came from just behind them. From inside the terminal building.

Charlie forgot all about the old man instantly, because there wasn't supposed to be anybody inside the building at all.

"Shit," he said, reaching for his walkie-talkie. All the night watchmen on each pier were on the same channel; there were two others on duty with him right now, and then there was the Port Authority Police command post, way down by Pier 1. Cruz was on duty tonight.

Charlie pressed the button.

"Command, this is one-four. Over."

"Charlie, that you?" That was Cruz.

"Yeah. Listen, I just heard somebody in the terminal. Over."

"What?"

"I'm telling you, I just heard someone in the terminal. Over."

"Stop with the over shit," Cruz said. "You heard someone. Is the door open?"

Charlie looked up, the bum at his feet momentarily forgotten.

Shit. The huge warehouse door was, in fact, open.

"Roger that," he said, and then realized he hadn't pressed the walkie-talkie button in. He did now.

"Yeah. The door is open."

"Okay. Stay where you are. Do not go in. Understand me, don't be a hero."

"Don't worry about that."

"I have two guys with me, we're on our way. Cruz out."

"Right," Charlie said. "Over and out."

He put the walkie-talkie back on his belt. Well, that was that. Now he just had to wait, and hope whoever was in there didn't come out before Cruz and the others got here, because all he had to defend himself with, thanks to the Authority's stupid rules about private guards carrying weapons, was this bat, and—

Shit.

He wasn't supposed to be carrying the bat. The Authority wanted him to use the nightstick, which was back in his hut. Damn.

He was about to set the bat down on the ground when he remembered the bum.

"Hey, buddy," he said, turning back to the figure underneath the blanket, who hadn't moved an inch since Charlie had switched on the walkie-talkie to speak with Cruz, "get out of here, will you? Things are going to get pretty hairy around here in a few minutes—lotta cops, and you don't want to be here, okay? Just move on."

The guy stared at him expressionlessly, like he hadn't heard a word Charlie had said.

*Never mind,* Charlie thought. Fuck it. Not his problem anymore; he had better things to worry about, and it didn't smell like the guy had crapped himself or anything like that, so they'd haul him out of here in a little bit and no one would be any the wiser for it. Not his problem.

From the shadow of the warehouse, the biggest man Charlie had ever seen in his life stepped out.

He had to be six and a half feet tall, shit, make that seven feet tall, and he was built like a goddamn rock, guy was wearing a sleeveless T-shirt and had muscles on his muscles. He had long, scraggly hair, and in one hand he had some kind of nasty-looking gun—an automatic weapon.

The man looked right at him, and Charlie pissed himself and dropped the bat.

"Shit," Charlie said.

"We got the watchman here," the man said, raising his gun, and then another man, not as big as the first, but almost, slid out silently from inside the warehouse too.

"What are we gonna do with him?" the second man asked.

"I didn't see anything," Charlie said. "I don't know anything."

The second man frowned. "We gotta assume he's called it in, right?"

"Right," the first one said.

The second one turned back to the warehouse. "Hurry it up in there!" he shouted, and then turned back to Charlie.

"Why do they always pick the fat ones as the watchmen?" he asked.

"He's not that fat," the first man said. "Drop him in the ocean, I bet he sinks."

He was looking at Charlie as he said it, but then he looked past Charlie and frowned.

"We got another problem, too," he said, pointing with his gun. "Look."

Charlie knew without turning they were talking about the bum.

"Two-for-one night," the second man said. "I'll take fatty here, you take the bum."

"Guns?" the first asked.

"No, too noisy. We want to surprise whoever's coming in after fatty." The second man drew something from his belt then. It glinted in the light of the setting sun. A knife.

"Oh, please," Charlie said, backing away, holding his hands out in front of him. "I got a family, I got a mother who worries about me night and day, if you—"

The second man laughed. "A mother. He's got a mother. Jesus Christ, that's the first time I heard that one, a mother."

Both men advanced, the second toward Charlie, the bigger man toward the bum.

"Say good-bye to Mama," the second man said, thrusting his knife forward, smiling.

"Hey," Charlie heard the first man say. "What are you—"

The second man looked over Charlie's shoulder and stopped smiling.

"What the—" was all he got out before Charlie heard a loud crack, and a scream, and then another, even more sickeningly loud crack, and a thump, like something soft hitting something hard, or vice versa.

"Fuckin' sonuva . . ." the second man began, dropping the knife and raising his gun again, walking past Charlie like he wasn't even there and at the same time cursing a blue streak,

"You're a dead man, you are a walking dead man," and Charlie spun in time to see—

Bam.

The bum, making like Willie McCovey, and the second man, looking a lot like that poor old seagull from a week earlier, lying motionless on the pier not far from his equally motionless friend. There was a lot of blood, and a lot of other stuff, and up above, the seagulls started making a racket all over again.

The bum dropped the bat.

"Walking dead man," he said, in a gravelly, echoey, almost not-human kind of voice that made Charlie's hair stand on end.

The bum walked past him then, heading toward the pier entrance, and Charlie realized that the man was both bigger than he'd thought, as big as the guy with the scraggly hair maybe, and also a lot younger, that what he'd taken for an old man's weathered, wrinkled face was actually, when seen up close, something else entirely, the face of someone scarred by disease or genetic deformity? Or maybe even an accident. Something with chemicals, or perhaps a fire.

*Would have had to have been a helluva big fire, though,* Charlie thought.

The bum was maybe fifty feet from the pier entrance when Cruz and his men came running toward him, weapons drawn.

"Hey, hold on!" Charlie yelled, running toward them. "He's one of the good guys."

There had been three others in the warehouse, all of whom Cruz and his men caught easily. It looked like a twin of the robbery that had almost cost Brody his job a few months back, which meant that there was still someone crooked on the inside, someone with pull and power in the Authority. Cruz didn't want to think about that right now.

He was still trying to sort out this business with the bum.

Charlie was in the office with him, next cubicle over, changing his clothes, talking as he got dressed.

"So then the bum—"

"Yeah, I didn't see all of it, but the bum apparently just got the drop on this guy, and clocked him with the bat. Then he did the same with the other one—the one that was gonna gut me."

Cruz frowned. "So where'd the bat come from?"

Charlie was silent a moment.

"I don't know," he said finally.

"Is it the bum's bat, you think?"

"Guess so. Whose else could it be?"

Cruz stood up and looked over the divider.

"Charlie . . ."

"All right, all right." Charlie zipped up his pants and frowned. "My bat."

Cruz shook his head. "What are you, stupid? Did we not have this conversation last month?"

"Yeah." Charlie sighed.

"Lose the bat."

"It's gone, believe me."

The door from the hall swung open, and the bum walked in.

He looked even bigger in the light. Even scarier, for that matter, the burns on his face and neck . . . nobody who caught a good look at this guy would ever, ever, think about fucking with him, even if they had an Uzi and a five-second head start.

This guy was trouble. This guy was dangerous.

"You all right?" Cruz asked the bum.

The man nodded.

"Good. I just wanted to thank you again for what you did back there. You saved the Authority from considerable embarrassment. And you saved Charlie's life here, I'm sure of that too."

"Yeah," Charlie put in. "Thanks."

The man nodded.

"Not gonna be any charges against you, by the way," Cruz continued, exaggerating just a little for the moment. "Definite case of self-defense. And I gotta tell you—no one's going to need help defending themselves from those two guys for a long, long while."

The man nodded again. He looked like he could care less. There was nothing in his eyes—not even a flicker of interest.

*Damn,* Cruz realized suddenly. *That's weird. The guy's eyes . . . they were two different colors.*

"So you mind if I ask," Cruz continued, "what you were doing out there?"

The bum didn't say anything.

"Let me take a guess. Looking to jump on the next ship out of here—one of the long-term cargo ships, probably. Am I right? You got that look to me, of somebody on the run."

The bum cleared his throat then.

"I'm not a crook."

His voice had a weird, husky kind of scratchiness to it—like it hurt him to talk. Cruz made note of that.

"I didn't say you were. Just said you had the look of somebody running away from something."

A flicker of something crossed the man's eyes then—feeling. Pain.

*Bingo,* Cruz thought.

"How much money you got?" Cruz asked, and then, before the man could answer, went on. "Not much, is my guess. Otherwise you wouldn't be sleeping on a pier in the first place, right?"

No response.

"Here." Cruz gave the man a hundred bucks he'd taken out of petty cash. "Little thank-you from the Authority."

The man looked at the money like he didn't know what it was, like he hadn't seen any in a long, long time.

"Thanks," he said finally.

"There could be more where that came from," Cruz said. "If you're interested."

The man looked up, inquisitively.

"What I mean is," Cruz said, "I might have some work for you. Just temporary work. A lot of valuable cargo passes through here, and there's a lot of unscrupulous people out there who wouldn't mind getting their hands on some of that cargo. Which is why we need someone like you—to dissuade them from trying to pull a job like tonight's. Somebody to stand guard."

"Hey, wait a minute." Charlie came bounding over from the next cubicle. "You giving this guy my job?"

"Relax, Charlie," Cruz said. "This is a supplemental position. Temporary, like I said."

He looked at the man again.

"So, you interested?"

"What's the pay?"

"Fifteen an hour."

The man nodded. Cruz could see the wheels turning in his head.

"It's temporary?"

"Yeah."

The man managed a small smile; he looked a lot younger when he did that, Cruz saw, which made him wonder how old the guy really was. Thirties? Younger? Not that he cared; the guy was obviously old enough to take care of himself.

"Okay," the guy said.

Cruz smiled. "Good. You be here at four tomorrow, okay?"

"Yeah."

"We can fill out the paperwork then."

The man nodded, and turned to go.

"Hey, buddy," Cruz called after him. "You got a name?"

The man, already at the door, hesitated.

Cruz could see the wheels turning in the guy's mind. He was trying to think of an alias, probably. No matter. Cruz wasn't really interested in the name, any more than he was really going to give the man a job. All he was interested in was the guy's picture, which they now had on the CCTV camera that ran 24/7 in the office here.

He'd send that, and the fingerprints he was sure they'd get off the bat, to NCIC, find out who this guy really was, and what he'd done. From how deep he'd been in hiding, Cruz guessed it was something really awful indeed.

"Yeah. I got a name," the man said. "Kane."

Behind Cruz, Charlie cleared his throat. "What's that—first or last?"

The man shook his head.

"Both," he said.

"Kane," Cruz said again. "Just Kane."

"That's right," the man replied.

And then he was through the door and gone.

Kane.

That was how he thought of himself now. That was his curse, that was his name. He'd come to understand that, come to know his place in the world these last few years.

What he didn't know was why he had talked to those people back there. His throat still hurt from the effort—it would hurt for hours to come yet, he knew that from painful experience. And he realized he was thinking about going back, the man had promised him a job, money . . . he didn't understand that, either. He didn't need money. He didn't need a job, or any of the other things the man, or the world, had to offer. He had no needs, no wants, no desires. All that was dead in him, dead and buried years before. Nothing had changed. So why had he done those things?

In the shadow of the vast seawall, he huddled in his blanket, searching for warmth. But the questions continued, racing through his mind without pause until at last, he fell asleep, and as always, dreamed of fire.

He stood outside the house, and watched his family burn.

He fled across the desert, chased by a monster with Paul Grimm's face and a fireball in its hand.

He stood on the edge of a cliff, and watched a car fall.

"Katie!" he screamed, and the car exploded, and he jumped after it into the fire that it had become. And the fire raged around him, but he felt nothing, and it burned the skin from his body, and he ignored it, and it set the forest on the cliffside ablaze, and he dragged himself through it, his body burned and bruised, broken and bleeding, but he couldn't save her, and when he woke—

"Excuse me."

Kane blinked.

The sun was bright in his eyes. He raised a hand to shield his face from it, and saw a woman standing over him.

"Are you all right?"

He didn't say anything.

"The tide's coming in, that's all. I just wanted to let you know."

She was right, he saw. His pants were already wet. The bag . . .

He stumbled to his feet quickly and checked the bag inside his coat.

The papers and the mask were safe.

He breathed a sigh of relief and turned to thank the woman.

But she was already backing away from him, an expression of mingled shock and fear on her face.

He didn't blame her.

The man with the gun had gotten it exactly right.

He was a dead man. A walking dead man.

# chapter
## sixteen

Mr. McMahon worked the dead man angle for all it was worth.

Organ music. Casket matches. A funeral urn that supposedly contained the ashes of Mark's dead parents. It was over the top; sometimes Bearer feared they'd gone too far. But the crowd ate it up. Undertaker moved from a mid-card attraction to a headliner; he wrestled the biggest names, Hulk Hogan, Hit Man Hart, Lex Luger, the biggest wrestlers, Giant Gonzales, Giant Kamala, the four-hundred-pound Japanese wrestler Yokozuna. He fought ten men at one match; in one he rose from the dead to reclaim his identity from an impostor, a fake Undertaker. Nothing seemed beyond him.

Paul Bearer loved it too. He became part of the action himself; ringside, he held Undertaker's urn high in the air, providing "mystical energy" for Mark to draw on at critical moments in the matches. He fought with the other wrestler's managers, sometimes with the wrestlers themselves. People recognized him on the street occasionally—it was marvelous. He ate steak. A lot of steak. And ice cream. His favorite was Ben and Jerry's—anything with chocolate in it. He had a pint with him now, in his overcoat pocket, burning a hole in it, you could say. He shut the door to his hotel room behind him, and set the pint down on the kitchenette counter. He'd eat in a minute, but first there was a phone call he wanted to make. He had an idea, looking at all the different Ben and Jerry's flavors in the 7-Eleven. What about Undertaker ice cream? Little fudge caskets, red hots . . . chocolate ice cream, of course. He could just about taste it. Perhaps he could be on the label too, alongside the Undertaker. His own ice cream . . .

He shivered with delight.

Bearer had the phone in his hand and was about to dial when he realized that there was someone else in the room with him. Sitting in the chair at the kitchenette table, not five feet in front of him, shadowed in darkness. A big—a very big—someone.

"Mark," he said.

"Paul." Mark leaned forward in his chair, so that the light caught his face.

Good God, he was still wearing the Undertaker makeup.

The apple doesn't fall far from the tree, Bearer thought, thinking about poor crazy Susanna Kane for the first time in quite a long while. He wondered again if he should have gotten Mark professional help when the man was younger. If he should have discouraged the boy's belief in the curse, told him the truth about those particular stories. On the other hand, if he had . . .

They might be sharing a room in a Motel 6, rather than occupying separate suites in the Marriott. Which set him to wondering how Mark had gotten into his room—probably just told the clerk he needed to wait for his manager. Fame had its advantages, after all.

"So," Bearer said, setting down the phone. "What can I do for you?"

Mark looked angry. "You can tell me when you're going to renegotiate my contract."

*Ah.* Bearer nodded.

"I'm sorry. I just assumed you would want me to handle the details of all that—as usual."

"You assumed wrong."

"Well. I—"

"I'm not a kid anymore, Paul," Mark said, getting to his feet. "I want to be involved in my career."

"Of course, of course," Bearer said. "From now on you will be, I promise you."

"I'll hold you to that."

"Would you like some ice cream?" Bearer asked.

Mark shook his head. "I want to see the contract."

"Ross is having it drawn up. I'll get you an extra copy."

"Good."

The man didn't seem mollified in the slightest by Bearer's promises. He was still angry. Spoiling for a fight. This was about more than the contract, Bearer realized. This was about control. Mark had said it himself; he wasn't a kid anymore. Wasn't going to ask how high when Bearer said jump. In a way, this was the teenage rebellion Callaway had never had.

Bearer wondered just how far that rebellion was going to go, and what he should/could do to keep it under control. Talking was always an option, of course, and keeping the lines of communication open was important, but conversation, in his experience, didn't always produce the desired results.

Chemicals were much more precise.

He had a sampling of several in the refrigerator, in the case he carried with him, and wondered now whether or not giving any to Mark (offering him something from the mini-bar and spiking it) would be a way to keep things—keep Undertaker—under his control. He decided against it. Massive doses might be needed, and they could incapacitate his wrestler. Incapacitate his cash flow. He couldn't have that. He had grown used to this lifestyle. He wasn't going to give it up.

For the moment, Grimm decided, he would have to try and work with Mark. Until he could come up with another alternative.

"Come on, Mark," he said, taking two spoons out of a drawer. "Let's have some ice cream."

\* \* \*

The NCIC had come back with nothing on the bum. His fingerprints weren't on file, his picture didn't match up with anything in the database . . . it was like the guy didn't exist at all. Maybe the guy really was just what he seemed, a good Samaritan. Maybe not.

Cruz decided to take the charade another step further, really give the guy that job, so that he could have a little longer to check him out. Or at least that's what he told himself, anyway. It had nothing to do with the fact that Charlie Latrell was worse than useless.

When the guy came back the next day, Cruz helped him fill out the paperwork—no big deal, just a couple pages, standard employee hire form. They got stuck on the first line.

"Name," Cruz said, pen poised to write.

"Kane."

"Right. Is that first or last?"

"I told you. Both."

Cruz looked up. "That's not funny."

"It's not a joke."

"Hey, listen. I need your full name, buddy. Without that, you can't work here. Without that"—he smiled—"I can't pay you either. Right?"

The man nodded. Cruz could see the wheels turning in his head.

"A name," he said again. "Let's go with Dean."

Cruz frowned. "Dean. What happened to Kane?"

"Dean," the man repeated.

Cruz sighed. "Okay. Dean. Is that first or last?"

"That's last."

"Okay. And your first name is . . ."

"James."

Cruz looked up at him. "Come on. Cut me some slack."

"That's my name."

"James Dean." Cruz rolled his eyes. "You got ID to prove that?"

The man smiled for the first time. "I can get it."

"Yeah. I bet you could. Okay," Cruz said, starting to write. "James Dean."

They paused a couple more times, when they got to height (seven feet exactly), weight (320 pounds), and birth date (November 2, 1970), the last of which made Cruz's head snap up in surprise.

"You're only twenty-four?"

The man nodded.

Cruz shook his head in disbelief. "That's unbelievable. You look . . ."

"Older."

"Yeah." Cruz rubbed the side of his own face, where the man's burn marks were particularly bad.

"Mind if I ask what happened?"

"You can ask," the man said, in a way that Cruz immediately knew meant he wasn't getting any answers.

He handed the man back the form to sign.

"All right," Cruz said, taking it back once his John Hancock was on it. "That's it, then. You start tonight. Charlie'll show you the ropes. Meet him at the entrance to the pier—you remember where that was?"

The man nodded.

"Right. Welcome aboard, then—James."

Cruz held out his hand to shake, but the man had already turned his back and was on his way out the door.

*That's gratitude for you,* he thought but didn't say.

This guy was an odd duck, that was for certain. Best to not say anything to upset him.

Best to keep an eye on him as well.

*       *       *

The job was only temporary, Kane told himself. A few months work to save up some cash, and then he would be off again. Where to, he didn't know exactly, but he knew one thing for certain, there was a reason he was still alive, why he'd managed to avoid the horrific disasters that had taken everyone and everything he'd ever cared for away from him, and whatever power had saved him would show him that reason soon enough. Kane was certain of it. A few months here in Galveston, that was all.

A year later, though, he was still on the job.

He fell into a mindless, mind-numbing routine; work until midnight, dream until dawn, then up and out of the apartment to wander the streets of Galveston before starting the cycle over again.

He had no friends, no interests, no possessions beyond a few clothes and the death mask. And the scrapbook, of course. He'd read the papers over so many times by this point that he'd memorized them; he could trace his family all the way back to Rebecca Kane without a second thought. There were a lot of stories, and he knew them all. A lot of paper, a lot of research. He marveled at how his mother had managed to find the time to do all that research, hunt down all the arcane bits of information she needed, how she even knew what to look for, given the fact that she'd never finished high school. She was a smart woman, clearly, smarter than anyone gave her credit for. And driven—perhaps in the same way that he now felt driven.

Driven to understand both the purpose of the Kane family curse, and by knowledge of her own eventual fate.

Kane punched in at the command center, and began wandering all over again. Pier 12, 10, down to the new cruise ship terminal, and back up to number 14, and Charlie Latrell's hut. He heard the TV blasting from ten feet away, and almost—almost—decided not to go in. But one thing about Charlie . . .

His fridge was always full. And he always had good coffee. Kane pushed the door open, and entered.

"Yo, Jimmy." Charlie smiled, and Kane smiled right back, not so much because he was happy to see the man, but because Charlie was just putting on a fresh pot of coffee.

"You gotta check this out," Charlie said, nodding toward the TV.

Kane sighed. The coffee was just starting to brew; looked like he didn't have much choice but to check out whatever it was Charlie wanted to show him. A couple nights back, it had been this cartoon show, with this Homer guy. Charlie kept laughing, Kane just kept edging toward the door. And the night before that, or thereabouts, it had been this old World War II movie. TV was this guy's life, it seemed to Kane, which struck him as an even sadder kind of existence than his own.

"Okay, look at this." Charlie was back in his chair now, nodding at the screen. "This guy here—Hart, Bret Hart—he's gonna whip the big guy's ass, even though he's so much smaller. You mark my words."

Pro wrestling. Kane studied the screen, interested in spite of himself, remembering that time at Chip Walker's house, the nights in the Harrisons' motel when he would sometimes watch matches as well. Wrestling always had an allure for him, and before too long, he was more than interested, he was absorbed. Sure enough, Charlie turned out to be right. Hart—Bret "Hit Man" Hart, as the announcer kept referring to him—pounded the other wrestler mercilessly, despite their size difference. Hart reminded Kane, for a second, of Manuel Santos back in Marfa, but he didn't dwell on it. He never let his mind dwell on Marfa for too long.

The match was over quickly; Kane stood, and went to pour himself a cup of coffee from the pot. "Be back around eleven."

Charlie nodded, and then all at once leaned forward in his chair and smiled.

"Oh, here we go. Bearer's making it official now."

Kane took his cup and headed for the door.

"Back around eleven," he repeated.

"Him and Undertaker, splitsville. I seen it coming, but man . . ."

Undertaker. Kane was intrigued, despite himself. Undertaker?

He turned back to the TV.

And then he dropped his coffee cup to the floor, and his mouth opened in shock.

"Ah, for chrissakes," Charlie said. "Look at that. What a mess. I'll get a towel for you."

Kane barely heard him.

On the screen, the two announcers had been joined by a third man, who sat between them now, a man who looked like . . .

"No." Kane shook his head. It couldn't be him. The man on screen was much bigger—fatter—than the man Kane was thinking of. Same dead-white skin, though. Same shifty look to the eyes, same sneer to the mouth . . .

But it couldn't be.

"Who's that guy, Charlie?" he asked.

"That's Vince McMahon. He's the boss of the whole company—the big Kahuna. You never heard of Vince McMahon?"

Kane had heard of McMahon. He shook his head.

"Not McMahon, the fat one, in the middle."

"Oh. That's Paul Bearer, the guy I was talking about. He's

Undertaker's manager—or at least he was. Now it looks like they're finished."

Paul Bearer. Kane wished he could get a better look at him.

As if on cue, the camera obliged, zooming in for a close-up of the man.

And now Kane was certain. The man on-screen was some-one Kane hadn't seen in almost twenty years, a man he thought never to see again. A man, Kane realized, that he had been brought to Galveston, brought to this pier, this job, this hut this very night, to find.

Paul Bearer was Paul Grimm.

And Charlie was right. Bearer was finished . . . though not in the way Charlie meant.

In a much more permanent, and quite likely, much more vi-olent way.

He headed for the door.

"Whoa. Where you going?" Charlie asked.

"Cleveland," Kane said, remembering where the match had been aired from.

"What does that mean?"

"That means I quit."

"That's it? You quit?" Charlie shook his head. "What am I supposed to tell Cruz?"

"Whatever you want. Start with the fact that I quit."

"Whoa, whoa, whoa," Charlie said, stepping in front of him. "Not so fast. Who's gonna clean this mess up?"

He nodded toward the puddle of coffee behind Kane.

"You are," Kane said.

Charlie looked at his eyes and nodded.

"Right. I am."

Kane walked out without another word.

# chapter seventeen

The end had come at *King of the Ring* back in June, during a match between Mankind and Undertaker. Bearer definitely bore the brunt of the responsibility for the incident, he was willing to acknowledge that. His fault, all his fault, he'd accidentally hit his wrestler with the urn, cost Mark the match, a result of not keeping his head in the game, but as he'd told Vince McMahon, problems between the two of them—between him and Mark—had been building for a long time. If it hadn't been the incident with the urn, it would have been something else. Mark was determined to be his own man now; the split between the two of them was inevitable, and Bearer was fine with that. Really, he was fine.

He finished his first pint of ice cream, and started in on the second.

Vince appreciated all his efforts, at least. Vince had hooked Bearer and Mick Foley up after *King of the Ring*. And the two of them got on like gangbusters. Foley liked ice cream too. Almost as much as Bearer. And Foley had the ability to leave what happened during a match inside the ring, unlike Mark, who still, once in a while, had trouble separating reality from the Undertaker fiction. Probably Foley could distinguish between his private persona and his public one because he wrestled under several different names—Cactus Jack, Dude Love, and Mankind, his best-known—and best-loved—identity.

Hmmm, Bearer thought. What about a Mankind ice cream?

Chocolate, of course, with fudge hearts. And red hots. Or vanilla and chocolate mixed together. Racial harmony. He liked it. He would make a phone call later. Tomorrow morning.

Bearer decided to save the second pint for after breakfast. He was hungry for something more substantial now. Truth be told, he was also a little restless, a little tired of sitting in his hotel room. He wondered if Mick—Mankind—was still awake. He checked the clock: 1:15 A.M. Probably not. Mark, he knew, was still up. Mark always stayed up late—the longer he took before going to bed, the more likely he was not to dream, Bearer knew from all the years they'd spent together on the road.

But of course, he couldn't go knocking on Mark's door. Not anymore.

Which made him a little upset. After all the time and energy and chemicals he'd put into Mark's career, into building Undertaker up into arguably the most popular character the organization had ever had, Mark decided to go out on his own? To take away that lucrative paycheck that Paul Bearer had spent so much time and effort earning? It wasn't right. It wasn't fair.

Something would have to be done about it.

Bearer went down to the hotel bar to get a drink. But the hotel bar was closed. Bearer decided to go for a walk instead. Clear his head, and think of a plan. A way to get back the money that was due him. A way to get back at Mark. What he needed was leverage. The curse came to mind, although right at the moment he was having a hard time seeing exactly how he could use that to his advantage. Still . . . it was a weakness he could exploit. Nothing Bearer liked better than exploiting a weakness. He would talk to Foley in the morning, too, he decided. Perhaps that would spark some other ideas.

He turned back in the direction of the hotel and stopped.

A figure stood before him, between Bearer and the hotel. A big man. Had to be a wrestler.

"Who's that?" Bearer frowned, and walked toward the man. He didn't recognize who it was. "Mick? Is that you?"

The man didn't respond.

"Shawn? Bret?" Bearer frowned again, and shook his head. "Austin?"

It couldn't be Austin, could it?

"Wrong, wrong, and wrong," the man said then, stepping out of the darkness.

Bearer saw his face and gasped.

He was looking at a dead man.

It was him. Whatever small shred of doubt had remained in Kane's mind was gone now.

He was staring at Paul Grimm. An older, heavier Paul Grimm, one who for some reason seemed happy to see him.

"Glen?"

"No. Not Glen. My name is Kane."

"Glen." Grimm said again, ignoring Kane's words. And then he smiled. The bastard smiled at him. "Glen. How in the world—"

Kane grabbed him by the shirt collar and slammed him against the wall.

"What were you doing there?"

"What's the matter with you?" Grimm said. "Let go of me."

Kane's free hand found his throat.

"You set the fire, didn't you? That's why you ran."

"Wait," Grimm choked out, trying to catch his breath. "That's not—"

"It was you," Kane said. "You killed my parents. You killed my brother."

The man's two hands pawed ineffectually at Kane's one.

Grimm's face began to change color. He went purple.

"Stop it," Grimm gasped. "Please."

Kane thought of Chris Hightower turning purple, and smiled.

*Not this time,* he thought. This time he wasn't stopping for anything, for anyone, for any reason.

"You left the front door open, asshole," Kane said. "After you set the fire, you left the front door open."

"Didn't." Grimm shook his head. "Wasn't me."

"Right. Sure."

"Ark," Grimm said.

Kane laughed.

This really was a fitting end to the curse. The last Kane would deliver death, and then—sooner rather than later, he suspected—welcome its embrace himself. What was the point of being alive when you had nothing to live for? When your whole family was gone?

"Ark," Grimm said again. "'Was im. E left door open."

"What?"

Grimm made a choking noise in his throat. Kane relaxed his grip, ever so slightly.

"What?" Kane repeated.

Grimm nodded, and swallowed, and then he said, "Mark left the door open."

Kane frowned. "Say that again."

"Mark left the door open. The night of the fire." Grimm tapped on Kane's hand, still tight around his neck. "Let go. Please."

Kane ignored his request. "That doesn't make sense. Mark left the door open and then went back upstairs to burn?"

"That's not what I said. Please." Grimm tapped on Kane's hand again.

This time, he let go.

"Thank you." Grimm straightened his collar, collected himself. Then he looked up at Glen and shook his head.

"I don't understand how you're alive. I read the papers. That car—"

"Tell me what you meant," Kane interrupted. "That Mark left the door open."

"That's just what happened. Mark ran out of the house and left the front door open."

"Ran out of the house." Kane shook his head. "No. Not possible. They found his body. They . . ."

His voice trailed off.

They hadn't exactly found Mark's body, had they? He remembered Melissa Vick telling him something about that, how they were having trouble with the ID. How they'd never really been able to confirm it. But still . . .

It didn't make sense. Mark left the front door open? He ran out of the house? He left Mom and Dad and me to die?

"He was a kid. He was terrified. He ran."

Kane realized he must have spoken out loud.

"He ran?"

Grimm nodded. "That's right. He ran."

"Wait a minute. You're saying he's alive?"

"Yes."

Kane blinked. His brother, alive? Mark was alive?

"Where is he? Where did he run to?"

"Why don't you come up to my hotel room"—the man nodded behind him, down the street—"and I'll explain everything to you?"

Kane hesitated.

"Come on," Grimm said, and smiled again. "I have ice cream."

\*     \*     \*

Bearer was glad to see him, of course. Glad that Glen was alive, genuinely glad, in ways and for reasons that he didn't quite know how to begin telling Glen about, but (and here he couldn't help himself, it was just his nature) beyond that gladness . . .

Seeing one brother reminded him yet again of the other, and the anger he'd felt earlier in the night. The beginnings of an idea began to take shape in Bearer's head. A plan. A way to exact the revenge he sought. The two would need to talk about it, though. *Or perhaps,* Bearer thought, talking was not the way to go. He'd tried talking with Mark, and look where that had gotten him. What that had gotten him. Nothing. Perhaps he should take a lesson from that experience, and supplement his talking with methods a bit more . . . precise.

He got the key to the mini-bar and opened it.

"You said Coke?" he asked Glen.

The man, who was sitting on the couch reading a wrestling magazine, reading all about his brother, grunted in the affirmative.

Bearer took out the Coke and went to the refrigerator. He got ice. He got out a glass. He looked over at the couch, made sure Glen wasn't watching, and then got out his kit. Mixed Glen up his drink. Coke with a little something extra. A very little something. A prod. Just to make sure the man reacted in the proper way. Bearer felt a little guilty about it—this was, after all, something of a family reunion. He wished the deceit wasn't necessary, but as his dad always used to say . . .

You couldn't make an omelette without breaking a few eggs.

Or in this instance, heads.

Bearer brought Glen his drink. Glen drank it down, greedily, thirstily. Bearer studied him. He was big—bigger even than Mark. And strong. He remembered the feel of Glen's hand around his throat. Bearer had felt hands around his neck before, had felt chokeholds and sleeper holds and death grips of all kinds from the strongest fighters in the world. He couldn't recall any of them having a grip like Glen's: like a vise, hard and unyielding as steel.

"Undertaker." Glen shook his head and set down his drink. "I guess that's fitting."

"It was his idea," Grimm lied. "A way of paying his respects to your father."

"That's bullshit." Glen—or Kane, as he'd already told Bearer several times was what he preferred to be called—tossed the magazine aside and got to his feet. "Paying his respects? He left my dad to die. He left all of us to die."

"That wasn't his intention," Grimm said.

"But that's what happened."

The man prowled the room like a caged tiger, pacing back and forth, his anger growing with each step.

"He could have saved us," Kane said.

"Well." Bearer shrugged. "I don't know about that. He was just a child."

"He should have tried."

"He was scared."

Kane turned and glared at him.

"Don't make excuses for him."

"I'm not. I'm just telling you how it was."

He went on to tell Glen the story of how he'd found the young Mark Callaway running from the house, running from the fire, how he'd taken the boy in. Of course he'd left out some details, but Glen was too angry right now to be interested in details. Glen didn't want to talk, not really.

He wanted to take action. Decisive, violent action.

"Where is he now?"

"He's got a couple weeks off," Bearer lied again. "Probably gone to this ranch he has, Outside Texas."

Kane turned to go.

"Glen." Bearer put a hand on Kane's shoulder. "What are you going to do?"

Kane glared. "Get your hands off me."

"What are you going to do?" Bearer repeated.

"I'm going to find him. I'm going to ask him why he ran out. Why he left us to die."

"And after he tells you? What are you going to do then?"

"I'm going to kill him."

"How?"

"I'm going to break off his own arm and beat him to death with it." Kane shook his head. "What does it matter how?"

Kane's eyes were pinpricks of red-hot rage.

"You'd better bring a gun."

"Why's that?"

"And you'd better sneak up on him."

Kane glared. "What are you talking about?"

"You can't beat your brother in a fair fight."

"Is that so?"

"Yes, that's so. Your brother," Bearer said slowly, "has been fighting professionally for almost ten years. Your brother"—he met Kane's eyes—"beats people up for a living. And he's good at it. He's very, very good at it."

"That wrestling shit?" Kane snorted. "Everyone knows that's fake."

"Really?"

Kane stuck his jaw out. "Yeah."

Bearer took a deep breath then, and before he could talk himself out of it, delivered a punishing elbow right to Kane's gut.

The man gasped for air, and bent over double. For a second.

Then he straightened and drew back his first for a blow that—Bearer was certain—would have knocked his head off.

"Don't. I was just proving a point. Look at me." Bearer

took a step backward and spread his hands. "I'm fat. I'm old. I have no muscle."

"Yeah?"

"So imagine what the elbow would have felt like if somebody who did that sort of thing for a living did it to you."

"It would hurt," Kane admitted. "But you sure that stuff isn't fake?"

"Sometimes it is," Bearer admitted. "That's true. But sometimes—they're out for blood. Sometimes, they genuinely want to hurt the other person in the ring. And for your brother, Glen . . . there is no sometimes. Every match he's out there, fighting, it's with everything he's got. It's to the death, as far as he's concerned."

For the first time, a flicker of hestitation appeared in Kane's eyes.

"You're strong, I can see that. Maybe even stronger than him. But in a fight . . ." Bearer shook his head. "In a fight, he'd finish you off in minutes. Maybe less."

"What's your point?"

"My point is that you can't just walk in on him, and expect to beat him."

"What would you suggest, then?"

"Do you speak Spanish?" Bearer asked.

"What does that have to do with anything?"

Bearer smiled, and explained.

# chapter
## eighteen

Not for the first time since arriving in Madrid, Kane wondered what he'd gotten himself into. Training? Why did he have to train in Spain? What was so special about Spain? What was he training for, anyway? Why hadn't he just called Mark up on the phone and talked to him? Why did you run away, Mark? Why did you leave us to die?

He'd acted before he thought, Kane realized. That was the problem. Bought the plane ticket that very night, after he and Grimm/Bearer had finished talking, had paid the man another few hundred dollars to get a passport in James Dean's name, and was on the way to start his wrestling training in earnest within a week. Why? What had he been thinking? Or more to the point, why had he let Bearer do his thinking for him, talk him into this course of action that in retrospect seemed very, very rash indeed?

Why didn't he call Mark right now, and talk to him? Besides the fact that phone service in Spain was terrible—as he'd discovered when trying to call Bearer to let him know he'd arrived safely—and very, very expensive? Everything here seemed expensive to him; food, his hotel, transportation . . . never mind how he felt about Bearer, the man had been generous with his money. Kane couldn't have afforded this trip without his help. And yet . . .

Something about the whole situation felt wrong to him. Felt off.

He stopped in his tracks, and looked up.

The number on the building in front of him matched the number on the piece of paper in his hand.

He was here.

Here was an old yellow brick industrial building, with a dingy, steep stone staircase off to the side of the main entrance, leading down to a half-rotted wooden door.

Kane took a deep breath and took the steps. He knocked hard. A minute later, the door creaked open and a short, balding man looked up at him and frowned.

"*Sí?*"

"Bearer sent me. I'm here to see the Spaniard."

"You're Kane?"

"That's right."

The man nodded and stepped aside.

Kane entered the building and followed the man down a dark hallway, ducking broken light fixtures as he walked. In the distance, he heard the muffled roar of a crowd. The man behind him suddenly began chattering away in Spanish. Glen turned and saw he had taken out a cell phone and was speaking into it.

They kept walking. There was paint peeling off the walls, garbage scattered everywhere; a dead plant lay across the ground, its dirt covering the floor.

They came to a door, a big, solid-looking thing in front of which a man sat. He looked up at their approach, saw Kane, and his eyes widened.

He was talking on a cell phone too.

A few steps further on, Kane realized that the man was seated because he was wheelchair-bound.

The man was thin and tan, and despite the darkness of the building, he wore sunglasses atop his gelled hair. As Kane approached, he stopped talking and put the phone on his lap.

Kane suddenly noticed that the man behind him was quiet, as well.

They'd been talking to each other, he realized.

"Welcome, my friend," the man in the wheelchair said in a thick Spanish accent. "Welcome very much. You are the one they tell me about. You are the American, no?"

"Yes," Kane said quietly.

"Big man, small voice," the man said, smiling. "My name is Javier."

"The Spaniard."

"They call me that too."

He extended his hand to his guest. Kane bent over to shake it.

"I'm Kane," he replied.

"I know. Come with me," he said. He turned his wheelchair around and propelled himself down another hallway, this one just as dark, but much cleaner. The buzz of the crowd was growing louder. "Mr. Kane—"

"No Mr. Just Kane."

"I hear nice things about you. I can't wait until you fight next week."

"I want to fight tonight," Kane shot back.

"Tonight?"

Kane nodded.

"You're not ready."

"I'm ready."

"You ever wrestled before?"

"No."

"Then you're not ready."

"I'll take that risk."

Javier studied him a moment, and then without replying, continued on down the hall. He pulled out a key and came to a stop near a black door. He unlocked it and motioned for

Kane to enter first, then followed the American inside. The room was flooded with light.

"Okay," he said. "You want to fight, you can fight. Stay here. I'll call you when it's time." He frowned. "Mr. Bearer told you the rules—Americans can't fight here without a mask?"

"He told me."

"So you brought one?"

Glen unzipped his bag and pulled it out.

Randall Callaway's death mask.

Javier reached for it; Kane hesitated a second and then handed it over.

The man turned the mask over in his hand, feeling it, and then saw the inscription. He studied it a moment, and nodded.

"This will do. You have maybe thirty minutes. Maybe forty," Javier said, handing the mask back to him, beginning to back out of the room. "I'll call you."

"Javier?"

"Yes?"

"The man I'm fighting. How big is he? Is he my size?"

The Spaniard laughed. "Mr. Kane, I never see anyone your size before."

Kane stretched.

He shadow-boxed. He did push-ups, and sit-ups, and stretched some more. From time to time, he would hear howls of excitement or groans of disappointment. He imagined himself in the arena, imagined the sound of the crowd as he entered the ring.

He flashed back then to Marfa High, to the game against Alpine, to Ty Crowell and Luis Campos and Frank Walsh and Katie Vick, jumping high in the air, leading the cheers. Shouting his name.

He saw her in his mind's eye again, leaning up on her toes to kiss him.

Buckling her seatbelt as they prepared to drive down the mountain.

Trapped in her car, reaching out for him, screaming out his name. Glen. Save me. Glen. Glen.

He punched the air before him again, and she disappeared.

His name was not Glen. Not anymore.

A full-length mirror hung on the wall. He picked up the death mask and pulled it on over his head.

He cracked his knuckles.

Another man, one he hadn't seen before, entered the room. "Mr. Kane?" he asked.

He turned away from the mirror. "That's me. I'm Kane."

"It's time," the man said.

The man led Kane down the hall, in the opposite direction from which they'd come in, toward a large double-sized steel door.

"You sure about this?" the man asked.

In response, Kane bulled past him, and pushed the door open.

The crowd noise, which up until that moment had been a dull muffled buzz of conversation and laughter, suddenly trebled in intensity, became a loud, overwhelming roar.

Kane was looking at what must have, at one time, been the main floor of the factory. There were several rows of benches in front of him, arranged in a rough circle, and that was where the crowd was, or where they mostly were, rather, because there were more people than places to sit. The audience—mostly men, but some women too—were everywhere he looked, sitting, standing in groups, talking to one another, and gradually, he saw, taking notice of him.

Gradually, the crowd fell silent as he walked into the room. The fans closest to him remained in their seats, slack-jawed, wide-eyed; others stood to get a better look at him.

"Kane!"

He looked ahead, past the faces staring at him, and saw Javier in the very center of the room. The man was next to a steel cage, whose footprint was the size of a wrestling ring, perhaps a little bigger, and whose chain-link walls extended perhaps twenty feet upward.

The floor, Kane saw, was spattered with blood.

Kane couldn't help but smile. Bearer had told him the Spaniard's methods were extreme, but effective, that if he wanted to learn how to fight quickly, there was no better teacher. Kane was beginning to get a handle on what the man had meant.

"You're in a hurry, I see."

"I'm ready to fight, if that's what you mean," Kane said.

"You have any questions?"

"What are the rules?"

"Rules? No below the belt. No biting. No weapons. That's all. You fight until you can't fight."

"Last man standing."

"Yes. Last man standing. You go inside, you don't leave until fight is over, okay? If you quit, you lose." He looked up at Kane then, and made eye contact. "You lose," he repeated, "and you never fight here again."

Kane nodded.

"Good luck," Javier said, and nodded to the announcer, who sat at a nearby table.

All at once, a spotlight flooded the room, and found Kane. Those few in the crowd who hadn't seen him before now roared to life. He heard his name, and then, all at once, saw the opening in the cage. He entered it, and awaited his opponent.

The spotlight swung away from him then, and back around to the entrance he had just come through.

Two men emerged. The first appeared to be Spanish, tall and lean with cropped black hair. The other was masked and muscular; another American.

Kane found Javier's eyes and nodded.

No one as big as him, huh? He supposed the man had decided to even things out. Fair enough.

He studied his opponents as they neared the cage. The masked one paused at the door while the Spanish man entered the ring warily. He entered talking nervously under his breath, then approached his opponent.

They were scared of him, Kane realized, and all at once whatever shreds of nervousness he had disappeared.

These men were nothing to him. Stepping-stones on the way to his brother.

So he would step on them, and not think twice about it.

*"¿Hablas Espanol?"* the Spanish referee asked. *"No entiendes, gringo?"*

Kane didn't respond. He waited until his masked opponent had entered as well, and the cage was locked behind the both of them.

*"Yo soy el arbitro,"* the man continued. *"Te daré las reglas de la pelea."*

In his mind, Kane saw the front door of his house, standing open, and swung at the man standing before him. His punch connected with a thud and knocked the man to the floor.

He twitched once, and lay still.

Kane turned toward the other man, the masked American, who had run to the corner of the ring and cowered there now, his back up against the steel of the cage. Even behind the mask, Kane could see the fear on his face.

He saw something else too.

He saw himself, hiding under the bed as Margaret Barrow called his name, and he roared his anger to the crowd, which roared back in approval.

The masked man came out of the corner in a fighter's stance, feet dancing from side to side and fists held high. Kane stalked him as the man shuffled from one side of the cage to the other. The crowd began to hiss at his cowardice.

Kane backed him toward the corner, and just as he was about to attack, heard a roar from the crowd, and felt himself pushed forward.

The Spaniard was up again.

Kane advanced toward him, but the Spaniard followed the same tactic as the masked man, using his quickness to stay out of harm's way. And then, using some subliminal signal that Kane missed, the two men attacked.

Their charge, though, was off by milliseconds. The masked man got to Kane just a little ahead of the Spaniard, and as he cocked his hand back to throw a punch, Kane raised his leg and booted him in the face. The American crumpled to the ground so quickly that Kane was able to turn and face the Spaniard charging at him from the other side of the ring without distraction.

The Spaniard realized what was happening, and tried to stop his momentum. He was too late.

Kane reached out with a right cross that caught the man's nose and jaw, drawing blood from the former, catching enough of the latter to send him flying through the air to crash against one wall of the cage.

The chain-link fence rattled.

The crowd roared its approval.

The masked man got to his feet, and Kane started after him again.

The Spaniard rose as well, but instead of attacking, he ran

to the cage door and started screaming: *"¡Abre la puerta! ¡Abre la puerta!"*

Kane ignored him and continued advancing on the American, who started his dance again. This time, though, he was too slow.

Kane caught him by the throat, then picked him up and slammed him against the side of the cage. The man's eyes rolled back in his head.

Kane sensed movement behind him and spun just in time to see the Spaniard flying toward him, right leg thrust straight out, right foot pointing toward his head.

Kane swung the masked man around like a rag doll; the Spaniard's foot caught him instead, right in the breadbasket. The man gasped and wheezed for air.

Kane grabbed the Spaniard with his left hand, and then lifted both men high off the ground.

He roared again, and saw Undertaker in his mind, and slammed his luckless, barely conscious opponents down on the cage floor.

The spectators exploded in hysteria.

Javier unlocked the cage, and raised his hand in triumph.

"I told you I was ready," Kane said.

Javier shook his head.

"Those men were nothing. A test. Tomorrow," he said, looking up at Kane and smiling, "tomorrow, we start your training for real."

Bearer had been right after all.

Kane knew nothing about fighting. But over the next few weeks, he learned.

From Javier and his trainers, he received instruction in a variety of methods of unarmed combat—from jujitsu to krav maga to zipota, from kung fu to kickboxing to wrestling. He wasn't the only one learning from the Spaniard, but he was far and away the most dedicated. He lived and breathed for the forms, the holds, the rules of each discipline. When the others broke for meals, or socialized, he remained in the dingy factory, pumping weights, practicing forms, punching the bag.

Always, in his mind, the questions burned. *Why did you leave us, Mark? Why did you leave me?* With each workout, his anger increased. Now he wanted that face-to-face confrontation; wanted to demand and if necessary beat the answers out of his brother. He bottled up that rage, storing it for later, letting it out in little drabs only when there were practice matches, when he faced an opponent—or two, or once, even three—in the ring, or the cage.

Bearer called twice, to see how he was doing. Kane peppered him with questions about Mark—he learned his brother had returned, was on the verge of being granted a title match. The thought fueled Kane's rage even higher. It made him careless.

"No, no, no, it's wrong now!" Javier said, excitedly pushing himself upward on his wheelchair handles like a gymnast on parallel bars. "Kane, you're too big! Big target. Get small, or get hit!"

Javier held his hands horizontally, a few inches apart.

"Crouch," Javier said. "Get low in your stance."

Kane tried it while sparring, but his punches lacked spark. After a minute of trying the technique, he returned to his upright style.

"Get small!" Javier yelled.

"I don't need to get small," Kane shot back.

"Then get hit!"

Kane shoved his opponent down. "I don't care about getting hit."

"You don't care."

"No. I don't feel a thing."

"Very well." Javier clapped his hands once, loudly, and suddenly everyone in the room was looking at him.

At which point he rattled off a phrase in Spanish, and every other fighter in the room turned toward Kane.

And then they attacked.

Kane took care of the first few, a kick to the stomach, an elbow to the head, a choke, but there were just too many of them, they just kept coming and coming and coming and eventually, it didn't matter that he was the biggest and the strongest, they got him down on the ground; three on each leg, two on each arm.

Javier wheeled over to him, and glared down.

"You don't care about getting hit?" he spat, and then pointed to the second biggest man in the room, another mask-wearing American.

The man walked up to Kane and ripped the mask off his head, then punched him hard in the jaw. Kane's head rocked backward.

"How's that feel?" the man asked.

"How's what feel?" Kane replied.

The man kneed him under the ribs, so hard that something cracked.

Kane's brow furrowed in anger.

"I'm going to remember this," he said, and was pleased to see an instant of fear flicker in the man's eyes. Then he started to punch Kane again, a flurry of jabs and crosses that lasted almost a full thirty seconds before the man stopped.

Kane could feel blood on his face, could feel where his skin was swelling up.

He glared at the man. "When do I get a turn, huh?"

A few of the fighters holding him shifted uneasily, loosening their grip for just a fraction of a second.

It was all the opening he needed. He swung his elbow backward, connecting with one man's nose, and lunged forward, breaking free.

First, he took care of the man who'd been hitting him. A single punch to the jaw, after which he grabbed the man's neck and squeezed it for a moment before hoisting him into the air and slamming him down hard to the ground.

Kane turned to face the others then, and smiled.

"Who's next?"

"Nobody. This is over." Javier rolled toward Kane, shaking his head.

"You are right," he said. "You don't care about being hit."

"Like I told you," Kane said. "I don't feel a thing."


A few more weeks passed.

One morning, Javier woke him up and handed him an envelope.

Inside was $500 cash and a plane ticket back to America.

"What's this?" Kane asked.

"You never seen a plane ticket?"

"Yeah, but . . . " He frowned. "I have to train, I have to be ready for—"

Javier shook his head. "I've never seen a fighter like you in my life. Whatever it is you want to do . . . you're ready."

Kane sat up on his cot, and nodded.

"May I ask you one question before I go?"

"Sure."

Kane nodded toward the man's legs. "What happened . . . why are you in a wheelchair?"

Javier was silent a moment before responding.

"I broke my back in a car accident a few years ago. I had just won my black belt in Hapkido. Fifth degree. I'm going home from seeing my friend, and a truck hits my car. Now, in my legs, I don't feel anything."

"That's a bad break."

"That's life. What can you do?" He shrugged. "Now, my turn. Why no matter how many times someone hits you, you never hurt?"

"Same as you," Kane said. "I don't feel anything. I'm not paralyzed, but throughout my body, I don't feel anything."

He explained his condition.

"It's a wonderful asset for a fighter, not to feel anything," Javier said. "Not so good for a person, though. Cuts you off from the world, from other people, I bet. Yes?"

"Sometimes," Kane admitted.

"You have to feel, Kane," Javier said, patting his heart. "That's what makes us all human."

"Don't worry, I feel," Kane said, picturing the fire, and the open front door, and his brother, dressed as Undertaker. "I feel plenty."

Javier nodded. "So where are you headed now?"

"Home, to see my family."

"That will be nice."

"Yes," Kane said, smiling. "It certainly will."

# chapter nineteen

Bearer looked himself over in the bathroom mirror and frowned.

He hadn't had the right chemicals after all.

The burns on the side of his face were just as evident as they'd been before he started the treatment. Perhaps he should have listened to the makeup person. They had recommended a certain salve, a healing ointment that also would help the injury fade. Bearer had researched that ointment, found it similar to certain fluids he'd used long ago during his days as an embalmer, and decided to create his own version of the salve, using his own higher-quality chemicals. It hadn't worked, though. His fault. His knowledge of such things, perhaps, was not as great as it had once been. Though of course, when you got right down to it, very little of the blame was his.

Mark Callaway—Undertaker—was responsible for the burns.

The accident had occured during a match a few weeks ago during the aptly titled Pay-Per-View event called *Revenge of the Undertaker*. The featured match had been a bout between Mankind and Mark. There were pyrotechnics (and Bearer did blame himself for this part of it, at least; the fire—another intended parallel to the curse—had been his idea). There was an accident—a particularly flamboyant display that got a little bit out of control. A burst of fire intended for Mankind that had instead hit Paul Bearer.

*Accident, my ass,* Bearer thought. Undertaker had it in for him. That was fine. He had a little something of his own to show Mark Callaway. A little something that was due back from overseas at any minute now.

As if on cue, the doorbell rang.

Bearer threw on his shirt, and opened the door.

Glen Callaway—Kane—stood on the threshold of Bearer's house, staring down at him.

"Good flight?" Bearer asked, leaving the door open and stepping inside.

Kane followed him in.

"Fine."

"Good. Something to drink? Eat?"

The man shook his head. He seemed even bigger to Bearer—bigger, and certainly in better shape. Cut. You could see it in his neck. The muscles on his arms were practically breaking through the shirt he had on. The hint of a stomach Bearer had seen back in Cleveland was gone.

He looked ready.

"What happened to you?" Kane asked, catching sight of Bearer's face for the first time.

"A little mishap during a match between your brother and Mankind."

"His fault?" Kane said.

"I certainly think it was deliberate," Bearer said. He turned toward the kitchen. "You sure I can't get you something to drink?"

"I'm fine. I want to see him now," Kane said. "Take me to him."

Bearer shook his head. "Let's not rush things. We have to set it up through Vince, we have to wait until the other contenders—"

"I'm not interested in any title matches, or any Vince, or

stuff like that. I just want to see my brother. I want some explanations."

Bearer studied him a moment, then nodded. "Of course. Explanations. Wait here a second."

Bearer walked down the short hallway to the kitchen and opened the refrigerator. He took out a Mountain Dew for himself, a Coke for Mark. A few other things as well.

"Here," he said, walking back into the living room, handing Mark his soda. "Drink up."

"I'm not thirsty."

"That's all right. It's got a lot of great chemicals in it."

Kane looked at him funny. But he drank anyway. Guzzled it down.

Bearer smiled, and sat down on the couch. He nodded to a chair opposite him, and Kane sat as well.

"The Spaniard told me you were the best natural fighter he'd ever seen."

"Yeah? So what?"

"Well. He's trained a lot of people over the years." Bearer went on to list a few names. More than a few, actually. A dozen almost, along with their match histories and as much personal information on them as he could remember. By the time he finished, Kane had risen from his seat, clearly impatient with all the talk. Anxious. Restless. Ready.

"You know, Glen—"

"Kane. My name is Kane."

"Of course. You know, Kane, I'd like to see some of that training for myself. Like to see if you're really ready to face your brother."

"You bet your fucking ass I'm ready," Kane spat out. "What do you want to see? You want to see me break that fucking table over your fucking head?"

The man's face was flushed. He was sweating.

Bearer thought perhaps he'd overdone the dosage a bit.

"No, no," he said quickly. "Nothing like that. I was wondering—would you be interested in a practice match or two?"

"Wrestling. Sure. Where do you want to do it? You name the place, I'm there. One of the local arenas? A gym? The living room here?"

Bearer smiled, and finished his own drink. The caffeine was hitting him now too. What a buzz. Chemicals. He loved them.

"The living room?" he said, getting to his feet. "Something like that, actually."

Kane ended up sleeping at Bearer's house that night. Passing out was more like it—the plane ride, the jet lag, must have taken more out of him than he thought. Right after the two of them had finished talking about the "exhibition matches" Bearer wanted to set up, Kane had felt a wave of exhaustion sweep over him. Bearer, unusually solicitous, had led him into the guest room, given him a pill for the raging headache Kane had also developed, and then shut out the lights.

He'd let Kane sleep the whole day through, in fact, though rather than feeling energized, by the end of that day Kane was just as tired as the beginning. He wanted to talk to Bearer further not just about the exhibitions, but about meeting Mark. Talking to Mark. There was a lot he wanted to talk to Bearer about, in fact, only the thing was . . .

He was having a hard time concentrating.

He woke up sometime during the night, made his way to the bathroom, and threw up. After that he felt better.

The next day, he took it easy. Watched TV, ate a little food, got his strength back.

That night, he slept like a log. And the morning after that . . .

It began.

\*     \*     \*

Bearer led him down to the basement. It was unfinished, partially framed out with two-by-fours in one corner, with boards and pipes and bricks and boxes scattered everywhere. There was a single lightbulb with a pull chain in the middle of the space.

"Kind of raw," Kane said.

"Good practice for you," Bearer answered, and went back up the stairs. Kane began his warm-ups, running through some of the exercises, the forms that Javier had taught him. He jogged in place awhile.

Bearer had left a pitcher of water as well. He poured himself a tall glass, and drank.

He imagined his brother Mark coming down the stairs, and pictured their encounter in his mind; what he would do to him, what he would say. Heard Mark's own meager, insincere responses, and began to get angry. Very angry.

He picked up a pipe and tapped one end of it on the floor.

"Kane?" Bearer called from the top of the stairs.

"Yeah?"

"You ready?"

"I'm ready."

Bearer flicked the switch, and the light went out.

Kane heard footsteps in the darkness, heading down the stairs. Tentative, unsure footsteps.

He smacked one hand into his fist and smiled.

This was going to be raw indeed. Very, very raw.

It went on for three days. Bearer sent down a series of fighters, the best he could find locally, with instructions to just survive. Anyone who could last more than ten minutes, he promised, would earn themselves $1,000.

Bearer kept his money, needless to say.

Of more concern to him became the health and well-being of the fighters he'd hired. He could tell from the sounds that emanated from below when his intervention was required. Then he would flash a light on Kane and back him away from his fallen opponent.

After a week of that, he decided the Spaniard was right. Kane was ready.

Now he had to go see Mark.

Bearer set up the meeting for the next night, at St. Jude's Cemetery, 9:00 P.M. He thought the venue choice inspired, given the subject matter at hand, given the history involved, the participants. The empty graves, the funeral home, death, resurrection . . .

Delicious.

Bearer got there fifteen minutes early to find Mark standing at the gates, waiting for him. Dressed as Undertaker, wearing the title belt. It glittered in the moonlight, beckoned him on, reminded him why he was there.

Bearer walked up to Mark, till the two men stood facing each other, maybe five feet apart. For one minute, then two, neither said a word.

At last, Bearer cleared his throat and began to talk.

"I want to deal."

The other man laughed.

"Deal what?"

"A deal. Between me and you."

"We're done."

"I don't think so."

The man glared at him. "What makes you say that?"

Bearer ignored the question, and plunged ahead.

"I want a lifetime contract with you, Mark. I want profit participation in all Undertaker-related activities, half of your cut, or more if you like—I want a formal, public apology for this"—he stressed the last word, and pointed to his face—"and I want—"

"Shut up," Mark said, advancing on him, balling one of the purple gloves into a fist, for show or for real, Bearer couldn't tell, but the man sure looked mad enough, mad in the angry sense, not the crazy one, mad enough to do something he might regret later.

Bearer took the mask out from under his coat and held it up.

Undertaker stopped in his tracks, a look of complete and total surprise on his face.

"Where did you get that?"

Bearer smiled, but didn't respond.

"The police had it, I thought. They found it in the motel, where we left it," 'Taker said.

"The police did have it," Bearer said.

"So how . . . ?"

"They gave it to your brother," Bearer said. "And then he gave it to me."

"I don't understand. He gave it to you . . . when? You said you hadn't seen Glen since before the fire." Anger sharpened 'Taker's features. "Are you saying you lied to me?"

Bearer shook his head. "No, Mark, I told you the truth. Then. Now the truth is a little bit different."

He waited a minute, for the man to catch up, and at last, he did.

"What are you saying?"

"I'm saying Glen gave me the mask, Mark." Bearer felt like laughing. "I'm saying your brother is alive. Glen Callaway is alive."

Undertaker shook his head.

"No. It's not possible. He died. The fire."

"The same way you did?" Bearer asked.

'Taker shook his head.

"I don't believe you."

"You should."

"Prove it."

"This is the proof." Bearer held up the mask. "Believe me, you don't want to see him. He knows what you did."

If it was possible, Undertaker paled even further. "What did you tell him?"

"That you were alive. He wants to see you, Mark. He wants to talk. He wants to know why you ran away that night."

The man closed his eyes, and sighed. In that instant, Bearer saw for the first time in years the scared little boy Mark Callaway had been two decades ago, the boy who'd run screaming from his house for help, who Bearer had intercepted and stopped from going to the police. It had been too late by then, of course—the house went up like kindling, the chemicals in there, the fumes, the flames . . . everyone had died within minutes, he had assured the boy. Which he had honestly thought was the case until they came back from Mexico a few weeks later and he found out Glen had survived. He'd thought Mark would be better off not knowing about that. His instincts, obviously, had been right, because now the wedge between the two brothers . . .

Well, it was leverage.

"A deal, Mark," Bearer said, pressing his advantage. "You and me, a team again. Together. Forever. Or I tell your brother everything."

Bearer could only guess at the thoughts running through the man's mind. The conflicting emotions, the regret, the anger, the pain . . .

The fear of exposure.

Undertaker swallowed once then, and opened his mouth to speak. No words came out for a second.

Bearer smiled. He knew right then and there, he had him.

Undertaker—and the title, and all that went with it—were his again.

With one Callaway in hand, Bearer didn't need the other. Not right away, at least. Of course he didn't want Kane to go flying off the handle, go seek out his brother, mess things up all over again. He needed to keep the man under control.

So Kane, unfortunately, got sick again. Too sick to leave Bearer's house. Too sick, sometimes, even to eat. He grew delirious. Bearer hired a nurse to watch him while he was away on tour. That didn't work out so well; he had no idea broken bones were so expensive to fix.

He locked Kane in his bedroom the next time. The man was so delirious he didn't even notice. He didn't even bother to eat. The chemicals were wrong, Bearer decided. He'd do better next time.

But there was no next time.

His reunion with Undertaker ended up lasting less than a month.

Which left Bearer with no choice, really. He wasn't just going to go away, wasn't just going to fade into the darkness and let Mark have sole possession of everything he'd worked so hard for too.

Bearer did exactly as he'd threatened; he told the world about the dark secrets hidden in the Undertaker's past. The family that had died because of his actions. Some of that had been known, of course, to wrestling insiders, to certain personages within the company. But now, Bearer let more of the truth out.

Not everyone in Undertaker's family had died. There was a survivor. A sibling, who shared not just the Dead

Man's name, but his prodigious fighting skill, his size, his strength.

Undertaker had a brother, who lived the curse the Dead Man embodied. His name was Kane.

And what he wanted—the only thing in the world he wanted—was revenge.

# chapter
## twenty

Inside the Kiel Center in St. Louis, the crowd—21,151 fans—was literally buzzing in anticipation.

Tonight's match was going to be a landmark.

A long-standing feud between Undertaker and Shawn Michaels would be decided in a steel cage with no way out. Unlike most Cage matches, where the combatants could escape by climbing over the side to the ground below, this new structure was enclosed by four chain-link walls and a reinforced ceiling. The door was padlocked. The cell stood twenty feet tall and stretched thirty-five feet across, encircling the ring and offering nowhere for the combatants—Shawn Michaels and Undertaker—to run.

Watching from the rear of the backstage area, waiting for Michaels and his brother to enter that cage, wearing a black bathrobe that covered him from head to toe, with a hood that hid all but his eyes, Kane thought the setup was perfect, though he wasn't thinking of the arena as a cage.

It was going to be Undertaker's coffin—a real Casket match, perhaps the last one the organization ever saw.

"You all set?"

Kane turned and saw Bearer smiling at him.

"Yeah."

"Feeling better?"

"Feeling great," Kane said, and he was; whatever bug had

knocked him on his ass the last few weeks was gone. He'd woken up this morning completely rejuvenated.

"Good," Bearer said. "Just a few more minutes."

Kane nodded. A few more minutes, and he would finally face his brother. He couldn't wait.

"You all done with that?" Bearer asked, nodding toward the soda can in his hand.

"Yeah," Kane said absently. "Finished."

"Good."

Kane nodded. He felt good. Ready to give the crowd a show. Get some answers, at long last.

Or maybe not.

Maybe he would pound the crap out of his brother first, and talk later.

He bounced up and down on the balls of his feet, wired beyond belief. He wanted to get in there before the ref ended the match. It wasn't going to take long, Kane saw. Ten seconds into the bout, and he could tell already it wasn't even going to be close.

His brother—Undertaker—walked slowly, ponderously, into the cage, reminding Kane of nothing so much as the Frankenstein monster, lumbering, but obviously very, very powerful. Michaels, who was half a head shorter, didn't even want to get into the cage with him, at least not by himself. Finally, Michaels was locked in, and the match was on.

Mark began by stalking the smaller man around the ring. He got a big boot in Michaels's face, sending him into the turnbuckle; the bigger man tried for a chokeslam, and Michaels kicked him in the shin. A little more cat-and-mouse, and then Michaels was on the mat, and then over the rope, and dazed.

"Make him bleed," some people yelled, and Kane was surprised to realize they meant Michaels, and he stopped watching the action long enough to take the measure of the crowd, and realized that his brother was the crowd favorite.

The thought made him see red, and he actually started punching the concrete wall by the entranceway. Two men walking past turned and looked at him.

He ripped off the hood on his head to reveal the death mask beneath, and their eyes widened and they hurried away, as fast as they could go.

Chickenshit cowards.

He smiled, and flexed beneath the robe.

Soon. His chance would come soon.

Shawn Michaels was a bloody mess. He had fallen from the top of the cell through the announcers' table, he had been chokeslammed from the top rope, and now Undertaker had drilled him in the head with a steel folding chair. Michaels crumpled to the mat, nearly unconscious. His defeat was imminent. Bearer knew what was coming next.

The Tombstone Piledriver. Undertaker would deliver the coup de grace, and then he would be world champion again.

Bearer's eyes went to Kane, an aisle away, and he saw that the robe was coming off.

He smiled in satisfaction. Everything was going exactly according to plan.

Katie Vick.

Jarvis Vick.

Susanna Kane.

Randall Callaway.

Kane mumbled the names to himself, even as the crowd around him was still chanting for Undertaker, chanting for the

Tombstone, the end of the match, the Dead Man's ascension, once more, to the very throne of professional wrestling's kingdom.

He caught Bearer's eye.

It was time.

"Undertaker!" Kane yelled, and at that moment, the lights in the arena faded to black.

In the cage, about to deliver the finishing blow to his opponent, Undertaker stopped, and frowned.

What was the matter with the lights? Where were the lights?

He looked to the announcer's table. Vince McMahon was on the mike, and he seemed as confused as anyone.

Then an organ began to play, and a murmur spread through the crowd. A murmur consisting of a single name.

Kane.

Undertaker turned and saw his fate coming down the aisle, walking toward him.

Kane reached for the door to the cage, and ripped it off. He didn't know his own strength, he supposed, studying the broken hinge for a second before stepping inside.

And then at last, he was face-to-face with his brother.

It was Glen, Mark knew that in an instant.

The eyes. Even behind the mask, he could see them. One brown, one blue. How this was possible, he didn't know.

But it was his brother. Bearer, at least, hadn't been lying about that.

Nearly twenty years had passed since they had last looked at each other face-to-face. Back then, Mark was a few inches taller and was more muscular. But time had changed them.

Now, Glen was taller, broader, more menacing. Not because of the mask, or the black and red uniform. Undertaker had seen wrestlers with masks and uniforms before. It was his brother's size. His attitude. The way he stood in the ring.

This was an opponent who would give no quarter, grant no mercy. Who sought, and would have vengeance for the past, for what had come before.

Mark Callaway closed his eyes for a second then, and thought of his parents, and their last moments as a family.

He'd gotten home late after hanging out with Paul Grimm again, late enough that his mom and dad sent him to bed with no supper. BFD is what he said; they probably didn't miss him anyway. They had Glen, poor little Glen, poor little shy Glen who Mommy loved to read to at night and tuck in, who Randall loved to take fishing. Nobody wanted to talk to him these days, they all wanted him to settle down and study and stop running around town like a crazy kid and getting into all those fights. They didn't understand; Mark just got so excited some times he couldn't sit still, he couldn't sleep. No one seemed to understand that—his mom and dad were content just working at the funeral parlor, same old thing day in and day out, put on your best suit and hold the door, set out the tissues for the families, don't smile, never smile, and for God's sake don't make so much noise outside when we have a ceremony under way in the parlor.

Mark hated it all, the sitting still, the stench of the chemicals, the endless parade of strangers in your own home . . . he hated it so much that he wanted to burn the whole place down.

And then, that night, he did.

It was an accident, of course. He'd been in the kitchen,

found a book of matches, lit one, and set the book ablaze before even thinking about what he was doing. He even watched the book burn in his hand for a moment—

And only when the flames actually licked his hand, and he dropped the matchbook onto the shaggy, tan carpet in the middle of the living room, and it started to burn, did he realize that there was a problem. Even then, he thought things were under control, thought he'd surely have time to run into the next room, take a pitcher of water out of the refrigerator, and douse the flames. Except that when he ran to the kitchen, there was no water in the refrigerator, and by the time he had filled up a pitcher out of the sink, the fire had already spread out of control, swallowing the curtains and climbing up the walls.

Frozen by fear, he screamed, trying to alert his parents and brother to the danger. His brother was on the other side of the funeral parlor. His parents were all the way upstairs.

He had to get help.

He ran through the parlor, stopping to grab his mother's papers—the Kane family papers—from the table where he'd been looking at them, and took his father's favorite mask off the wall, the death mask he'd brought back from Mexico, because he knew how important both things were to his parents, if they lost them that would be a disaster, and then he ran out the front door and found Paul Grimm parked at the end of the driveway.

"What is it, Mark?" Grimm asked. "What's the matter?"

In the ring, Kane lifted his arms to the sky. For a second, he stared at his brother.

Then he dropped his arms, drawing fire from the four ring posts.

The fire had been Bearer's idea. Kane had smiled at the

suggestion. It reminded him—as he knew it would remind his brother—of the curse.

And as Undertaker turned to take in the flames, Kane moved forward, a bolt of red and black lightning. He kicked Mark in the stomach, then scooped him off the ground and onto his shoulder.

And then he positioned Undertaker in place for a Tombstone of his own.

Kane held him for a few seconds, reflecting on this moment of redemption. He was going to make his brother feel pain like he had on that long-ago night; he turned to every side of the arena. If his parents were watching from the sky, he was going to give them a view.

He spiked his brother headfirst into the canvas. Undertaker crumpled to the ground. Michaels covered him for the pin.

Kane smiled, and caught Paul Bearer's eye.

Phase one—the first part of their plan, which Bearer had outlined to him a few days ago—was now complete.

Afterward, backstage, Bearer munched thoughtfully on an ice cream cone. Kane, as usual, had a Gatorade, though of course it was more than a Gatorade, it was an antidote of sorts, a way for the man and his nervous system to throttle down, which he clearly needed.

Ripping a steel door off its hinges, Bearer thought, shaking his head. He needed to adjust the dosage next time, or it was possible Kane would rip apart something much more fragile than a door.

The man held the Gatorade in his hand as if he'd never seen one before. The bottle looked the size of a Dixie cup in his massive paw.

"Drink," Bearer said, and at that instant a shadow fell across the room.

Bearer turned and saw Undertaker standing in the doorway, blocking the light.

"Glen," Undertaker said.

Kane raised his eyes. "I'm going to kill you," he said.

"Glen." Undertaker took a step into the room. "I don't understand. What are you doing? How is it you're alive? I thought—"

"What you thought doesn't matter," Bearer said, stepping in between the two brothers. "What matters is now. The here and now. And here and now, I want you out of this dressing room."

"I don't know what he's told you, but don't believe him," Undertaker said to Kane. "He's a liar."

"A liar." Bearer shook his head. "*Tch, tch.* It's not nice to call someone names. Especially when they're not accurate. Was I lying about him?" Bearer nodded to Kane behind him. "About your brother being alive? No. Of course not. Glen knows I'm not a liar. You ought to know that too, Mark. After all the time we spent together."

"What I know is that somehow you've managed to turn my brother against me. But I want to tell you, Paul, that's not going to last. Glen and I—"

"I'm going to kill you," Kane said again, staring straight at Mark. "I'm going to crush your bones and make them into soup."

Bearer ignored him and turned to Glen. "Drink your Gatorade, please."

When Glen had started drinking, he turned to the older Callaway again. "Bone-crushing is probably too extreme. But a fight . . . we definitely plan on a fight, Mark. After tonight, I think a lot of people would be very excited about a fight between you two, may the best man win and all that. I think Mr. McMahon will be very excited for that match as well, don't you? Mark?"

Undertaker shook his head. "I'm not going to fight him. I'm never going to fight him. He's my brother."

"We'll see what happens," Bearer said.

"I know what's going to happen," Undertaker said. "Glen, come with me. Let me help you. I can—"

Six security staff entered the room then, as if on cue. Actually, they were late. Bearer, suspecting that Undertaker might try to see Glen after the fight, had told them to be backstage, waiting, in case of that eventuality. At a nod from Bearer, the six moved into a rough semicircle around Mark.

None of them were as big as the older Callaway brother. But they were all at least six-two, all in pretty good shape, and they had nightsticks, and there was a rumor that one of them—the boss, a guy named Tramonte—had a Taser.

Bearer figured that at best, they'd slow down Mark for a few seconds, give him and Glen enough time to make it out the entrance, and to their car.

"You okay in here, Mr. Bearer?" Tramonte asked.

Bearer looked at Undertaker.

Undertaker glared back, looked down at Glen, at the guards surrounding him, and then shook his head.

"This isn't over yet," he said.

"Soup," Kane said.

With a last angry glance at Bearer, Undertaker spun on his heel and left the room, so quickly that the security guards all jumped.

"Gonna kill him," Kane said again, watching his brother go. "Soup."

Bearer frowned.

He wasn't so sure about killing. He had a pretty detailed plan, of which phase one was now complete. Kane, who Bearer had been building up to the audience in every way possible for the last six months, was no longer just a rumor.

Now Kane was solid, undeniable fact. A very, very bankable fact. A hot commodity. The two brothers would wrestle each other. Bearer now thought that despite Mark's vastly greater experience in the ring, Glen—the revenge-seeking Glen—would win that match. Win both of them a lot of money (although Bearer would bank Kane's share too; the man was hardly in the kind of mental shape necessary to handle large amounts of cash), win them both a measure of revenge. But death . . .

That wasn't part of the plan. Not that death scared Bearer—after all, he'd been an undertaker himself, once upon a time. He was used to the sight of dead bodies. Still, death in the ring . . . that was best avoided.

Crippling injuries, on the other hand . . .

"Let's worry about Undertaker later. For now," Bearer said, nodding to the Gatorade that Kane still held in his hand. "Drink. After all, you need to keep your strength up, don't you?"

"Yes." Kane nodded. "I need to be strong. I need to be the strongest one of all."

"That's right," Bearer said. "You need to be the strongest."

He smiled. Kane drank.

# chapter
## twenty-one

It was a good long sleep.

When Kane opened his eyes, he was in Paul Bearer's basement, only for some reason, there were posters up on the walls. The same posters he'd had in his room when he was a kid. Darth Vader. Danny White. Undertaker.

Undertaker?

Kane sat up.

The door at the top of the stairs was open.

His brother stood there, looking down at him. Dressed in his Undertaker finest.

"House is on fire," he said, and then walked away.

He was right: Kane smelled it now. Smoke. Bearer's house was burning too, just the way the funeral parlor had when he was a kid. And Mark was abandoning him again. Leaving him to die again, just as he had that night long ago. Anger surged through Kane.

He ran up the stairs, taking the steps two at a time.

He emerged into Bearer's kitchen, just as a man strode through the back door. An EMT, who looked very familiar to him. The guy was drinking a can of Coke.

"Aren't you dead yet?" the EMT asked.

Kane looked past him, out the back door, and saw Undertaker running down the street. Getting away.

He pushed past the EMT and outside.

Tumbleweeds blew across the backyard, blew in front of

his face, obscured his vision. He shoved them out of the way with his arms, and there before him was a sign.

Welcome to
MARFA, TEXAS
Home of the World-Famous Marfa Lights
*Giant* filmed here, 1951–1952

Paul Bearer stepped out from behind it.

"He's getting away," Kane said, pointing down the road. "Undertaker's getting away."

"He can't run forever," Bearer said. "We'll get him."

"We'll kill him," Kane said.

"Well. We'll see about that." The man held up a Gatorade. "Thirsty?"

"Always." Kane took the bottle and chugged it. Felt good. Strong. Energized. His vision sharpened. Off in the distance, a black speck resolved itself into the form of his brother. Undertaker was tiring, Kane could see. Slowing to a walk. Bearer was right: the man couldn't run forever.

Kane cracked his knuckles and smiled.

It was going to end here and now, back in Texas, back where it had all begun. He took a step forward. Bearer put a hand on his shoulder to stop him.

"What?" Kane asked.

Bearer held up a piece of paper.

You're Dreaming

It said.

Kane nodded. "I know," he said. "Even so . . . I could use the practice."

He raced down the road then, and caught up to his brother,

and lifted him like he was a child, and carried him to the graveyard where their parents were buried, and gave him a Tombstone Piledriver, planting him headfirst in the ground next to Randall and Susanna Callaway.

The man's legs, still visible in the air, twitched a few times before going still.

"That's that," Kane said, and then turned to his own gravestone.

GLEN CALLAWAY
1970–1988

Suddenly he was exhausted.

Kane dug for a while with his hands. When he'd dug a deep enough hole, he pulled the dirt down on top of himself, and went back to sleep.

Bearer shut the basement door behind him and shook his head.

The hospital had called: the man Kane had just finished beating to within an inch of his life was going to be fine. Nothing a few operations, a few pints of blood, and a few months of rehab couldn't cure. So that problem was behind him. That was going to be the last basement match as well, Bearer decided. He didn't need that kind of aggravation in his life right now. He had enough problems as it was. Dealing with Kane under the influence, and trying to find a way to proceed to phase two of his plan.

The problem was Mark. Undertaker. Over the last few months since the Hell in the Cell match, the man had stayed true to the promise he'd made that night, backstage. He wouldn't fight Kane, no matter what the provocation. It drove Bearer crazy. At match after match, Bearer had Kane appear in the ring, sometimes scheduled, sometimes unscheduled, always with the intent of forcing Undertaker's hand. Well, almost always. Bearer still didn't have the chemicals entirely right. Sometimes Kane acted—acted out—on his own.

Like the week after the Hell in the Cell match, when the Hardy Boyz were in the ring, waiting for their Tag Team opponents, and Kane, who'd been backstage with Bearer, somehow made his way to the arena and proceeded to toss the two fighters out of the ring like they were nothing. Bearer had to act quickly to explain that one away.

And a couple weeks after that, he had to do it again, when Kane interrupted a match between the British Bulldog and Dude Love. And then in November when he took on Ahmed Johnson while Johnson was waiting to start his match with Steve Austin. It all worked to Bearer's ultimate advantage—fed the public's image of Kane as a masked madman, a scarred monster waiting to take his revenge. Of course the scars underneath that mask were anticlimactic—Bearer actually made Kane keep the mask on most of the time, even when they were back at his house, because the fewer people who knew Kane's scars were not that much worse than a bad sunburn, the better.

The voicebox was another nice touch. Bearer had gotten the idea after one of Kane's basement matches, which he was still having the man do, to keep in practice. A few weeks back, an unfortunate soul named Gene Snitsky had gone down to the cellar to try and win Bearer's thousand dollars. He'd had no more luck at that than the others, but Snitsky had actually managed to hurt Kane a little, struck him on the throat with an elbow. Kane had trouble talking for a while after that—Bearer ended up taking him to a doctor friend of his, Dr. Kovar over at Presbyterian, to see what they could do.

"Old injury," Kovar announced after the examination, in a

heavily accented voice. "Is going to be problem for this man's whole life. Get hit here"—he made a chopping motion at Kane's throat—"and injury aggravated. Swelling. No way to fix."

Bearer frowned. His plan had been to have Kane start amping up the war of words between the two men the next time he entered the ring.

"We don't necessarily need to fix it," Bearer said. "Can't you give him something so the swelling goes down? So he can talk?"

"Mmm." Kovar frowned, shook his head. "Not such a good idea. Powerful drugs, powerful man . . . not a good combination. No."

All at once then, the doctor's eyes lit up.

"But . . . you want him to talk?"

Bearer had outlined his desires briefly to Kovar before the examination.

"Yes."

"Then we use Servo-vox."

"What?"

"Servo-vox. Wait. I be right back."

Kovar dashed out of the room then. Bearer shrugged, and put a hand on Kane's shoulder.

"Maybe he's got something. We'll see. I'm sure he'll be right back. He's a good man, Doctor Kovar."

Kane didn't respond. The man continued to sit on the exam room table, staring off into space, lost to the world. Bearer's heart went out to him. When this was all over, when the drugs were no longer necessary, he was going to send him on a long vacation. Let him detox in the warm sun, someplace tropical. Rio, perhaps . . . he'd go with him, of course, help Glen make the transition back to reality. Maybe then they'd be able to have a nice, long conversation about the past.

There was a thing or two, after all, that Bearer still needed to tell him.

"And here we are."

Kovar walked back in carrying a small cardboard box. He set it down on the counter near the exam room sink, ripped it open, and pulled out something that at first glance looked to Bearer like a little blue flashlight.

"Servo-vox," Kovar declared.

"Okay," Bearer said. "What's it do?"

Kovar smiled, and pressed the device to his throat.

"This is what it does," he said, only the sound that came out of his mouth was not Kovar's normal voice, but a harsh, mechanical, grating effect. It was an artificial voicebox, Bearer realized, and he remembered a time back when he was in high school, and a man had come to talk to them about the dangers of smoking. The man, it turned out, had throat cancer, and had to speak with the aid of a mechanical device just like the one Kovar was showing them. He sounded like a robot on one of those old TV shows, *The Outer Limits* or something. Bearer knew that sound was supposed to scare the kids into never wanting to smoke.

But it had made him laugh; he got expelled from the assembly.

"Produces tone that mimics vocal cord action," Kovar said. "Sound. So he can talk."

Bearer nodded.

"You want to try it?" he asked Kane, gently touching the man's shoulder.

Kane didn't respond, just continued to stare off into space.

Bearer put the device up against Glen's throat.

"Try to talk," he said. "Say something, Glen."

The man turned and looked at him then.

"My name is Kane," he growled, and it came out sounding

like a pronouncement of doom, like the words of a creature stolen right from every thirteen-year-old boy's worst nightmare.

Bearer grinned.

"Wrap it up," he said to Kovar. "I'll take it."

Needless to say, the voicebox was a big hit with the fans. Kane's every appearance—even the promise of an appearance— began to draw cheers.

In the meantime, the war of words between Bearer and Undertaker continued, their private feud played out on a public stage. It really got to Mark, Bearer was pleased to see, especially when he would get on the ring microphone and publicly denounce the man as a murderer. It made the man in black furious, obviously, and yet . . .

He still wouldn't rise to the bait.

Even when Kane climbed over the ropes and entered the ring during a match between Undertaker and Jeff Jarrett, not only disrupting the flow of the fight but walking right over to his brother and slapping him in the face. Slapping him like a girl.

Even after he did it again the next week—twice.

Even after Bearer publicly called him a coward, and repudiated their entire, lengthy association. Nothing seemed to be able to stir Mark to action. And what really got to Bearer . . .

The week after that, when seven wrestlers, tired of Kane's antics, interruptions, and continual distracting appearances during their matches, attacked him, Undertaker actually climbed in the ring to help his brother even the odds a bit. Undertaker helped Kane, and afterward, even told the stunned crowd that he would burn in hell before he fought his brother.

Bearer realized that perhaps, phase two was never going to happen. At least, not the way he'd planned it out. So he made a new plan.

Undertaker fought Shawn Michaels again, at the *Royal Rumble* in January 1998. A Casket match, for the title. It got a little crazy. A lot of wrestlers ended up in the ring, Kane among them. For a second, it seemed like Kane was returning the favor his brother had rendered weeks before—helping him out against overwhelming odds.

But once Undertaker's other foes were vanquished, Kane turned on him. In his weakened condition, Mark was no match for his younger brother. Kane stuffed him into the casket without breaking a sweat. Bearer entered the ring then and locked Undertaker in, and then together, he and Glen took hold of the wooden box and began to wheel it offstage.

Behind them, the ring announcer declared Shawn Michaels the winner of the Casket match—and still the champion.

Bearer smiled to himself as the crowd roared, as Michaels soaked in the applause.

*Enjoy it while you can, Shawn,* Bearer thought, *because soon . . .*

He looked over at Kane, on the other side of the casket, muscles bulging in his neck, his back, eyes fixed dead ahead, face frozen in an expression of grim, implacable determination—

*Soon that belt is going to be in other hands.*

The crowd was yelling and chanting his name, screaming as he wheeled the casket past.

"Kane! Kane! Kane!"

A boy in the front row was pumping his fist into the air, shouting at the top of his lungs. A few seats down, a woman in her fifties gave him a big thumbs-up.

Ty Crowell sat next to her.

"Way to go, Glen. Way to go, buddy," he said.

Kane blinked, and Ty disappeared, changed into a fat man in a checked sport shirt.

*That was weird,* he thought, and started pushing again.

He'd been feeling weird a lot lately—a little disoriented. Not quite himself. It was a good thing Bearer was so good with medicines, with chemicals. Otherwise, Kane didn't know if he would have been able to fight. Been able to go after his brother at all. To gain revenge. And revenge was everything to him. When he slept, he dreamed of it, awake, he planned it in his mind, visualized the action, the moves he would make, the Tombstone, the pin, the crunching of the bones. The making of the soup. Undertaker soup. The one thing he couldn't visualize . . .

What the soup would taste like, going down his throat.

The veins in his forehead throbbed. His vision blurred again, and again for a second, he saw Ty in the crowd.

"It's our time now, Glen," Bearer said. He was on the other side of the casket, helping wheel it down the aisle. "Our turn to take revenge for what happened twenty years ago."

Kane nodded. Revenge.

Ty smiled at him, gave him a thumbs-up.

Kane blinked, and Ty was gone.

His head began to hurt. His steps slowed.

"You all right, Glen? You okay, honey?"

He looked up. His mom was sitting on the casket, legs dangling over one side, looking at him with an expression of concern on her face.

She reached over and put a hand on his forehead.

"Hmm. I think you have a fever, honey. You're burning up."

He was hallucinating, obviously. His mom was dead. He blinked again, shook his head.

But his mom was still there.

"You know what, Glen? I don't feel well either now. Maybe I have it too. Maybe it's a family thing."

Smoke began rising from the top of her head.

"Some kind of curse," she added, and burst into flame.

Startled, Kane made an involuntary noise, and jumped backward from the casket.

"You all right?" Bearer asked.

Kane nodded, but inside he thought: No. No, I'm not all right. People who were all right didn't hallucinate this way. It was probably because he wasn't getting enough sleep. All those dreams. He would have to ask Bearer to give him something—a pill from his stash. He certainly had a big stash—early the other morning, after a particularly hard night, Kane had wandered upstairs from the basement, looking for something to do, someone to talk to, anything to break up the monotony of his existence, and somehow found himself in a room literally overflowing with pills. He had no idea what they were all for, and hadn't really had a chance to ask. Bearer had heard him shuffling around, come downstairs, and promptly had escorted him out of the room. Was very suspicious of Glen, and his motives.

"What are you doing?"

That was just what Bearer had said, in fact.

"I said, what are you doing?"

But that wasn't Bearer. That was a woman's voice.

Kane looked up and saw Margaret Barrow, sitting on a horse right in front of him, right in the middle of the aisle, blocking their way forward.

"What am I doing," he repeated dumbly. "I'm—"

"You're not using the reins to steer," she snapped. "You have to use the reins—you do remember that, don't you?"

"Yes, but—"

"God." She shook her head. "Don't make me hit you again, Glen. I don't want to have to hit you."

"Okay," he said, because he couldn't think of anything else to say.

"That's far enough," Bearer said, stepping in front of the casket. Margaret and the horse vanished. "Go get the ax."

Kane turned and looked at him, confused for a second. Ax?

"The ax, Glen. Remember?" Bearer looked at him expectantly.

"Right," Kane said, nodding. "The ax."

He turned and walked to the entranceway that led backstage. The ax was there, leaning against the wall, just where they'd left it before entering the ring.

He picked it up, and turned back to the casket.

Katie Vick stood in front of him, dressed in her cheerleader's uniform.

Kane dropped the ax.

Katie raised her pom-poms and started cheering.

"Kane, Kane, he's our man, if he can't do it—"

"Kane!"

He blinked, and Katie was gone, and Bearer was glaring at him, holding a big red can—gasoline—poised above the casket.

"Come on."

Kane picked up the ax again, and started walking.

A car came roaring down the aisle toward him, a sports car, and in it he saw a young man whose face looked awfully familiar, and the man smiled and gave him a big thumbs-up and yelled—

"Curse? What curse?"

And the car flipped over and exploded into flames.

"End it here," Bearer said, and it seemed to Kane for a moment as if the fat man stood inside a ring of fire himself. "End it now."

Kane hesitated.

"Do it," Bearer said. "Go on. Do it."

Kane pictured his brother when the two of them were kids.

Pictured them standing together, standing next to each other as Denton Young and his gang ran away as fast as they could.

"Chickenshit cowards," Mark said. "Teach 'em not to mess with a Callaway."

Kane looked into the fire, and saw the posters in his room burning. Saw the open front door. Saw Marfa Cemetery, and his parents' graves.

He brought the ax down once, and then again. The lid began to splinter.

In his mind, he heard a scream. He couldn't be sure if it was his own, or someone else's.

Gasoline splashed on his arm. Bearer pulled him back a safe distance from the casket.

"Revenge," the man said, and lit a match, and threw it.

Flames burst forth from the casket. It burned.

It smelled like chicken.

"It's over," Bearer said. "At last, it's over."

But it wasn't. It was only just beginning, in fact.

Somehow, Mark had managed to escape from the casket. He didn't return for two months, but when he did . . .

He was angry. He was out for blood. For a little revenge of his own.

Undertaker was, at last, ready to fight his little brother.

# chapter twenty-two

The match was set to take place at *WrestleMania XIV*. It was not a title bout, nothing larger than victory was at stake, and yet it was arguably the most eagerly anticipated event of the year. Pete Rose was picked to be special guest announcer. The company touted the encounter for weeks beforehand, teasing audiences around the country with a recap of Undertaker's and, to a lesser extent, Kane's history. Reminding them of the fire, of the loss both men had endured, of Undertaker's cowardly exit the night of the blaze. Both fighters (and Paul Bearer as well) became regulars at every bill, touting themselves, denigrating their opponent, promising viewers a fight to the finish.

Unfortunately, the bout itself was entirely anticlimactic.

To the world, it seemed as if Undertaker's skill and experience was just too much for Kane to handle. The man in black won the match handily, although afterward (with a considerable amount of help from Bearer) Kane attacked his brother again, and inflicted a lot of damage on him. Which didn't change the outcome in the slightest.

It was the medication, Bearer knew. The chemicals. He'd used them too freely, too often. They'd dulled Kane's reactions, blunted his fighting instincts. He'd have to take the man off them entirely, either let him go cold turkey, or . . .

Find new ones.

The first option didn't sound entirely promising to Bearer,

and was potentially quite risky as well, to his own safety. If Kane ever got in his right mind again, and found out what Bearer had been doing to him . . .

That was the problem with keeping secrets, the fat man thought, which he was doing quite a bit of here. Not just regarding the chemicals; regarding his relationship with Susanna Kane. There were aspects of that which sooner rather than later required a bit of truth-telling to be done, though perhaps not the entire truth, as the entire truth might be quite upsetting to Glen. As the entire truth about the chemicals would be. Which was really a much more pressing matter at the moment.

Bearer went into his study then, and spent the remainder of the night studying.

In the morning, a little earlier than usual, shortly after seven, he went down to the basement and rousted Kane from what was obviously a restless sleep.

"Katie?" the big man said, sitting up and blinking.

"Shhh. It's just me," Bearer said. "I brought something for you."

He held out a glass.

"Yeah." Kane nodded. "You read my mind. I need a little something. A pick-me-up."

"This is a new something," Bearer said. "A protein shake."

"Protein. That's good for you, isn't it?"

"We'll see," said Bearer, crossing his fingers.

Bearer kept up his merciless verbal humiliation of Undertaker; every time he took the microphone in the ring, he called the man a murderer, impugned his skill, his courage. It was clearly all Mark could do to keep from ripping his head off when they passed backstage. Bearer went beyond talk too— one Monday night in April, during *Raw,* he and Kane brought out replicas of the coffins Randall and Susanna had been buried in, and started to burn them. Undertaker freaked; even though no match was scheduled, he charged the stage. He and Kane fought on top of one of the replica coffins until they both were bleeding and dazed.

Bearer liked what he saw from his fighter: Kane seemed on top of his game. And so he scheduled another match between the brothers: an Inferno match. The first person to set their opponent on fire would be the winner.

They set the bout for the end of April. During *Unforgiven.* It started off well for Kane; he attacked Undertaker without mercy. The two ended up fighting in the aisle, which was when Vader, another wrestler, jumped out and started in on Kane as well.

Kane fought as best he could; but it was no use.

Before long he was down, and out.

And moments later, Undertaker, Mark Callaway, did to him intentionally what he had unwittingly done to their parents.

He put fire to his brother's arm, and watched him burn.

Bearer felt like his own chemicals were off a little bit that night.

Helping Glen back down to the basement, looking at the charred flesh on the man's arm, he felt a sudden attack of conscience, of remorse for what he had done through his actions and his inaction.

"Another match," Kane said, beginning to pace across the bare concrete floor. He kicked a metal pole out of his way. It clattered across the space with a harsh, metallic echo. "Set it up."

"Let's talk about that later," Bearer said.

"He cheated," Kane said. "Using Vader. I can beat him. I can kill him. I'm going to kill him."

Bearer studied the man a moment. The new chemicals were definitely helping in terms of his ring ability. But they were a little harder to come down from, clearly. Adjustments, once again, would be required.

"I understand how you feel," Bearer said slowly, calmly, trying to get Kane to relax just a bit. "But for now, the important thing is to—"

Kane spun and slammed one fist into the hard cement wall in front of him.

"The important thing is another fight. As soon as possible. Right? Another fight?"

Kane towered over him. His knuckles, Bearer saw, were bleeding. Not that it mattered. The man couldn't feel anything, obviously. As witness the oozing, cracked skin on his arm where the fire had touched him. The man's burns were more severe than anyone ringside had initially suspected. He needed antibiotics, probably. And soon. But before that . . .

Bearer wondered about getting a sedative into him. Another protein shake, perhaps.

"You need to calm down, Kane. You need to—"

"I'll calm down when he's dead. Dead and buried, like my parents. He killed them," Kane said. "My mother, my father. He set the fire, he killed them both, and he is going to—"

And then, before Bearer could stop himself, the words were out of his mouth.

"That's not actually true," Bearer said.

The big man frowned.

"What?"

Kane stared. Bearer stammered.

"Ah . . ."

For the first time in a long, long while, the fat man hesitated. He had spoken without thinking, which he never did. Even so, easy enough to take his words back. He didn't have to tell Glen the truth, did he? What did he gain by telling him the truth?

Well . . .

A point worth considering, wasn't it?

Kane continued to glare at him.

"What do you mean, that's not true? He didn't kill my parents?"

*The fire killed them,* Bearer thought. That's what he could say. And that would end it. All telling the truth would do would be to clear his—Bearer's—conscience. Except that honestly speaking, Bearer had no conscience. He had occasional attacks of conscience, but for the most part, Bearer was an amoral, selfish person, just like every other person on the planet, the only difference being he was honest with himself about it. So his conscience wasn't a factor. What was, then? What would telling Glen the truth gain him?

"Bearer. I'm waiting."

Bearer looked him over. The man was on the edge of collapse, that was evident. Physical collapse, prompted not just by the hard match he'd just fought but by the war going on inside his body, his systems versus the chemicals Bearer had given him. It couldn't go on this way. There were only so many different stimulants, and soon his body would develop an immunity to all of them. And the toxicity . . . no, in the long run, chemicals would not only end up being ineffective, they would likely kill Kane. But without the chemicals, Bearer wondered, how could he control the man? He had no edge. No leverage.

Ah.

Here then was a reason to speak the truth.

"Mark didn't kill your father, Glen," Bearer said then. "I'm your father."

Kane blinked.

Kane frowned.

Kane sat down hard on the mattress in the middle of the floor.

He must have heard wrong. Paul Bearer, his father? That was impossible.

He looked down at the skin on his right arm. Charred, and burned, and underneath it, flesh pink and raw, just as it had been the night of that long-ago fire at the funeral home. He remembered running through the parlor, slumping down at the foot of the staircase, burned then as he was now, trying to find a way up the stairs to his family, to find his brother and his mother and . . .

Kane looked up.

"You're my father."

Bearer nodded. "That's right."

"How is that possible?"

The man's eyes glinted, and all at once, Kane remembered a time—several times—when he'd found Bearer and his mother alone in the office, "working," talking about the curse, talking to each other, laughing. Bearer's hand on his mother's knee. Her dress rumpled, lipstick smeared. How was it possible that Bearer was his father?

*What a stupid question,* Kane thought. What a stupid, unnecessary question.

He blinked, and looked down at his arm again. Boy, he thought. If I could feel that, it would hurt like hell. Except of course, that he couldn't feel it. He couldn't feel a thing.

"So what do we do now?" Kane asked. "Another fight? Or do we . . ."

His voice trailed off. His shoulders slumped.

The fat man smiled.

"Don't worry, son," Bearer said. "Don't worry about a thing. From here on out, I'll handle all the details. You just leave it to me."

Kane, suddenly feeling more alone than he had ever felt in his life, forced himself to smile in return.

\*        \*        \*

No one believed Bearer's latest claim; the company didn't want to advertise it, at least initially. They wanted proof. Bearer wasn't surprised by that. He had them do a DNA test. It came back positive, as he knew it would.

"I'm not the little boy who hollered 'Wolf!' " Bearer told the crowd at ringside that night. Kane stood next to him, arms folded across his chest, glaring out into the crowd. "I'm the fat man who told the truth!"

The crowd roared.

"I told Undertaker that his brother was alive, and here he is!" He pointed to Kane, and the crowd erupted again.

"I told the world Kane was my son, and now you have proof." The crowd roared a third time, and then a moment later, a fourth, the loudest roar of all, after Bearer gave them a few choice words about Undertaker's father. They roared so loud, in fact, that Bearer (who was also trying to gauge Kane's reaction to his words about Randall Callaway) completely missed Undertaker climbing into the ring. Kane somehow missed it too, and the man in black made them both pay. A chokeslam on Kane, and then a vicious beating of Bearer that the fat man felt all through the next few days. Still, Bearer decided, it was worth it.

Kane had been off the chemicals entirely—cold turkey—for a couple weeks, and showed no signs of any independent initiative, of wanting to reconcile with his brother, of wanting out from underneath Bearer's thumb. And why should he? They were, after all, father and son. Could there be any closer relationship in the world? Of course not.

There was no doubt in Bearer's mind; Kane would do what he said, when he said to do it, in exactly the manner he wanted it done.

Now—and quite possibly forever—the man was his.

# chapter
## twenty-three

Over the next few months, things between Undertaker, Kane, Paul Bearer, and the World Wrestling Federation (in the person of Vince McMahon) got complicated, chiefly because there was a new edge to Undertaker's actions, an edge that hadn't been there before. He seemed to have been thrown off-balance by the fact that his brother was no longer really *his* brother—or rather, that Bearer had a legitimate claim on Kane's allegiance which Undertaker could not dispute.

So Undertaker found a new focus for his anger: Vince McMahon and the company. At the June 1 *Raw* show, he stalked into the ring and berated McMahon for giving Bearer a forum to air the Callaway family's tragic past, for encouraging the feud between himself and Kane, for rewarding all his years of loyalty with a slap in the face. Undertaker demanded a shot at the title again: McMahon came out then, angry himself, and told Undertaker all he had to do was win his fight that night, and he'd be the number-one contender. He'd get his shot.

If he beat Kane.

But that match wasn't even close. Undertaker was off his game; Kane was at the top of his. Glen won handily, although not before Mark had managed to grab hold of Bearer and give him a beating. Bearer had to spend the next few weeks convalescing at home. Kane, meanwhile, began prepping for his first shot at Steve Austin, and the heavyweight title. Spending extra hours down in the basement, spending extra time at the ring nearest Bearer's house, honing his moves. The man seemed more driven, more devoted to his wrestling, than ever before. Probably because he didn't have anything else in his life.

Kane took his newly honed skills to the ring several times that month. Bearer was still unable to accompany him, so he sat home and watched the show on TV. He had just finished watching Kane manhandle the Road Dogg, was in fact giving his reaction to that fight live via satellite, when Undertaker showed up at his home . . . and beat the crap out of him all over again.

Another week to heal. And then it was time for *King of the Ring.* June 28, 1998. Kane vs. Stone Cold Steve Austin, a First Blood match for the title.

It was a mess.

Mick Foley, in his Mankind guise, tried to enter the fight on Kane's side. Austin got Mankind with his signature move—the Stone Cold Stunner. Then Undertaker came to the ring, and tried to take out Mankind with a chair. He missed. He hit Austin, who began to bleed.

And that was the match.

Kane—Glen Kane Callaway/Grimm—was the heavy-weight champion. The best wrestler on the face of the planet. Even though the formal presentation of the belt would happen the next day, Mr. McMahon let Kane take it home for the night. Get used to the feel of it. Vince clapped him on the shoulder as he said that. McMahon was happy; he was over-joyed to see someone else besides Steve Austin with the belt. Bearer was happy. Both men tried to get Kane to go out that night, to celebrate.

Kane begged off.

He went home by himself, opened the door to Paul Bearer's basement, and then shut himself inside.

\*   \*   \*

The belt was a beautiful thing, *the* championship belt. It stood for something too, Kane thought, all the hard work he'd put in, all the sweat and blood and training he'd put in, down here in Paul Bearer's basement, and in Madrid, and in the ring. It had all paid off now.

BFD, as his brother used to say.

Because sitting here in the basement of Paul Bearer's house (even though over the last few months he'd made the basement over into something like an apartment for himself, built out the raw space into a bedroom with a desk in the corner where the stack of two-by-fours had been), fingering that belt in his lap, he was reminded more than anything else of that day long ago when he'd held another trophy in his hands, when he and the rest of the Shorthorns had won the state championship. Of course that had been small-time, compared to this. Small potatoes. And yet . . .

When he'd won that trophy, he had someone to share it with. Katie, Ty, and Luis, and Coach Walsh, and Pete and Alma, who he now realized had been more like parents to him than anyone else in his life. He'd even had the memory of his parents then to hold on to, Randall and Susanna, and his brother, whereas now . . .

Now he had nothing.

His whole life had been a lie. His dad wasn't his dad, his mother had been just what Bearer had called her on national television, a whore, and his brother was a murderer. Kane had no past. This—Paul Bearer's basement—was the grim reality of his present. And as for his future . . .

*I should have died a long time ago,* Kane thought. In fact, I was supposed to die. The fire. The curse.

He felt, he realized, the same way he had after Katie Vick's car had gone off the mountain. Lost. Completely and utterly lost.

He had a hard time sleeping that night.

For the first time in a long while, he dreamed about running through the desert, being chased by fire.

The next night, in a match hardly worth the name, Kane lost the belt back to Steve Austin.

Over the next few days, Bearer noticed a change in Kane's attitude. A lack of desire, of drive. When he asked the man what was wrong, Kane's answer was evasive. Bearer couldn't pin him down to anything. He decided a change in Kane's diet was called for. One day as champion? Ridiculous. Bearer had in mind a much longer, more successful, more lucrative reign.

"Try this," he said to Kane at lunch the next day, setting down a tall glass with a slightly foamy, orangish pink liquid inside it next to the man's plate.

"What is it?"

"Mostly juices," Bearer said. "Freshly squeezed. Carrot. Orange. Pineapple. A little bit of this. A little bit of that."

Kane eyed it curiously. For a minute he looked like he was going to say something, then he shrugged his shoulders and picked up the glass.

He drank.

That afternoon, much to the discomfort of his newest sparring partner, a young man named Hawk who had been working on the semi-pro circuit in Nashville, Kane had a particularly energetic, fast-moving, violently brutal workout.

Bearer went to sleep with a big smile on his face.

Kane woke up with the taste of Bearer's juice concoction in his mouth and the image of Katie Vick and her car toppling off the side of the mountain and bursting into flames in his mind.

He was sick, he realized. Nauseous.

He closed his eyes and waited for the feeling to pass. But it didn't.

*Fresh air,* he thought. That'll do the trick.

He got out of bed and climbed the basement stairs. But that turned out to be a bad idea. The nausea turned into full-fledged, stomach-churning vertigo. His head spun. His vision swam.

Now what he needed was not just fresh air, but the bathroom. And quick.

He went down the hall, and opened the door, and—

Found himself staring into Bearer's office. The light above the desk was still on—Bearer must have just gone to sleep, forgot to take care of it. Not his problem at the moment. What he needed was the bathroom.

What he needed, all at once, was to throw up.

For the next half hour or so, he did just that. He'd never been so sick in all his life. Luckily, he made it to the bathroom in time to prevent a total disaster. Lucky too that after he got sick, he felt almost instantly, all-at-once better. Well enough to go downstairs, get a good night's sleep, and in the morning—

He passed by the door to Bearer's office, and stopped.

He'd never been in Bearer's office before. It looked nice—big cherry desk, bunch of fancy-looking bookshelves, lined with all sorts of books and magazines and . . .

Pills. Of course pills. Kane remembered the other room he'd been in. Bearer had a lot of pills. What were they all for, he wondered?

He stepped into the room, and shut the door behind him.

He walked to the nearest shelf, pulled a bottle down at random, and read the label.

Sample: Not for Sale

Huh.

He put that back, and looked at another.

Experimental: Not Approved for Use with Humans

*My father,* Kane thought, and shuddered. It seemed like the newly discovered side of his family had as many problems as the old.

He put that bottle back on the shelf, in front of a whole row of identical-looking books, an entire set called *Grudberg's Principles of Basic Chemistry,* and as he did, his glance fell on a small, much older-looking volume near the end of the shelf. *Primal Persecution: The Salem Witch Trials.*

Kane pulled that book out, saw a dog-eared page, and flipped open to it. The paper was yellowed, and crinkled; the corner he touched crumbled to dust and fell to the floor.

Halfway down the page, there was a break in the text. A headline. The story of Rebecca Goody.

Kane read a few lines and frowned. He read some more, and shook his head.

Rebecca Goody's story was Rebecca Kane's story, right down to the words she'd said on the stake as she burned. Every detail was exactly the same. But how . . .

He looked at the bookshelf again. Next to the empty space where the *Witch Trials* book had been was an oversize volume, red binding, black lettering on the spine. *Go West, Young Americans!* by Sidney Cassel. There were two dog-eared pages; the first marked the beginning of the story of Jedediah Bromwell, a man who'd moved west from Binghamton New York, to the Dakota Territory in the late 1800s, whose entire family—wife, and ten children—perished in a freak fire that started in the middle of a hailstorm, when a candle tipped over.

Kane knew it as the story of his great-great-uncle, Jedediah Kane.

"This isn't right," he said out loud.

The second bookmark began the tale of the great St. Louis railroad fire of 1843. The story of Aloysius Worth, which was also the story of Aloysius Kane. Except that wasn't possible, any more than Rebecca Kane's story could be the same as Rebecca Goody's, or Jedediah Kane's the same as Jedediah Bromwell's.

Something was off here. Something was very, very wrong indeed, and as Kane began going through all Bearer's bookshelves, and the man's filing cabinet, and found more books, more stories, old newspaper articles, and magazine clippings, all of which were at once hauntingly familiar to him and completely, shockingly different, he began to realize just what that something was.

Finally, he stopped reading. He sat in Bearer's office chair for a long, long time, until the sun came up and he heard footsteps coming down the hall. Until he heard the door behind him open, and the labored breathing of the man who was his father behind him.

"Glen? What are you doing in here?"

Kane shook his head and spoke without turning.

"You made it all up. The entire curse. You made it all up."

"Glen. I—"

Kane spun in his chair, and met his father's gaze.

"You made it up."

For a second, Bearer looked angry. Kane thought the man was going to deny everything.

Then he shook his head, and a crooked smile crossed his face.

"Well . . . you have to admit. It's a hell of a story."

"A story," Kane repeated disbelievingly. "A story. Is that all it is to you?"

"It's what your mother wanted to hear."

"And you had to tell her that."

"What harm did it do?"

Kane shook his head. What harm? He thought of Katie Vick, and the years of his life he'd wasted avoiding her, avoiding happiness because of the lies this man had told. He thought of the terrible dreams that had plagued him for years, of his mother's fevered imaginings and the fears her beliefs had instilled in an entire town. And then he thought of his brother. He remembered Mark as a young boy, convinced that he was doomed to die, a bad seed, cursed from the moment he was born. He thought of his brother as he was now, Undertaker, an outlaw, and wondered how much of the man Mark Callaway had become was due to the boy he had been, and the things he believed.

Then Kane sighed, and shrugged, and managed a small, crooked smile.

"You're right," he said to his father. "It's all water under the bridge."

"Exactly." Bearer smiled back. "That's very mature of you to realize that, Glen. I'm very proud of you."

Kane shrugged again.

"Come on," Bearer said. "I'll make us breakfast. Some eggs, some bacon—wash it all down with a protein shake, okay. What do you say to that? Breakfast and a protein shake."

Kane shook his head, and met his father's gaze dead-on then.

"No, thanks," he said. "I'm not hungry right now.

# chapter
## twenty-four

Kane trained extra hard that week. His motivation was back. Bearer noticed, and he was pleased. He was glad not to have to use the chemicals anymore. Glad to have the relationship between him and his son clean, and above board.

After Kane's workout, Bearer suggested the two men grab some dinner. Kane declined.

"I'm going to hang here for a while," Kane told him. "Hit the weights again."

"You've been hitting the weights all week," Bearer said. "All work and no play . . ."

"Time for play when I have the title again. Don't you think?"

Bearer nodded. What could he say? The boy was right. First things first. He smiled. A real chip off the old block, that's what Glen Kane—Glen Grimm, Glen Bearer, whatever you called him—was.

"I'll see you at home then. Son."

"Yep," Kane said, and Bearer had his back turned, so he couldn't quite see the way the man's jaw tightened at Bearer's use of the word *son*. "See you at home."

Kane watched the man drive off.

Then he showered, and dressed, and made a phone call.

"Yeah?"

"You all set?"

There was a pause on the other end of the line.

"I still don't see the point of this."

"Trust me."

"I don't."

"Then why are you doing this?"

Silence again.

"Okay. See you there," the voice said, and then hung up.

Kane hung up too, and made a second call.

"Dad. It's me, Kane. Something's come up. I'm not going to be home tonight. Not till late. Maybe not at all. I'll see you tomorrow at the gym, though. Okay? Good night."

He was about to say, "I love you," but decided against it.

That was pushing it. That particular lie, he might choke on.

Kane hung up, collected his things, and drove to the airport.

He caught the last flight out. A small plane that landed in Austin at close to 8:30 P.M. He rented a car, and pushing it, made it all the way to the outskirts of town by midnight. He passed the sign—

Welcome to

MARFA, TEXAS

Home of the World-Famous Marfa Lights

*Giant* filmed here 1951–1952

—and a few minutes later, pulled up to the graveyard.

His brother was there already, waiting.

"Mark."

"Glen. What's the point of all this?"

Kane took a deep breath. He looked around at the graves surrounding them, the headstones and footstones and markers that all bore the name Kane, and then he looked down at the one in front of Mark, Randall Callaway's stone, and he thought of the fat man and his house, and the lies he'd told, and he thought about Pete Dominguez, and Red Barrow, and in his mind, all at once, he heard Red's voice once more, heard again what the old man had told him on Glen's first night at Aurora:

"I'm not your dad, am I? Randall Callaway was your dad."

And then Glen Callaway—that was his name, Glen Callaway, that's what it said on his tombstone now, and that's what it would say on the real tombstone, the one where someday he really would be buried—turned to his brother and said:

"Here's the point of all this, Mark. We gotta stop fighting each other. We're all that's left. Out of all the Kanes and Callaways in the world, it's just me and you."

Mark looked puzzled for a second, then angry. "Yeah. And a fucking cup of coffee is seventy-five cents. So what? I knew that already. What's your point?"

"This is my point," Glen said, and then proceeded to tell him what he'd discovered the night before, in Paul Bearer's office.

The two brothers took the same plane out of Austin the next morning.

The whole way, they talked.

Curious things were happening in the ring.

It had started last week, at *Raw,* July 6, 1998. Mr. McMahon had scheduled a Three-Way match between Kane, Undertaker, and Mankind, winner to be named number one contender for the title. Ringside, Undertaker never showed. Kane and Mankind fought. Kane seemed once more to be at the top of his game. He pinned Mankind in the center of the ring, then stood and, to the surprise of everyone watching, took off his mask.

Bearer (as well as everyone else watching) got another, even bigger surprise then.

The face underneath was not Kane's after all.

Underneath the mask was Undertaker.

After that match, Bearer confronted Kane.

"Where did he get the mask?"

"It's not the real one," Kane said. "I have the real one here."

He showed it to Bearer. The writing was right there, on the inside: *Mascara de la Muerta Negra*. Mask of the Black Death.

Bearer handed it back to him. "Well, where were you, then? Why didn't you show at the match?"

"I told you," Kane said. "I didn't feel well. I called it in."

"I didn't get the message."

"I don't know what to tell you."

Bearer looked at Kane. Kane looked right back.

"Dad," he said. "I swear. I'm telling you the truth."

"Okay," Bearer said. "Okay."

But it wasn't okay. Something was going on. Just now, he'd watched Undertaker vs. Vader, seen Mark Tombstone him pretty good, get the win, and Mankind had come in the ring while he was distracted and was about to nail him with a chair, only Kane had taken the chair away from him and nailed Vader instead. Which didn't really prove anything, Bearer supposed, except . . .

There was a chance for Kane to get Undertaker good. To get a little revenge on Mark for the way he beat me up, at least, Bearer thought. And Kane hadn't taken that chance.

Vince had pulled Bearer aside before the match, told him he thought that maybe Undertaker and Kane were in cahoots, which had made Bearer laugh. Undertaker and Kane in cahoots? That would be the day, he told Vince. And yet . . .

Curious things were happening inside the ring.

A couple weeks later, Undertaker was at the root of a strange series of events that ended up winning a match for Kane and

Mankind that only seconds earlier, they had seemed on the verge of losing.

The week after that, Bearer entered the ring with Kane to again denounce Undertaker. To mock the man, to call him a coward and a murderer. The whole time Bearer was speaking, he had the oddest sensation in the pit of his stomach. It took him the longest while, until late, late in the evening, lying at home, in bed to identify it.

Fear. Even with Kane standing at his back, Bearer realized, he'd been afraid in the ring.

He got up then, and locked the door to his bedroom.

Curious things started happening outside the ring as well.

Bearer came home one afternoon to find Kane had emptied the bank account he'd set up in the man's name. Bearer had provided the man with a way to make withdrawals, of course, so it was all aboveboard, but still . . .

"We were supposed to consult on your spending," Bearer said.

"Sorry," Kane said. They were in the gym; Bearer had gone hunting for his son after he'd found out about the money. He hadn't had to look hard; this was the first place he'd come.

"I just thought it was time for me to have my own place."

"Your own place."

"Uh-huh. Can't stay in the nest forever, after all. Isn't that right? Dad?"

Kane smiled.

Bearer forced himself to smile back, but in the pit of his stomach . . .

That fear was back.

Bearer woke up in the middle of the night, sweating. He had the strangest dream.

He was back in Texas, running down a highway. Being chased by fire.

He took some chemicals, and went back to bed.

In the morning—the late morning, he overslept, something must have been wrong with how he'd calculated the dosage, he realized—Bearer went in the kitchen to eat and found Kane sitting at the table waiting for him. There was a blender full of an orange-and-pink drink sitting in the middle of the table.

"Protein shake?" Kane asked, holding out a glass to him.

Bearer shook his head.

"Actually, I don't feel well," the fat man said. "I think I'm going to go back to sleep."

He felt Kane's eyes on him the whole way back to his bedroom.

A few days later. Monday, August 10, 1998. It was all Bearer could do to make it to the ring. He and Kane met backstage, entered the ring together. Kane didn't say a word the whole time; it was just like back in the old days, with the voicebox. Vince was in the ring when they got there. He was upset, for some reason.

He pointed a finger at Kane.

"That's Undertaker under that mask!" he said. "It's Undertaker!"

"What?" Bearer looked closely. Kane smiled at him.

Vince reached for the mask, and the lights in the arena went out.

When they came back up, Mark was there, and he had McMahon by the throat.

Bearer ran from the ring as fast as his fat little legs would carry him.

\*     \*     \*

The next week, it was more of the same. Only this time, it was Glen—Kane—dressed up as Undertaker. He arrived in a hearse. He fought Austin. Stone Cold unmasked him, managed to stuff him back inside the hearse, was ready to drive off with him, except that there was already someone in the driver's seat. Mark. The real Undertaker.

The brothers and the hearse disappeared into the bowels of the arena.

Bearer watched it all from backstage.

That night, he had quite a few dreams. Quite a few very scary, fire-filled dreams.

When he woke up, he knew Vince was right, and he was wrong.

Mark and Glen were back together again.

The brothers Callaway were in cahoots, and he was the target.

August 23, 1998.

Backstage, Glen Callaway adjusted his mask.

Seated on a bench next to him, his brother, Mark, straightened one boot, and stood.

Tonight was the night. They were coming out together at last. Kane and Undertaker, working as one.

"You ready for this?" Mark asked, turning to his brother.

Glen nodded. "I'm ready. Let's go get 'em."

"Yeah. Chickenshit cowards."

Glen smiled.

They walked down the long tunnel leading to the arena, and emerged into the auditorium.

The lights went up. The music began.

The two men walked down the ramp together, side by side, headed for the ring.

\*     \*     \*

Bearer put on a good show.

He stalked to the ring himself a few minutes after Glen and Mark, demanded that Kane do one last thing for him. Destroy Undertaker. As if that was really going to happen.

Kane turned his back on Bearer, and then Undertaker took it to him one last time.

A month and a half later, Paul Bearer invited Mark Callaway to his house. "An attempt to reconcile." Mark reluctantly agreed. They toasted the future. A special wine, a bottle that Bearer had been saving for a very special occasion.

It had a nasty aftertaste, Mark Callaway thought. Gave him a bit of a headache.

He ended up spending the night at Bearer's house, too sick to drive home.

A few weeks later, Undertaker turned on his brother once more.

# epilogue

In 1998, Paul Bearer developed health problems that necessitated a long departure from the ring.

As of this writing, his relationship with both Kane and the Undertaker—Glen and Mark Callaway—remains strained.

Mark Callaway has continued his career in WWE, where he is the most respected Superstar in the organization, and a four-time WWE Champion. A true legend of the sport, he is considered a surefire Hall-of-Famer.

He is now married with children and lives in Texas, not far from Marfa. He and his brother have attempted many times to heal the scars of the past, with some success, but their relationship is still best described as strained.

Denton Young, who was twelve years old when he fought Glen Callaway in Marfa, Texas, died in a rock-climbing accident in 1996 while rappelling off Devil's Tower National Monument in Wyoming. He was thirty-one.

Javier Antonio Marquez still resides in Madrid, where he continues to teach martial arts and fighting techniques.

In June 1998, tipped off by one of his students, he ventured to a local bar that broadcast American television over a satellite feed. It was 4:00 A.M. local time when at his request, the bartender switched the channel to *Raw.*

"Mascara de la Muerte Negra" was staring back at him, wearing the Championship title.

Melissa Vick saw "Mascara de la Muerte Negra" on TV as well. She recognized his story and, even behind the mask, recognized the man. She called Glen shortly thereafter, and he told her the truth of what had happened on Senior Skip Day so long ago. The two reconciled, and made plans to meet. Tragically, before they could do so, Melissa was diagnosed with an advanced stage of amyotrophic lateral sclerosis (ALS—more commonly known as Lou Gehrig's disease). She died in January of 2003. In her last letter to Glen, she wrote, "I realize I am coming to the final days of my life, but instead of it being a time of sorrow, I am looking forward to seeing my daughter again. And I will tell her the success you turned out to be. Be well."

Kane quietly paid for her funeral. She is buried next to her husband and daughter.

Kane has continued his career as one of the most physically dominant wrestlers in history. In June 1998, he won the WWE Championship, and has also won several Tag Team titles. In early 2004, he was selected as one of the fifty greatest WWE Superstars of all time, and in October of 2004, *Smack-Down!* magazine readers voted him the Greatest Wrestling Villain of All Time.

He has no known address, living life wherever the day takes him.

In 2003, Kane seemed to be opening himself up to the world. The injury in his throat had at last been properly diagnosed and corrected by surgery, and the fans seemed to be warming up to him.

Later that same year, Kane was forced to remove the mask

that had protected him from the world for so long. It opened up a new chapter of violence and brought back a flood of memories about his tragic past.

No longer a believer in the curse, Kane is a man who survived a deadly fire, overcame a life-threatening condition, lived through physical and mental abuse, and survived unspeakable tragedies to become one of the sport's most enduring figures. He has captured all of the major titles in the sport and has spawned a legion of loyal fans. Deep down, they hope their cheers will heal him. Kane lives in his own private hell, and the reason fans love him is simple: continually, every day of his life, he fights to escape it.

Printed in the United States
By Bookmasters